Big Lake Tragedy

By Nick Russell

Nick Russell
1400 Colorado Street C-16
Boulder City, NV 89005
E-mail Editor@gypsyjournal.net

Also By Nick Russell

Fiction
Big Lake Mystery Series
Big Lake
Big Lake Lynching
Crazy Days In Big Lake
Big Lake Blizzard
Big Lake Scandal
Big Lake Burning
Big Lake Honeymoon
Big Lake Reckoning
Big Lake Brewpub
Big Lake Abduction
Big Lake Celebration
Big Lake Tragedy

Dog's Run Series
Dog's Run
Return To Dog's Run

John Lee Quarrels Series
Stillborn Armadillos
The Gecko In The Corner

Standalone Mystery Novels
Black Friday

Nonfiction
Highway History and Back Road Mystery
Highway History and Back Road Mystery II
Meandering Down The Highway; A Year On The Road With
Fulltime RVers
The Frugal RVer
Work Your Way Across The USA; You Can Travel And Earn A
Living Too!
Overlooked Florida
Overlooked Arizona
The Gun Shop Manual

Author's Note

While there is a body of water named Big Lake i
of Arizona, the community of Big Lake and all p
only in the author's imagination. Any resemblanc
persons, living or dead, is purely coincidental.

Also By Nick Russell

Fiction
Big Lake Mystery Series
Big Lake
Big Lake Lynching
Crazy Days In Big Lake
Big Lake Blizzard
Big Lake Scandal
Big Lake Burning
Big Lake Honeymoon
Big Lake Reckoning
Big Lake Brewpub
Big Lake Abduction
Big Lake Celebration
Big Lake Tragedy

Dog's Run Series
Dog's Run
Return To Dog's Run

John Lee Quarrels Series
Stillborn Armadillos
The Gecko In The Corner

Standalone Mystery Novels
Black Friday

Nonfiction
Highway History and Back Road Mystery
Highway History and Back Road Mystery II
Meandering Down The Highway; A Year On The Road With
Fulltime RVers
The Frugal RVer
Work Your Way Across The USA; You Can Travel And Earn A
Living Too!
Overlooked Florida
Overlooked Arizona
The Gun Shop Manual

Keep up with Nick Russell's latest books at
www.NickRussellBooks.com

Author's Note

While there is a body of water named Big Lake in the White Mountains of Arizona, the community of Big Lake and all persons in this book live only in the author's imagination. Any resemblance in this story to actual persons, living or dead, is purely coincidental.

To Roberta. I told you I would.

Prologue

"I'm telling you, Jimmy, you should have been there. You missed one hell of a show! That old gal must have weighed 300 pounds. She had half a dozen T-bone steaks shoved up under her shirt and you couldn't tell the difference. But talk about being light on your feet! That woman could've been a ballet dancer or something. Poor Jordan here managed to get one 'cuff on her wrist before she took off running down the aisle of the grocery store, and this poor kid was hanging on to the other end of those handcuffs for all he was worth. I swear, I don't think his boots ever touched the floor!"

Jordan Northcutt, Big Lake's newest deputy, took the ribbing good-naturedly and asked, "What else was I supposed to do? You sure weren't any help!"

Buz Carelton spread his hands and replied, "I'm sorry kid, but what could I do? I was so busy laughing I couldn't move. Besides, I thought you'd turned into one of them superheroes and could fly."

"It's a wonder she didn't tear his damn arm off," Dolan Reed added. "I had just rolled up and was walking in the door when I saw them coming at me. By then the kid had got his feet back down on the ground, and I'll give him credit for trying, because he damn sure was. If you go in that store, Jimmy, you will see skid marks from his boots all the way down aisle seven. It's a wonder he's got any soles left on them."

"Well, one thing I learned when I was in the Navy was that you have to have a big enough anchor to hold down whatever you're trying to keep in one place," FBI agent Larry Parks said. "That's the problem, Jordan, you just weren't enough anchor for the job. You pack on another couple hundred pounds and you might be able to slow somebody like that down next time around."

Jordan laughed along with the rest of them and added, "All I can say is, I'm glad you showed up when you did, Dolan. I believe if she'd have gotten out in the parking lot she wouldn't have slowed down until she was back in Albuquerque."

"Hell, kid, I didn't do anything. I think she just saw me and decided she was surrounded, so she gave up."

"Where is she now?" Sheriff Jim Weber asked.

"Back in one of those new holding cells we just added on for women and kids," Buz said. "I told her she was our first guest there, but she didn't seem all that thrilled with the honor." Buz had acquired his nickname back in high school, a result of his skinny neck and hawk-like nose. The kids used to say he was part buzzard. In his mid-40s now, Buz was an experienced deputy, and among the coolest heads when trouble reared its ugly head, something that happened all too often in Big Lake. That's why the sheriff had assigned him to be the new deputy's Field Training Officer. And now that the last day of Jordan's probationary period was finished on such a stellar note as the arrest of the woman shoplifter who had added resisting arrest and disorderly conduct to her original violation, it was time to let the new guy spread his wings.

"So, do you think you're ready to handle patrol on your own, Jordan?" the sheriff asked.

"Oh, yeah, I'm looking forward to it."

"Well, you've done a fine job with him, Buz. I'm proud of both of you."

"Thanks Jimmy, but it wasn't much work at all. This kid is a natural."

"Of course he is," Dolan said. "We don't take nothing but the best around here."

Jordan blushed slightly at the compliments, but Weber could tell he appreciated the praise.

Unfortunately, he didn't get to enjoy his moment in the spotlight for very long, because the door to the office slammed open and a tall, skinny man with blood spattered clothes and a wild look in his eyes burst inside.

"Sheriff, you gotta come quick. Somethin' awful's happened."

"Carl? What's going on?"

"The hogs ate Duncan!"

Chapter 1

The smell of the hog farm was bad enough from the highway, but it was overpowering when Weber crawled out of his Ford Explorer. He and his deputies donned paper masks that covered their noses and mouths and pulled on coveralls.

Weber had seen a lot of horrific things in his time and was no stranger to violent death, but the gruesome sight before him on this cold October morning was enough to make him glad he had not eaten much for breakfast.

In life George Duncan had been a large, ruddy faced man with a strong work ethic and a good sense of humor, but death had reduced him to a torn, half devoured body that hardly looked human. Weber let go of the edge of the blue plastic tarp someone had put over the dead man and stood up. Behind them, he could hear one of his deputies retching. He didn't know which one and it didn't really matter. The sheriff was close to doing the same thing himself.

"What the hell happened to him?"

"I think the bull got him first," Duncan's son Sonny said. "It looks like he drug himself over here by the hog pen and climbed in there to try to get away from it. When we found him in there me and Carl pulled him out here and covered him up."

"Maybe if you would have been out helping your father this wouldn't have happened," a woman shouted shrilly. "But no, where were you? Laying there in bed sleeping off a drunk, like you do every morning!"

"Shut up, Rosanne. Just shut the hell up!"

"Don't you tell me to shut up, Sonny Duncan. Your father may have put up with your sinful ways, but I can tell you right now, those days are over!"

"Go to hell, bitch. You got no right to tell me what to do."

"Right? I have every right. You're going to find out just who makes the rules around here from now on, buster!"

"My dad's dead, which means there's no reason for you to be here anymore. So pack your shit and get on down the road."

"This is my place now. You're the one who's leaving!"

"Whoa! Everybody just calm down," Weber said, stepping between them.

"Officer, I want this man off my property right now.

The woman looked to be somewhere in her early 40s, with a medium build and curly red hair. She tried to push past the sheriff when Sonny said, "Your property? I don't think so. You're nothing but a whore."

Weber held her back and turned to Sonny and said, "Okay, that's enough of that talk. You both need to settle down right now. This isn't the time for this nonsense."

"Nonsense? It's not nonsense that I want this loser off my..."

"Shut up!"

The woman looked startled at the sheriff's outburst and took a step backward, clamping her mouth shut. Weber didn't like shouting at people, but it seemed to have had the desired effect.

"Okay, ma'am, I don't know you, but I'm Sheriff Weber. What's your name, please?"

"Rosanne. Rosanne Duncan. I'm George's wife. Or least I was until this morning." She wiped tears from her eyes with the back of her hand.

Weber had heard that Duncan had found himself a wife a while back, but he had never met the woman until now. There had been a lot of speculation in Big Lake about the hog farmer's new wife. The gossip mill said she was some kind of mail order bride from the Philippines, or maybe Russia. It had to be somebody from a place like that, because who else would want to live out there in the middle of nowhere, with all those smelly hogs? But compared to wherever she came from, it was probably an improvement.

Of course, some said, some women would put up with anything for the right price. And don't forget, Duncan was also filthy rich. He owned a hundred odiferous acres seven miles from town, filled with fat hogs that he raised and sold to meat processors across the Southwest. He also had his own butchering operation and supplied restaurants from Show Low to Springerville, and all the way to Gallup, New Mexico with pork chops, hams, and sausage. Everybody knew about the big wad of bills wrapped up in a rubber band that he always carried in the pocket of his bib overalls.

More charitable souls asked what did it matter where she came from? Didn't Duncan deserve some happiness in his life, too? It had been twelve years since Eleanor died, God rest her soul. Duncan may have been coarse and unpolished in his own way, and yes, he smelled of pig shit. But he was always nice to everybody and always tipped his cap when he saw a lady. Who are we to judge?

Rosanne Duncan obviously wasn't a Filipina, and Weber didn't think she was from Russia either, given her lack of any accent. But wherever she was from, it was clear she didn't plan to go anywhere else just because her husband was now dead. And it was just as obvious that there was no love lost between her and Duncan's son. But that was none of Weber's concern at this point. The courts could decide who got what from the man's estate. His job was to investigate how Duncan had died.

"All right, Mrs. Duncan. What I need you to do is go in the house with this deputy here and give him a statement. Just tell him everything you can about what happened."

"My husband is dead! That's what happened. And it's all your fault, Sonny!"

Weber raised his hand to stop her and said, "Just go with Deputy Northcutt, okay?"

He nodded at Jordan, who led the woman away. Weber turned to Sonny and said, "Okay, start at the beginning and tell me what happened."

Sonny stared at Rosanne's retreating back and shook his head. "I don't know why my old man got messed up with that bitch in the first place. If she thinks I'm leaving, she's crazy."

"Like I said, right now we've got more than that to worry about. When was the last time you saw your father alive?"

Sonny turned to look at the blue tarp and shook his head. "I don't know. Sometime yesterday, I guess."

"Sometime yesterday?"

"Yeah. I don't live in the house. I'm in one of the trailers over there with the rest of the hired help," he said bitterly.

5

Weber turned to look toward the four mobile homes located about fifty yards from the main house. They weren't new, but they looked to be well-maintained.

"Which one is yours?"

"I guess they're all mine now," Sonny said.

"No, I mean which one do you live in?"

"The one on the left end. The one with the green trim."

"Okay, who lives in the others?"

"The one next to me is empty right now. José Barela and his wife and a couple of their kids lived there until last month. She ran them off."

"She? Rosanne?"

Sonny nodded his head. "Yeah. She likes to pretend she's so religious, runnin' off to church a couple times a week, but that's all for show. She don't like Mexicans, and as soon as she got here she was after my old man to get rid of José. He wasn't having any of that. If you knew my old man, you know how he was. He didn't care what color your skin was, just that you were honest and a good person."

"And this José was a good person?"

"Damn good. He was a hard worker, and Carmen, his wife, was a sweetie. Always smiling and doing whatever she could to make people happy. She used to cook and clean the house for us, before Rosanne showed up. But she put a stop to that real quick. She told the old man it was because she wanted to take care of him. Said that was a wife's job. Well, I'll tell you what, Sheriff, you go in the house and see what a good job she did taking care of him. Place is a mess! It was never like that when Carmen was here."

"So how did she run them off if they were such good people and your dad liked them?"

"Rosanne was jealous of Carmen. She thought her and my old man had something going on. Even accused her of it, right in front of José."

"And that wasn't true?"

"Of course not," Sonny said hotly. "You know my dad. He wasn't like that. I mean, he'd compliment Carmen and tell her how good her cookin' was and what a good job she was doing around the place, but that was it. But after that blowup, José said they needed to move on. Dad tried to talk him into staying, but José said no, and they shook hands and that was it. They packed their stuff up and were gone."

"What about the other two trailers?"

"Leonard Bowers lives in the next one. Him and his wife Mona. And the other one is where Carl Turner lives."

"Turner? That's the guy that came into town?"

"Yeah. Rosanne's been trying to get rid of him, too."

"What's the problem with him?"

"Nothing's wrong with Carl at all," Sonny said. "I mean, yeah, he's kind of a halfwit. But he's a hard worker and he'd do anything my dad asked him to. But Rosanne don't like him because he's different."

"What do you mean by different?"

Sonny shrugged his shoulders. "Like I said, he's not too bright. When my dad brought her up here for the first time, after they got married, and introduced her around, Carl just gave her a big old hug. That's the way he is. He hugs everybody. He didn't mean nothing by it, but right away Rosanne got all pissy and pushed him away and told him to keep his hands off her. After that she kept calling him dummy all the time. Dummy Carl. Ain't that a nice way for a so-called Christian lady to be talkin' to somebody?"

Weber didn't reply, just shook his head. He had learned a long time ago that you couldn't take anything at face value, especially with people who obviously disliked each other as much as Sonny and Rosanne did.

"Okay, let's talk about this morning. Tell me everything you know about what happened to your father."

Chapter 2

"We found him right there," Sonny said, pointing at the hog pens. He led the sheriff to the spot where his father's body had been found. A fence made of steel pipes enclosed the pen. Pipes that were stained a dark color from the victim's blood.

Weber could see the bodies of several hogs lying inside the pen. "What happened to those hogs?"

"I shot them. Shot every damn one I saw."

"You said 'we found him.' Who was with you?"

"Me and Carl. We came out to help with the feeding, like we do every morning. When we came walking up we saw all the blood there and looked inside and there he was. Or what was left of him, anyway. The damn hogs were..." Sonny choked up and closed his eyes. Weber put a hand on his shoulder to comfort him.

"Like I said, the damn hogs were eating him. We grabbed his arms and tried to haul him out of there and a couple of them were hanging on. We had to kick the hell out of them to make them let go. We got him out here, and it was obvious he was gone."

"What did you do then?"

"I ran up to the house and tried to use the phone, but the damn thing isn't working again. It's down about half the time. Rosanne started yelling at me for coming in the house without knocking. Like I don't belong there or something. I told her what happened and she started screaming and carrying on. I went outside and I told Carl to get to town and get some help and he took off."

"Then what happened?"

"One of those damn hogs was standing up on its hind legs, like it was trying to get over the fence and get back at him. That just set me off. I went back to my place and I grabbed a rifle and I just started shooting those bastards. I killed every one of them I could see."

"How do you think he got in there? You said something about a bull."

"Yeah. I killed it, too. I kept telling my dad to get rid of that big son of a bitch. Told him over and over it was dangerous. But he just wouldn't listen to me!"

"But what does a bull have to do with pigs doing what they did?"

"Every morning my dad went out and messed with that damn bull. That was the first thing he did. He'd toss it a couple of apples and that bull would paw the ground and snort and wave its horns around. My old man just thought that was funny as hell. He'd act like he was a matador or something. I kept telling him that bull was going to kill him one of these days, but he'd just laugh and say that they were buddies. After we found my dad, after we got him away from the pigs and I shot them, I saw that blood trail over there and followed it into the pasture where the bull stayed. The gate was open and it was standing there with blood all over its horns. I figured out then what must've happened. I think the bull finally got him, and my dad managed to get out of the pasture and stumbled this way until he got to the hog pens."

"But why would he have crawled into the pen?"

"I don't know," Sonny said shaking his head. "Maybe the bull was still coming after him or something. All I know is what I told you."

"Okay. Listen, I'm sorry for your loss. Your dad was a good man. Do me a favor. Go back to your trailer now, and let us process things here."

"Still got lots of hogs that need feeding over that way," Sonny said. "I reckon I need to get to them."

"That's fine, if you're up to it," Weber told him.

"Don't matter if I'm up to it or not, it needs done."

"Yeah, I understand," the sheriff said. And having grown up on a small ranch outside Big Lake, he did. It didn't matter if it was raining or snowing, or a holiday, or your birthday, or if somebody had just died in such a tragic way. If you had livestock, somebody still had to attend to them.

Once Sonny had left, Weber went to where three of his deputies stood at the open gate leading to the pasture.

"What have you got, guys?"

"Looks like the bull gored him first," Deputy Chad Summers said, supporting Sonny's theory. "Got blood on one of its horns, and there was a pool of dried blood over there. And we found this."

He handed Weber the green feed store baseball cap Duncan always wore. "Do you want to see the bull?"

"Not really, but I guess I ought to."

Chad led him a short distance into the pasture to the body of the animal. One of the bull's massive horns was covered in blood, and there were two bullet holes in its skull.

"He sure was a big sucker."

"I guess," Weber said. "What do you figure he weighed, Chad?"

"You probably know better than I do, Jimmy. You're the one grew up on a ranch. I'm guessing a couple thousand pounds at least."

"Show me the blood pool."

"Right over here," Chad said, leading him a few steps away. "You can see where he got up and stumbled a couple of times."

Weber really couldn't, but he took Chad's word for it since he was an experienced big game hunter and had spent a lot of time tracking animals in the wild.

"Follow along here, Jimmy, you can see his progress." The deputies had stuck small triangular shaped orange flags mounted on stiff wires into the ground where they had found blood spots or other evidence of Duncan's last moments on earth. Outside the pasture there wasn't much grass, mostly bare earth.

"It looks like he fell here, then got back up. And there's a hoof print over there."

"You think the bull was following him?"

"Could be. Or it could have been made some other time fairly recently. Hard to say."

A few steps further, Chad pointed to a dark wet smear in the dirt. "I think he fell down again here and laid there for a little bit. Then he got up, or at least enough to crawl, and made it over there to the hog pen. And when he got in there the hogs finished him off."

"Jesus, what a way to die."

"No kidding. I'm surprised he made it that far with all the blood he lost. I think by the time he got to the hog pen he was pretty much gone. I'd like to think so, rather than him being in there and them eating him while he was still alive."

11

Both men shuddered at that thought. An ambulance had arrived and the two paramedics stood over the body with Dolan and Buz. One of them knelt down and gingerly lifted the tarp, then quickly dropped it and turned his head away.

Weber walked over to them and said, "This is a bad one, guys."

"Yeah, we saw," Rusty Heinz replied. A stocky bald man with a shaved head and a goatee, Rusty wore a silver hoop in his left ear. He and the other EMT, Pat Price were both good, compassionate men who saw as much misery and carnage as the deputies themselves did, and they all worked well together.

"Is it okay to transport him?"

"Yeah, we've got all the pictures of the body we need," Dolan said. "The problem is, I can erase a camera's data card, but this is going to be in my mind for a long, long time."

"Where are we with things at this point?" Weber asked.

"We're still measuring and taking pictures, Jimmy. But it looks like it happened about like Sonny said. Duncan got careless with the bull and it stuck him, and he managed to get over there by the hog pens and some way or another got in there."

"What was it? Twenty, thirty yards? That's a long way to go when you're bleeding out."

"It is," Dolan agreed. "But Duncan was a tough old bird. If anybody could do it, he could. You know about the time he shot himself, don't you?"

"Shot himself? No, I never heard anything about that."

"I guess that was probably back when you were away in the Army. Duncan was turkey hunting and he stepped over a log and right on top of a rattlesnake. I don't know who was more scared, him or the snake. It didn't bite him, it just went slithering off in one direction while Duncan was jumping in the other. But somehow while he was doing that he dropped his shotgun and it went off. About half the charge caught him in the shoulder. He was hunting alone, so he stuck a bandanna in the hole, wrapped his shirt around it as tight as he could, and drove all the way into town to get to a doctor."

"Damn. That's a hell of a story."

12

"Like I said, he was a tough one," Dolan said.

Watching as the paramedics eased Duncan's mangled remains into a plastic body bag and then onto a stretcher, Weber couldn't help but wonder if fate had been all that kind to the old farmer by letting him survive his hunting accident so long ago, only to die this way.

Nick Russell

Chapter 3

It took hours to process the scene and interview everybody on the property. No one had actually witnessed what had happened to Duncan. His wife said she was still asleep when he got up and left the house early in the morning, as was his habit. She had been awakened by the sound of Sonny coming into the house screaming and making all kind of noise. She had gone downstairs and he was trying to get the telephone to work, but the lines were apparently down again, which happened quite often. Not knowing what had happened, she ordered him out of the house. Roseanne said the next thing she heard was the sound of gunshots and when she looked out the window Sonny was shooting the hogs. She said that she thought her adult stepson had gone on a rampage and locked herself in her bedroom, fearing he would come after her next.

"Did you have any reason to believe he would do something like that?" Weber had asked her.

"He drinks a lot. Who knows what somebody's going to do when they're like that?"

"But had there ever been any kind of violence? Any threats of any kind made?"

"No, nothing like that. But Sonny and George argued a lot."

"What did they argue about?"

"What do you think? Sonny's drinking and him not pulling his weight around here."

"You said arguing. Did it ever get physical?"

"No, but it was just a matter of time," she said.

"Why do you say that?"

"Because he's a drunk. In your line of work, surely you know how drunks are. You can't trust them."

"Roseanne, do you think Sonny had anything to do with his father's death?"

The woman stiffened slightly and said, "I would prefer you call me Mrs. Duncan, Sheriff. We are not on a first name basis."

Chastised, Weber said. "Well okay, then. *Mrs. Duncan*, do you think Sonny had anything to do with his father's death?"

"Of course he did. I said that before. It's because of him that my George is dead!"

"When you say because of him, do you think he did something to your husband?"

"What do you mean?"

"Do you think Sonny physically harmed his father?"

She looked at him and her eyes narrowed. "Are you asking me if I think Sonny killed George?"

"Yes, ma'am. You said Duncan was dead because of him."

"Oh, no," she said shaking her head. "No, I didn't mean that. I meant George is dead because Sonny is so lazy. If he had been out there helping like he was supposed to, this wouldn't have happened. But instead he was still in bed, like he is every morning."

"Okay, I understand now. But I'm kind of confused. First you said it was only a matter of time before something *did* happen because of Sonny's drinking, but yet you're sure he didn't have anything to do with what happened this morning."

Roseanne shook her head again. "No, that's not what I meant. I think you misunderstood me. I meant it was only a matter of time before George had enough and knocked him on his rear end. If you ask me, he should have done that a long time ago. Spare the rod and spoil the child, the Good Book says in Proverbs 13:24. Sonny never had any discipline growing up. That's why he turned out the way he did. I blame Eleanor for much of that."

"Eleanor? Duncan's first wife?"

"Yes, Sheriff. I know it's not right to speak unkindly of the dead, but she coddled Sonny from the day he was born. She was always making excuses for him. And that's why he grew up to be a spoiled, lazy, good for nothing drunk."

Listening to her, Weber was reminded of another Bible verse about not judging others lest you yourself be judged, but he kept the thought to himself. Instead he asked, "When did you find out what happened to Duncan?"

"Please don't call him that. His name was George. George Duncan."

"I'm sorry," Weber replied. "To be honest with you I didn't even know his first name was George. Everybody has always just called him Duncan for as long as I can remember."

"I know, and I hated it. It just sounds so... I don't know, redneck, maybe?"

That line about judging others came to mind again, but Weber didn't say anything.

"After the shooting stopped, I kept calling George's name," Roseanne said, recalling the events of the morning. "Finally I went to the door and opened it enough that I could peek outside. That's when I saw something covered up out there by the hog pens. Mrs. Bowers was talking to Sonny and I called out and asked her what was going on. That's when she came to the door and told me..." Rosanne's voice broke and she buried her face in her hands as she sobbed. After a moment she looked up again and wailed, "she told me that my George was gone!"

She began crying again and Weber sat next to her for a while, wishing there was some way to comfort the woman, but knowing there was nothing he could do to ease her grief.

When he left Jordan with Roseanne and went back outside, Chad was talking to a short heavyset woman and introduced her as Mona Bowers.

"How is Mrs. Duncan doing?" she asked, looking toward the house with concern in her eyes.

"About as well as can be expected under the circumstances," Weber told her.

"I've been talking to Mrs. Bowers here about what happened this morning," Chad said. "Ma'am, would you mind telling Sheriff Weber what you told me?"

"There's not much to tell, really," she said shrugging her shoulders. "I mean, I didn't see a whole lot. Leonard, that's my husband, left early in the refrigerated truck to make deliveries in Springerville, then he was going up to St. John's, making the loop over to Show Low, and back here. I offered to get out of bed and make him breakfast, but he said no, he'd grab something at McDonald's in Springerville. He kissed me and I rolled over and went back to sleep. I woke up a little later when I heard someone yelling and then gunshots. I looked outside and Sonny was standing by one of the hog pens shooting into it. At first I thought a coyote or maybe one of those gray wolves had gotten into the hogs, but then Carl came pounding on my door and said that Duncan was dead."

"What happened then?"

"I pulled on some clothes and ran outside. By then Sonny's gun was empty, but he was still pulling the trigger. I don't think he even realized he had run out of bullets. Until then I hadn't even seen poor Duncan. I mean, I guess I saw the blue tarp, but I didn't realize what was under it until he told me."

The woman was crying as she told her story and Weber gave her a moment to compose herself. "He was such a nice man, Sheriff. Why did something like this have to happen to him? He had so much heartbreak in his life, what with losing Eleanor and all. I had hoped things would be better for him once he married Mrs. Duncan. But..." She shook her head and didn't finish.

"When did you first see Mrs. Duncan this morning?"

"When I was out there talking to Sonny. She opened the door and asked what had happened. I had to tell her. I hated it, but I didn't want her coming out here and seeing it."

More than once Weber had been the one to deliver terrible news to surviving family members before and knew how hard it was.

"I imagine it must have hit her pretty hard."

"She cried a lot, that's for sure. I tried to put my arm around her and comfort her, but you don't do that with Mrs. Duncan."

"What you mean by that?"

"Oh, don't get me wrong, Sheriff. I don't mean to imply anything bad about her. She's just... different, I guess."

"What do you mean by different?"

"What's the word I'm looking for? Not stuck up necessarily, although that's what Leonard says about her. But... aloof. That's it. Aloof. There's a distance between her and people like us, and she makes sure to keep that distance. I tried to put my arm around her, just so she would know someone was there for her. But she kind of pushed me away and stood up with her back to me and just thanked me for telling her, and that I could go. I told her I was happy to stay with her, so she wouldn't be alone. But she just said that wasn't necessary, She said she was never alone, God was always by her side. I could tell she didn't want me there, so I left."

"Where was Sonny while this was going on?"

"He was over there next to his father, down on his knees crying."

Weber had left Deputy Tommy Frost at the farm's gate a quarter mile away to keep out the morbid curious who always seemed to show up when something bad had happened. His portable radio crackled to life. "Sheriff, I've got a man named Leonard Bowers here. He says he lives there at the farm."

"Send him in."

"10-4."

A couple of minutes later a large cargo truck with a refrigeration unit mounted on the front of the box pulled to a stop and a man jumped out. He ran to his wife and she met him halfway, throwing her arms around him and sobbing into his chest.

"What the hell happened here?" he demanded.

"Mr. Bowers, I'm Sheriff Weber."

"Yeah, I know who you are. What's going on?"

"I'm afraid there's been an accident, sir. Duncan's been killed."

"An accident? How? What?" He looked around, then back at the sheriff. "An accident on the highway?"

"No, sir. We're not exactly sure what took place yet, but it looks like his bull gored him."

"Montezuma?"

"Sir?"

"Montezuma. That's what he called the bull. Oh Lord, I told him to stay away from that thing. I don't know why he bought it in the first place. I kept telling him not to go in there messing with it, that it was going to hurt him someday. But Duncan would just laugh and say something about he wasn't afraid of Montezuma's revenge."

"You say he would mess with the bull? What exactly do you mean?"

The man pushed the bill of his ball cap back and shook his head. "Duncan treated that damn bull like it was a pet. He'd go out there every morning and feed it and give it apples and talk to it like you would a dog or a horse or something. And that bull would snort and bellow and lower its head like he was going to charge. Duncan thought that was funny as hell. He'd pull out his big red handkerchief and wave it at Montezuma like he was daring him to do something. I kept telling him he was playing with fire, but he just wouldn't listen."

There were tears in Leonard's eyes. "I wish I would have been here. Maybe I could've..."

"There's nothing to be gained by going down that road," Weber told him. "And I'm afraid there's more. And it's not going to be pretty to tell, or for you to listen to."

Chapter 4

While his wife was short and plump, Leonard Bowers was close to six feet tall and broad shouldered. His body was hardened from a life of working on a farm, but he started to shake and almost collapsed when Weber told him what the hogs had done to his employer.

"Oh, my God. No!"

Chad took his arm to steady him as Leonard cried, moaning Duncan's name. It was obvious to see that he was close to the dead man, and the loss was hitting him hard. It was several minutes before he could talk again.

"Where's Sonny?"

"I tried to send him back to his trailer, but he said he needed to feed the hogs first," Weber said.

"Please tell me he's not the one that found his father."

"I'm afraid so."

"No," Leonard moaned, shaking his head. "That poor kid."

Mona put her arms around her husband, holding him while he sobbed. He managed to get control of himself to ask " What about Mrs. Duncan? Is she okay?"

"She's okay, honey," his wife said. "I'm the one that had to tell her what happened. She took it as well as could be expected."

"This has to be a bad dream or something."

"I wish it was," Weber told him. "Listen, folks, instead of standing out here, do you mind if we go over to your to house and talk?"

"Sure, no problem," Mona said.

"I need to check on Mrs. Duncan first," Leonard said.

"She's okay, I've got somebody in there with her," Weber assured him.

"I tried to stay with her," Mona added. "But you know how she is, Leonard. She just told me I could go after I gave her the news."

He looked at the house and shook his head, then led Weber and Chad to his mobile home. Once inside, Mona made coffee for everybody, and Weber nodded gratefully when she set a thick mug in front of him.

"I have to ask you a few questions," Weber told the couple. "And I really need you to be open and honest with me when you answer, okay?"

"Sure," Leonard said. "We don't have anything to hide."

"No, I didn't mean it that way," Weber said holding up his hand. "This is about how Duncan and Sonny got along."

"What do you mean?"

"Well, according to Mrs. Duncan, there was quite a bit of friction between the two of them."

"Between Duncan and Sonny?"

"Yes."

"Oh, they butted heads now and then. What father and son don't? I know my two boys and I did, but it all worked out. One of them is in the Air Force and making a career out of it, and the other is a long-haul trucker."

"Did they ever argue about Sonny not helping out more around here?"

"Not that I ever heard. Sonny grew up working hogs and he never made any secret of the fact that he'd rather be doing just about anything else in the world. But he pulled his weight. He's not afraid of hard work, no question about that."

"So that's all it was between Duncan and Sonny? Just typical father-son stuff?"

"Yeah, I'd say so," Leonard said, looking at his wife. "Don't you think so, honey?"

Mona nodded her head, then stopped and thought for a moment and said, "Well, it was like that until Duncan got remarried. I think maybe things changed after that."

Before Weber could say anything his radio crackled again and Tommy said, "Sheriff, there's a Reverend Jacobson here to see Mrs. Duncan."

"Hold on a minute," Weber replied, than keyed his radio again and asked, "Jordan, is Mrs. Duncan up to company?"

There was a pause, then Jordan replied, "10-4, Sheriff, she wants to see him."

"Okay, send him in," Weber told Tommy over the radio, then asked Chad to meet the new arrival and brief him before taking him to the house.

With that done, he turned back to Mona. "You said things changed after Duncan got remarried? How did they change?"

"Oh, it's probably nothing."

"Maybe so, but I'd like to know, if you don't mind."

She sighed. "Listen, Sheriff I'm probably making a mountain out of a mole hill. It just seemed like after Mrs. Duncan got here, things between Sonny and Duncan weren't the same."

"How so?"

"Well, for instance, Sonny moving back into the trailer. He lived there when he was married to Claudia, but after she left he moved back into the house with his dad. Duncan said he understood young newlyweds wanting their own place and some privacy, but after she was gone he said he was glad to have Sonny back in the house to keep him company. But the new Mrs. Duncan wasn't here more than a week before he had moved back into the trailer."

"We just figured older newlyweds needed their privacy, too," Leonard said. "But I think maybe Sonny felt like he'd been displaced or something, I don't know."

"Aside from Sonny moving back into the trailer, was there anything else?"

"Well now, it's not our place to be talking behind anybody's back," Leonard said.

"I understand that," Weber told him, "but you have to understand, Duncan didn't just die in his sleep. When something this unusual happens, we have to cover all the bases."

"Now you wait just a minute, Sheriff," Leonard said sternly. "If you're thinking Sonny had anything to do with his father's death, you need to think again. Like I said, they butted heads once in a while like any father and son do, but that boy loved his daddy and he would never do anything to hurt him. No sir, you're way off base there! Mona and me, we've lived here close to nineteen years. We were here when Eleanor was still alive, and we watched Sonny grow up. There is no way that boy would ever lay a finger on his daddy. I told you, that old bull was dangerous. I told Duncan that

23

more than once, and so did Sonny. I wasn't here, so I didn't see what happened, but I know this was an accident. A terrible accident, but that's all it was."

"I believe you," Weber assured him. "Like I said, this thing is different from most accidents. We just need to make sure we dot every i and cross every t. That's all."

"I don't mean to step out of line with you," Leonard said. "But living this close and working together every day, we've always been kind of like family out here. Least we were before Mrs. Duncan showed up and things changed. I know Sonny, and I knew Duncan. He was probably my best friend in the world, aside from Mona, here. He loved his boy, and Sonny loved him right back."

"You're not out of line at all," Weber told him. "And I understand what you're saying. This thing here is just tragic all the way around. But let me ask you this, if I can. You said things changed after Duncan's new wife arrived. How did they change?"

Mona refilled her husband's coffee cup, and when she turned to Weber he shook his head and held his hand over the top of his to indicate he didn't need any more.

"Like Leonard said, we were all kind of family. Duncan and Sonny, and us, Carl, and the Barelas. Sometimes we would all eat together up at the big house, or we'd barbecue something together and throw horseshoes, or bring out the trap thrower and shoot clay pigeons. Or Duncan would stop by of an evening and have a cup of coffee and shoot the breeze. But after he remarried, that ended real quick. I told you before, she's kind of aloof. She kept to herself and Duncan didn't socialize with us as much. Not that he was rude or anything, but he was focusing his time on her, which is to be understood. But it was just different."

"You mentioned the Barelas. How well did you know them?"

"They were just part of the family, too. Wait, did she say something about them?"

"No, Mrs. Duncan didn't," Weber replied. "But Sonny said there was a problem that caused them to leave."

Mona's lips tightened in a frown and she said, "What happened with them was just wrong. Totally wrong, and that's the one bad thing I will say about Duncan. He should have put a stop to that right then and there."

"Put a stop to what?" Weber asked.

"Carmen is a very pretty lady," Mona replied. "And she would cook for Duncan and clean house, and he'd pay her for it. But that's as far as it ever went. But just a few days after Mrs. Duncan moved in, Carmen came to me crying and said that Mrs. Duncan had accused her of doing things with Duncan."

"Things?"

"You know what I'm talking about, Sheriff. That was absolutely wrong, Duncan would never do something like that, and neither would Carmen! But the next thing we knew, they were loading their pickup up and said they were moving."

"We tried to talk them out of it," Leonard added. "I even went and talked to Duncan myself. Like I said, I considered him and me to be friends. I could tell he was hurt by all of it, and he tried to smooth the waters over and make things better. But that wife of his, she wasn't having any of it. She told him if those greasers stayed, she was gone. That's a hell of a thing for anybody to say, and she said it right in front of them."

"Do you know where they went when they left here?"

"I think they had some kinfolk up around Holbrook," Leonard said. "José said they were going to stay with them while he looked for work up there."

"Have you heard anything from them since they left?"

He shook his head. "No, not a word. I hated to see them go. We really did consider them part of the family. José was a hard worker and Carmen was just as nice as could be."

"One more thing. Mrs. Duncan said there had been some problems with Sonny's drinking. That he and his dad had argued about that."

Leonard shook his head. "No, Sheriff, not that I ever knew of. The man enjoys a few beers now and then, but so what? I'll have a drink myself at the end of a long day. Duncan, too. But Mrs. Duncan, she's a real churchgoing type. Some might even say she's a fanatic about things. She put a stop to Duncan drinking the first time she saw him open a beer. Said that was the devil's own water and it was going to drown him and float him right to hell. She told him she wasn't going to live with no drunkard and he could either pour that out on the ground right there, or else she was gonna go inside and start packing. So that's what he did, and I don't think he took a drop after that."

"So you've never seen Sonny drunk?"

"No, I wouldn't say that. Sure, I've seen him when he had a snootful a time or two. But he's not a drunk, like Mrs. Duncan says, and he's never gotten out of hand in any way."

"You've heard her call him a drunk?"

"Trust me, *everybody* has heard her call him that," Mona said. "That and worse."

"Worse? Like what?"

"She was always saying he was lazy and worthless, things like that. It seemed like she didn't like Sonny from the first time she laid eyes on him."

"She said something this morning about if Sonny hadn't still been in bed sleeping off a drunk, he would have been up to help his father and this wouldn't have happened. What do you think about that?"

"That's bullshit," Leonard said, shaking his head. "Pardon my French, but that's what it is. Yeah, I don't doubt Sonny was still in bed when Duncan went out there. He was up before the crack of dawn every day of his life that I knew him. I can't tell you how many times I'd get up at daybreak and he would be out there drinking his cup of coffee and looking at the sunrise. He always said it was his favorite time of day, when the world was all peaceful. But we all get up pretty early. That's life on a farm. Three times a week I roll out of here before 5 AM to make my delivery runs to the stores and restaurants. And there's never been a time I haven't seen Duncan before I left." He stopped and wrinkled his brow in thought for a moment, then said, "Not until this morning."

"What do you mean by that?"

"I just realized, I didn't see Duncan this morning. It never entered my mind until just now."

"When was the last time you did see him?"

"Last night when we loaded the truck for today's deliveries." Leonard stared off into space for a moment, then looked at Weber with an expression of horror on his face. "My God, Sheriff, do you think he was laying out there, hurt already, and I drove right by and never saw him?"

"Oh, honey," Mona said putting her hand on her husband's arm. "No. Don't even start thinking like that. Don't."

But Weber could tell the man was already blaming himself for what happened to his friend and employer.

"Your wife's right, Leonard. This isn't anything you could have prevented or changed. Who knows why you didn't see Duncan? It could have been the one morning he decided to sleep in."

Leonard shook his head. "Duncan never slept in."

"Okay, so maybe he went inside and poured an extra cup of coffee. Who knows? He may have walked around the corner out of sight to relieve himself. Just because you didn't see him this morning doesn't mean what you think. Try to put that out of your mind, okay?"

He could tell the man wasn't accepting what he was telling him, but Weber didn't know what else to say. They heard the sound of a truck pulling up and Weber looked out the window to see Sonny Duncan and Carl getting out of the cab of a battered gray flatbed Ford. He drained the last of his coffee and stood up and said, "Thank you for the coffee Mrs. Bowers. And thank you both for your time. I know you were close to Duncan, and I'm sorry for your loss."

When he went out the door Leonard had his face buried in his hands sobbing, while his wife knelt next to his chair, her arms wrapped around him, trying to ease his pain.

Chapter 5

"How you holding up, Sonny?"

The man's eyes were red, and he looked worn out from a combination of hard work and grief.

"I feel dead inside," he replied.

"I understand."

"How can you understand what I saw out there this morning, Sheriff? How can anybody understand that? I don't even understand it myself."

"You're right," Weber admitted. "All I can say is, I'm sorry you had to go through that. Sorry anybody would ever have to go through what you did."

"Where is he? I mean, where did they take him?"

"He's going to be transported to Tucson for an autopsy. It may take a few days to get the results of that."

"What good is an autopsy going to do? You saw him. There wasn't much left to autopsy, was there?"

"They'll do the best they can."

"I just hope...," Sonny's voice broke and he had to turn away for a moment. When he turned back his eyes were wet. "I just hope if they can find anything out, it will be that he was already so far gone that by the time he got into the hog pen he didn't know what was happening to him."

"Me, too."

"When I was growing up, he used to always tell me to be careful around the hogs. Said they'd eat me up in a minute if they had a chance. Said to them, I was just food. That used to scare the hell out of me. Course, when I was older and started working with them, I wasn't scared anymore. But I never liked 'em, and I never trusted 'em. My dad used to always say that someday this was all going to be mine, and I'd tell him I didn't want no part of it. Do you know what it's like to carry the smell of hogs around with you everywhere you go, Sheriff? To try asking a girl for a date and see her wrinkling her nose and trying to make sure she stays upwind of you while she just laughs in your face and says no? What it's like to have other kids not want to hang out with you because no matter how many baths you take and how clean your clothes are, you still stink? My dad always said that was the smell of money, but it ain't, is it?"

"Well, Duncan made a pretty good living, as far as I know."

"Yeah, he made a lot of money. Enough that we could have lived in town and paid someone else to run this place. Leonard knows as much about it as my dad did. Him and Mona could have stayed here and ran things while we lived in town. I can't tell you how many times I begged him to do that, but no, my old man wasn't having any of it. He loved this stinking place. But I'll tell you what. Not me. Once this is all said and done, I'd just as soon shoot every one of those damn hogs and leave them all lay there and rot, and burn the place to the ground!"

"That I *can* understand," Weber told him. "I grew up on a little ranch outside of Big Lake, and once my parents were gone I couldn't wait to sell off the cattle and be done with it. It's a hard life under the best of circumstances."

"Yeah, it is," Sonny replied. "But at least cows don't smell half as bad as hogs do."

Weber saw Jordan coming out of the house and said to Sonny, "Why don't you go get cleaned up and try to get some rest. We're about wrapped up here."

"I'm dog tired, but I don't know if I'll ever sleep again," Sonny replied. "I think every time I close my eyes I'm going to see my dad."

"I wish I could tell you it's all going to be better someday, I really do. But we both know that's not true. Time passes and I guess you just learn to cope with things, one way or another."

"My dad always said you were a good man, Sheriff. Thanks for being here and doing what you have to."

Weber watched his back as Sonny walked away and knew the man was carrying the weight of the whole world on his shoulders.

Jordan joined him and said, "Man, I'm glad that preacher got here when he did. That is a weird lady."

"What do you mean?" Weber asked.

"I don't know, but if I was in her place and my husband got killed like that, I think I'd fall apart. But she's just... I don't know the word for it. Cold, maybe? I tried to talk to her, and she pretty much ignored me. So I sat there in a chair and she was reading her Bible for most of the time, except when you were in there talking to her. Then when that preacher came in, she changed completely."

"What do you mean by that?"

"Like I said, she didn't have two words to say to me and was just sitting there with her Bible. But as soon as he walked in the door she seemed to fall apart. I don't know, I guess maybe she was holding it in all along."

"I learned a long time ago you can never understand where someone else is coming from," Weber told him. "I've seen big strong men cry like a baby, and I've seen some of the weakest people I knew handle things you couldn't imagine. Hopefully her minister can give her some comfort."

Chad had been talking to Carl, and after he was finished he came over to Weber and Jordan.

"Did you get anything new out of him?"

Chad shook his head. "Basically the same story we heard from Sonny. They came out to start feeding the hogs and when they got to the pen they saw Duncan in there and pulled him out. He said they were both screaming, and after Sonny went in the house and found out the phone wasn't working he told him to get in the truck and get help as fast as he could. So that's what he did. I asked him why he drove all the way into town to the Sheriff's Office instead of stopping at the first place with a telephone, but he said he never thought of it. Not that it would have made much difference."

Weber pushed his hat back and looked around. Dolan and Buz were putting away their equipment, and then they approached.

"I don't know how people can live out here like this," Dolan said. "Every time I drove by this place I had to hold my breath because it smells so bad."

"I hear you," Buz agreed. "I don't think I'll ever get the smell out of my nose. There ain't nothing in the world smells worse than a hog farm."

"With a nose as big as yours, you might want to make sure one of those pigs didn't crawl up in there and hide," Dolan said. Everybody was used to how the two old friends badgered each other from time to time. The two deputies worked well together and were the best crime scene investigators the small department

31

had. Their friendship had been tested when young Gina Reed announced she was pregnant with Billy Carlton's child, resulting in a public fistfight between the two deputies that disrupted the breakfast crowd at the ButterCup Café. But once the young lovers were married, the birth of their grandson had solidified their friendship even further.

"So it looks to me like this is just a terrible accident," Weber said. "What do you guys think?"

"I don't see it being anything else," Dolan replied. "I think we need to have necropsies done on those pigs Sonny shot, though seeing all the blood on their snouts and heads pretty much tells me they're the ones that got to Duncan. What do you think, Buz?"

"I think I'm never going to eat bacon or pork chops again, that's what I think."

"Where can we even get a necropsy done?"

"Down in Tucson. I'll radio Mary and tell her to get it set up," Dolan said. "Chuck Fields has a daughter who lives down there. If we pay for the fuel he'll haul them down and spend the night with her."

Fields was one of the Citizen Volunteers who assisted the Sheriff's Department with everything from traffic control at accidents to checking summer cabins left vacant during the off season.

"Sounds good to me," Weber said. "Let's wrap this up. Buz, while Dolan is calling Mary, why don't you go over there to Sonny's mobile home and see if we can borrow a stock trailer or something and get these pigs loaded into it? Chad, you and Jordan might as well head on out, and tell Tommy to take off, too. I'm going to go check in with Mrs. Duncan one last time and give her an update on what's happening."

He found the bereaved widow sitting on the couch talking with her minister, who shook Weber's hand and identified himself as Reverend Patrick Jacobson, from the New Light Christian Church in Springerville. Jacobson was a small man with a noticeable bald spot that he tried to cover with a comb over, pale skin, and a damp handshake. Weber couldn't help noticing his heavy cologne. He wondered if the preacher always wore that much, or if he had put on extra in preparation for his trip to the hog farm.

"I'm sorry we had to meet under such circumstances," Weber said to him.

"Yes. God is certainly testing us today."

"I'm glad you came along when you did. Mrs. Duncan really needs some support right now."

"She has God. That's all anyone ever really needs, Sheriff."

"I suppose so," Weber said. "But having someone like you here for her helps, too."

He knelt down in front of Roseanne and said, "Ma'am, we're about to wrap things up here. Is there anything we can do for you before we go?"

She kept her eyes closed for a long moment, then opened them and said, "Yes. You can tell Sonny to leave. I don't want him here."

"I'm sorry, I can't do that. Not at this time," Weber replied.

"Why not? With my husband dead, this place is mine now. And I don't want him here. Not for one minute longer!"

"Mrs. Duncan, I'm not an attorney and I don't know what all the legalities are with something like this. But I can't just order the man to leave like that. And he just lost his father. It wouldn't be right."

"It wouldn't be right? It's not right that my husband is dead because that worthless son of his wasn't out doing his job! That's what's not right. I want him gone, and I want him gone right this instant. I won't stand for him being on this property one minute longer. I forbid it!"

Weber looked to the minister for some sort of support, but Jacobson just looked away.

"I'm sorry, there's nothing I can do about that. If you want to go to court and get some kind of an order from a judge evicting him, I'll send a deputy back to enforce it. But like I said, I'm not an attorney and I don't have the authority to just throw someone out because you don't like them being here."

"Get out of my house! Get out of my house and off my property," Roseanne said, pointing at the door. "If you're not going to do what I tell you to do, then you can just get yourself out of here right now."

Weber stood up and nodded his head. "Yes, ma'am. As soon as we get those hogs Sonny shot loaded into a trailer, we'll be gone."

"Why are you taking the hogs?"

"We need to have necropsies done on them. That's like an autopsy, except for animals."

"I know what a necropsy is, Sheriff. I have two college degrees. I'm not like the other women around here. I want some kind of a receipt for those hogs."

"A receipt, ma'am?"

"Yes, a receipt. They're worth money, aren't they? If they were butchered we could sell them. But we can't very well do that if you take them off for these necropsies you are talking about."

Weber dropped his jaw in horror.

"Mrs. Duncan, you can't butcher those hogs. My God, after what they did? Not to mention the fact that they've been lying out there for hours."

"Then I'm sure there must be some kind of insurance that Mr. Duncan had on them for a loss. I'll need a receipt to show what happened to them."

"I'm not sure this can be written up as a loss. Not when Sonny shot them."

"Whatever," she said, waving her hand at him dismissively. "Just get done and get gone. The next time I see you or any of your men out here, you'd better be bringing an eviction notice for Sonny."

Chapter 6

"Pee-ew! You guys stink," Mary Caitlin, Weber's administrative assistant, said when he and the deputies returned to the Sheriff's Office.

"Really? I hadn't noticed," Weber said sarcastically.

"How bad was it?"

"Imagine the worst you think it could possibly be, then multiply that by a hundred times," Dolan said.

"Make that a thousand," Buz added.

"How is Sonny doing?"

"He's holding up better than I would if I had been in his place," Weber told her.

Mary shook her head sadly. "Poor Sonny. First to lose his mama when he was still not much more than a boy, and now this. It makes me sad."

"You know Sonny?"

Weber wasn't sure why he was surprised by that. Mary was a walking, talking encyclopedia of all things Big Lake. She knew everybody in town. Not just by name, but also their family history and tidbits of useful personal information. Mary wasn't a gossip by any means, but Weber, who had been born and raised there, was amazed that she could always tell him who was married to who, which marriages were on the rocks, what bride had walked down the aisle a short six or seven months before giving birth, who had been in trouble with the law in the past, and who was struggling to get by in the town's often shaky economy.

"Of course I know him. I know him, and I knew Duncan and Eleanor both."

"How about Leonard and Mona Bowers? Or José Barela and his wife?"

"Leonard went to work for Duncan years ago. His father used to drive a semi and he was disappointed that Leonard would rather raise pigs than go on the road. But I think he saw his mother spending too many nights alone while he was growing up, and he didn't want that for his family. Mona used to be Mona Bancroft before they got married. She grew up over around Payson somewhere. They're good people. Raised two boys who anybody would be proud to call their own."

"And the Barela's?"

Mary nodded her head. "José's family is from up around Holbrook. I don't know him all that well. I haven't seen Carmen for a while, come to think of it. She used to do her shopping at the Thriftway, and she'd come around selling her homemade tamales, but she hasn't been around lately."

"That's because they're gone," Weber said, drawing a look of surprise from Mary. It wasn't often that anybody knew something about the locals that she didn't.

"When did that happen?"

"I guess not too long after Duncan got remarried. His new wife didn't much care for them and there were some accusations made about Carmen and Duncan."

"Accusations? What kind of accusations?"

"From what I gather, the new Mrs. Duncan suspected that the two of them had some kind of physical relationship."

"Are you kidding me? There's no way anything like that happened," Mary said indignantly. "Duncan may have smelled of pigs everywhere he went, but the man was a perfect gentleman all the time. There's no way he would trifle with a married woman."

"Yeah, that's what the Bowers said, too. But I guess the new wife wasn't gonna let it go. I think Mona said they were staying with family in Holbrook while he looked for some kind of work up there."

"And Duncan let them go, just like that?"

"Apparently so. Leonard said Duncan tried to talk José out of it, but it didn't do any good."

Mary shook her head in disbelief. "Wow. That woman must have really changed him. The Duncan I knew would never have stood still for that."

"What do you know about the new wife, Rosanne?"

"Nothing at all, really. Someone said he met her on some kind of online dating service or something like that, but I doubt it. I don't see Duncan as being the kind of fellow to go looking for a wife that way. In fact, I would've never expected him to get remarried at all. He and Eleanor were totally devoted to each other. I'm not judging him, don't get me wrong, Jimmy, but I just assumed that he was kind of like swans and eagles that mate for life."

"I don't know," Weber said shrugging his shoulders. "I guess if a man gets lonely enough he goes looking. Do you know how they got together?"

"No," Mary said shaking her head. "All I know is she's not from around here. And apparently she does her shopping in Springerville or Eagar, because I've never seen her in town that I know of. What did you think of her?"

"To be honest, not much," Weber said.

"What do you mean?"

"Mona Bowers said she was aloof, and if anything, I think that's an understatement. I made the mistake of calling her by her first name and she very quickly told me to refer to her as *Mrs. Duncan*."

"I noticed that Leonard and his wife both called her that, too, never Rosanne," Chad said. "I think the only one that called her by her name was Sonny, and it's obvious they don't get along very well at all."

"No, they don't," Weber said. "In fact, when I went up to the house to tell her we were getting ready to wrap things up, she wanted me to throw Sonny off the place right then. Said she didn't want him there."

"You're kidding me? She expects him to just leave because Duncan's dead? It's the only home he's ever known!"

"Yeah, and she was pretty ticked off because I wouldn't do it. Although, to tell you the truth, I don't think Sonny wants to be there anyhow. From talking to him and what the Bowers couple said, he never wanted to live out there. Sonny told me he asked his dad many times if they could move to town, but Duncan wouldn't consider it."

"Well, you know how these old-timers are. They love their land and their way of life," Chad said.

Weber knew how true that was. He had watched his own parents hang on to the family ranch that had been passed down through the years, sometimes barely able to make enough money to buy feed and pay the taxes, sinking further into debt all the time but stubbornly refusing to give up.

"Is there any reason to believe this was anything but a terrible accident?"

"No," Weber said, shaking his head. "It's just one of those things that happen sometimes."

"Well, you need to touch base with Paul over at the newspaper. He heard the radio traffic on his scanner and knew something was up, and then someone at the medical clinic called him and said Duncan's body had been brought in."

Weber wondered why his boyhood friend even continued to run his newspaper, as quickly as word-of-mouth spread through the small town.

"Yeah, I'll walk across the street and visit with him for a minute. Who's on duty now?"

"Coop and Dan just went on," Mary said.

"Okay, the rest of you guys go home and get cleaned up and get some rest," Weber told his deputies. "We can do reports and stuff tomorrow."

"Yeah, I need to go home and take a long hot shower," Dolan said. "But as for getting any rest, after what we saw out there today, I'm afraid to close my eyes."

~***~

Paul Lewis was sitting behind his desk eating a Subway sandwich when Weber walked in.

"Jesus, Jimmy, I don't mean to be rude, but your personal hygiene has taken a nosedive or something."

"If you spent the day where I did, you wouldn't smell too pretty, either."

Paul pushed his sandwich aside to join the piles of press releases, notes, and other paperwork that always seemed to live on top of his desk. "Man, I can't eat this with you sitting there stinking like that."

"That's got to be a first," Weber told his portly friend. "I always figured we would have to make sure your funeral was catered so you could reach out of the coffin and grab something to munch on while the preacher was doing his thing."

"Now that's hurtful right there. Those words cut me right to the bone. And you know I've got some pretty deep bones, Jimmy."

In spite of all he had seen that day, Weber couldn't help but chuckle.

"Seriously, you reek," the newspaperman said. "I don't know how you guys could have stayed out there that long. Whenever I drive by that place I have to hold my breath and floor it until I get past."

"Dolan said the same thing today," Weber said. "I'm surprised we don't have more accidents out that direction from drivers blacking out due to lack of oxygen."

"So, what can you tell me? And please," Paul said holding up his hand, "spare me the gory details. I really would like to finish that sandwich someday."

Weber gave him a rundown of what had happened at the hog farm, trying to keep from getting too graphic, but when he was done the newspaperman wrapped up what was left of his sandwich and deposited it in the trashcan next to his desk. "Okay, I guess today is as good a day as any to start my diet."

"Do you really think dieting is going to help, Paul?"

"What? You don't think I can lose weight? I'll have you know I've probably lost 500 pounds in my life. Of course, most of it came right back because my body and my fat have become really good friends and they missed each other."

Weber laughed and stood up. "I'm going to go home and spend the next three weeks standing under the shower."

Paul waved his hand in front of his nose and said, "Please, don't let me stop you. You'd be doing the public a great service if you did that."

Chapter 7

News of Duncan's death had spread quickly, and when Weber got to the office the next morning Mary handed him a stack of telephone messages and said, "Five TV stations and four newspapers want a statement on what happened out at the hog farm."

"Damned jackals," Weber said. "Always scavenging around for a story, and the more sensational it is, the better they like it."

"They're just giving the public what it wants," Mary replied, following him into his private office and setting a cup of coffee on his desk. "And you've got to admit, it's not every day somebody gets devoured by hogs. There's no way they're not going to pick up on that story. In fact, your buddy Lisa Burnham has already come and gone."

"That doesn't surprise me," Weber said. The pretty blonde anchorwoman from News Channel Six in Phoenix was a ball buster who had been a thorn in Weber's side for a long time. But they had made peace, and while he would never call her a friend, they had developed a working relationship that had proven mutually beneficial in the past. "Please tell me they're not going to go out and bother Duncan's family."

"Actually, two different new stations sent vans up to cover the story. Dan Wright is out at the farm now to make sure things don't get out of hand. I told him they can shoot footage from the road, but not to let anybody set foot on the property."

"I guess I need to prepare some kind of a statement, don't I?"

"No, you don't. I already have," Mary told him, pulling a sheet of paper out of a folder in her hand. "I just need you to look it over."

"What would I do without you?"

"I don't know, Jimmy. What would you do?"

"I don't even want to think about it," he said. Mary, the wife of Big Lake's former sheriff and Weber's mentor, had stayed on the job after her husband Pete retired to devote his time to fly tying and fishing for trophy trout in the deep, cold waters of the lake that had given the small mountain town its name. But she was much more than an employee; Mary and Pete were like a loving aunt and uncle, and had been there for Weber and his younger sister when their parents were killed in an automobile accident years ago.

He read through the press release and nodded his head. "Looks good. Go ahead and send it out. Anything else I need to know about?"

"Chet's called a couple of times. He's worried about what a story like this is going to do to the town's reputation."

"If Chet didn't wake up in the morning worried or aggravated about something, he wouldn't know what to do with himself."

"That's true. I don't suppose you want to call him back?"

"No, I don't."

"Okay then, how do you feel about getting together with Edith Carmichael? She wants you to come to the Women's Garden Club luncheon next week to talk about a fundraiser. They're trying to come up with enough money to install planters full of flowers to put along the sidewalk on Main Street."

"Didn't they try that a year or so ago?"

"No, that time around they were trying to put window boxes on all the stores. It didn't work out because a lot of the business owners thought they would just wind up being a place for people to throw cigarette butts and other trash in."

"Then what makes them think the planters won't wind up being the same thing?"

"The glass is always half empty with you, isn't it Jimmy?"

"I'll pass on the luncheon. Last time they suckered me into one of those things I wound up sitting next to Dorothy Englebretson and spent two hours listening to her talking about her gallbladder surgery and having her varicose veins stripped."

Mary drew a line through that entry on her notepad and asked, "Posing for pictures with dogs up for adoption at the animal shelter?"

"Pass."

"What? You don't like dogs?"

"I like hot dogs. Does that count?"

"I think they make them out of pork bellies or something, don't they?"

"Okay, now you've ruined hot dogs for me, too. What else have you got?"

"I've only got two things left, you have to choose one or the other."

"I have to? Why do I have to?"

"Because you're the sheriff and it's your job to put on a pretty face for the community now and then."

"I thought my job was to enforce the law and keep things peaceful around here."

"Nope, the deputies do that."

"Then what do I do?"

"Mostly you take up space, and try to get out of anything I ask you to do," Mary told him.

"Okay, what are the last two?"

"Going to the nursing home and..."

"Pass."

Mary shook her head. "You don't like old people, either?"

"I like you sometimes. Doesn't that count?"

"Watch it, smart ass. I'm not old. I'm mature."

"Isn't that just another word for old?"

"No, it's not. I'll have you know that I've just reached my sexual prime."

"Does Pete know about that?"

"No, and don't you dare tell him or he'll be chasing me around the house even more than he does already."

"There are some mental images I don't need to have running around inside my head, Mary. Can we move on?"

"Sure," she said with a Cheshire cat grin. "Since you don't want to do any of the other things I suggested, you get to go to the high school and talk to the kids for career day on Friday."

"Oh, you set me up," Weber said.

"Who? Me?" Mary asked innocently. "You had other choices, Jimmy."

"You know I hate going and talking to those kids."

"Don't you know our children are our future?"

"How about I take the nursing home instead? At least the old folks will fall asleep ten minutes into my presentation?"

"Sorry," Mary said with a satisfied smile. "I already put Chad down for that."

"I hated school while I was in it," Weber complained. "I can't believe you're making me go back there again."

"What do you have against kids?"

"Forget it, I'm not going. Send somebody else."

"Why? It's not like they're a bunch of inner-city hoodlums or something. They're just kids."

"It's not gonna happen, Mary. Forget it."

They had known each other and worked together long enough that she could pick up on the changing tone of his voice.

"What's wrong, Jimmy?"

He looked away and didn't answer.

"Jimmy? Talk to me."

He looked back at her in anguish. "The last time I was there a couple of them kids wanted to talk about me shooting Steve Rafferty. One of them just wouldn't let it go."

A look of concern crossed Mary's face and she shook her head. "I'm sorry, Jimmy. I didn't know."

Steve Rafferty was a teenaged sociopath who had helped murder a young gay man, and then shot one of Weber's deputies when they came to arrest him. The sheriff had killed him while he was trying to escape. It was an incident that still haunted him.

"I'll do whatever else you need, but I really don't want to do that, Mary."

She nodded her head. "I understand. How about..."

Before she could finish the question there was a knock on the door and Dispatcher Kate Copley stuck her head in. "Sorry to interrupt, Sheriff. But there's some kind of disturbance going on over at the courthouse."

~***~

Weber and Chad could hear shouting as soon as they opened the door to Big Lake's small courthouse.

"This is ridiculous. What do you mean your hands are tied? I want action and I want it right now!"

Weber looked at Chad, who shrugged his shoulders. They were in a small vestibule, with a solid oak door in front of them that opened into the courtroom. They went through it and followed the sound past the rows of chairs in the center and the jury seats off to the right side, past the witness stand and the judge's podium, and opened the door that led to the Court Clerk's office.

"I'm glad you're here," said Cindy Oswald. "I tried to tell her she needed an appointment to see the judge, but she barged right past me and into the judge's chambers, and she won't listen to a word he says."

Weber looked through the open door and was surprised to see that the woman in question was Rosanne Duncan. Judge Harold Ryman was trying to say something, but every time he opened his mouth to speak, she interrupted him.

"I know the law. I have every right to do anything I want. Arizona is a community property state, and now that my husband is dead I own everything out there. That man is trespassing and I want him gone today!"

"Mrs. Duncan, if you will just let me explain..."

"There's nothing to explain," Roseanne shouted. "Just sign the paperwork like I told you to!"

"Okay, how about you just calm down, ma'am? Nothing ever gets accomplished when people are shouting instead of talking."

At his words, Rosanne turned to Weber and said, "If you would have done your job like I told you to this wouldn't be a problem. I told you I wanted Sonny off that property yesterday, but you wouldn't do it. You're just as lazy and worthless as he is!"

"Rosanne... Mrs. Duncan, you need to calm down right now. I don't know what the problem is here, but you're way out of line."

"I'm out of line? I'm out of line? I'm out of line because I want a trespasser off my property? I'm out of line because you and this fool you people call a judge refuse to do your jobs?"

"I told you to lower your voice," Weber said. "And I'm not going to tell you again. I would really hate to arrest you for disturbing the peace, especially the day after your husband was killed. But if you keep this up, you're not going to leave me a choice. And I don't think any of us wants that to happen."

"You have *got* to be kidding me! You're threatening me with arrest because I expect you and this... this man, to do your jobs?"

"No, ma'am, I'm telling you that if you don't lower your voice and stop making a scene, I'm going to arrest you for disturbing the peace."

"Nobody needs to be arrested," Judge Ryman said. "I'm afraid Mrs. Duncan is a little upset because..."

"I don't need you to speak for me," Roseanne said vehemently, although in a lower tone of voice.

"Fine," the judge said. "But as I've tried to tell you several times already, Mrs. Duncan, I can't help you. I cannot give legal advice. I cannot talk to a person involved in a case without the other side present. That is an ex parte communication and not allowed by law. You need a lawyer. I can only hear cases and address lawsuits that come before me. I can't just order an eviction notice on your say so."

"Why not? It's my property, isn't it?"

"No, not necessarily," the judge said. Yes, Arizona is a community property state, but that doesn't mean Sonny doesn't have certain rights."

"What rights could he possibly have if his father's dead?"

"The way the law is written here in Arizona, community property is property acquired *after* a marriage took place. So anything that you and Mr. Duncan acquired together, after you were married, is community property. That can be real estate, automobiles, home furnishings, whatever the two of you acquired after the date of your marriage. However, property that was acquired prior to your marriage is legally defined as Separate Property. When a spouse dies, their Separate Property goes to the estate of the deceased person and is distributed to whomever is named in their will."

Rosanne stood with her arms folded tightly across her chest, tapping her foot as the judge spoke. Her body language made it clear to Weber that she wasn't going to accept anything Judge Ryman said that disagreed with what she wanted.

Continuing, he said, "The surviving spouse, which is you in this case, gets half of all Community Property and the other half goes to your husband's estate and passes to whoever he has named in the will. Do you know if Mr. Duncan had a will?"

"Of course he left a will. And he left everything to me in it."

"Do you have a copy of it with you?"

"No, I don't have it with me," she snapped. "My husband's attorney is out of town on some silly wilderness adventure or something like that and I haven't been able to contact him yet."

"Well, until you have a copy of the will in hand...

"I don't need a copy of some stupid will. It's my property and I want Sonny gone!"

"Yes, ma'am, you do need to have a copy of the will. And even then, Sonny, as your late husband's natural child, still has certain rights. Among them the right to contest the will."

"Why? The will says everything goes to me and that settles it. I know the law."

"You've told me that quite a few times already this morning, Mrs. Duncan. But while you may *think* you know the law, you don't. Your husband's will has to be probated, and we have to see what kind of considerations were made for his heirs, if any."

"This is ridiculous. Absolutely ridiculous. I know what this is, it's the good old boy network in action. You're probably all Sonny's drinking buddies, and I'm the outsider. Well, I won't just roll over and play dead for you. I know my rights and I can tell you right now, this isn't over!"

She was shouting again, and Weber said, "It's over for right now. Unless Judge Ryman has anything more to say to you, you need to leave, Mrs. Duncan."

"I've already said all I can say," the judge said. "I don't make the laws."

"No, but you interpret them to suit your needs. You're an idiot if you think you can stonewall me like this and just expect me to take it."

"Okay, that's it," Weber said. "You can go home, or you can go talk to your attorney, or you can do whatever you want. But you need to leave right now. Otherwise, you're going to jail."

"Fine," the woman spat. "But I'll be back. And when I do, I'll get action."

She shouldered her way past Weber and Chad and out the door, slamming it behind her so hard that a picture of the governor hanging on the court clerk's wall fell off.

"Now that is one ticked off lady," Weber said, shaking his head.

"She may be a lot of things, but she's not much of a lady," Cindy Oswald replied as she picked the picture up and hung it back in its place. "Can you imagine? Her husband just died and she's already in here trying to get Sonny evicted from the property and causing a scene like this?"

"I've seen a lot in the past 24 hours that I never could have imagined," Weber told her.

Chapter 8

"I'll tell you what, Jimmy, I've seen some really greedy people in my time, but that woman takes the cake," Chad said as they walked back into the Sheriff's Office. "Her husband's body, or at least what's left of it, isn't even cold yet and she's acting this way? Where the heck did Duncan come up with her, anyway?"

"Through her church," Mary said.

"Really? How did you find that out?"

"Because, while you two were out playing policeman, I was here playing detective," she said with a superior tone to her voice.

"And just what did you find out, Miss Smarty-Pants?"

"They met through her church."

"Really? I didn't know Duncan all that well, but he never struck me as a churchgoing man."

"I don't know that he was. But every year he donated a hog to her Church in Springerville for their annual picnic. I guess he did that for several organizations."

"Yeah, he did," Chad said. "Duncan was good that way. When I was a Scoutmaster he used to always donate one to us for our fundraising barbecue at Pioneer Days. He'd have it all cleaned and dressed and ready to go and bring it down to us so we could put it in the fire pit the night before."

"Anyway, according to Earl, she was on the church picnic committee, and that's how she and Duncan hooked up."

"Earl?"

"Yes, Earl Duncan. He's one of our Citizen Volunteers."

"I know who he is, Mary. I just didn't realize they were related, even though they have the same last name."

"They're cousins," she told him. "Earl's mother, Catherine, was Duncan's aunt. There are a lot of Duncan's all through this area, and they're all related one way or another."

"How is Earl taking the news about Duncan?"

"He was pretty shook up about it. He said they weren't real close, but even so, when somebody dies in such a terrible way, it's got to be hard to take."

"I'm curious, did Earl say anything about Duncan's wife? The new one, that is?"

Mary shook her head. "He said he never met her. Earl said he had heard about Duncan getting remarried, but had not talked to him in a while."

The door opened and a small dark-haired woman came into the office and said, "Hi y'all. Is Archer around?"

"He's more of an oval shape," Weber said. "How are you doing, Kallie Jo? I hear you've been making a lot of changes at the hardware store."

Contrary to local gossip, Roseanne Duncan may not have been a mail order bride, but Kallie Jo really was. The little fireball from Georgia had met Deputy Archer Wingate through an online dating service, and everybody was surprised when she showed up in town ready to marry the man she only knew through email. They were even more surprised when she actually went through with it after meeting Archer. The overweight deputy had gotten his badge only because his father, Big Lake's little despot of a mayor, had forced him on the sheriff. Since he joined the department, Archer had proven himself to be even more inept than anybody thought possible. It was hard to decide which of his many screw-ups were worse, but some of the top contenders were rear-ending civilian cars while in Sheriff's Department vehicles not once, but twice, and then there was the time he had tasered the sheriff. But to everyone's surprise, after marrying Kallie Jo, Archer had actually begun shaping up. Not physically, his belly still hung several inches over his belt buckle, but at least his shoes and gun belt were always shined and his uniform was clean and neatly pressed when he came on duty.

"Oh, I'll tell you what, Sheriff Jimmy, that place really needed some attention! Now I love Mr. Chet, Archer's daddy, don't get me wrong. But I've got to tell you, that man may be really good at runnin' a town, but he shore came up short runnin' a business."

Weber wanted to say that Mayor Chet Wingate probably wasn't going to win any awards for his civic duty either, but Kallie Jo was still talking. Kallie Jo was *always* talking. Weber had never met anybody who could talk nonstop as fast as Kallie Jo could. Listening to one of her lengthy monologues about the folks back home in Georgia or what was happening in town, the sheriff had always suspected that if a doctor gave the woman a thorough physical, somewhere under her clothing they would find gills that she breathed through.

"Do you know that Mr. Chet's idea of a file'n system was just to cram everything into one of them big old manila envelopes at the end of every month? And I do mean everything! Receipts, paid invoices, employee time cards, why, would you believe I even found a wrapper from a Hershey bar in one of them there envelopes? And the way he had that store laid out? You could go in there lookin' for tenpenny nails, and you'd think they'd be with the other nails, right? Well maybe so, and maybe not! It depended on where Mr. Chet was with them when the telephone rang or somebody came in the store lookin' for somethin'. Why, he'd just set them down on whatever shelf he was standin' in front of and leave them there!"

A few months earlier, when a series of cardiac episodes had convinced him he was now an invalid, the mayor had turned over the day-to-day operation of his hardware and lumber store to his daughter-in-law. As it turned out, Chet survived the medical scare in spite of the fact that he ignored his doctor's orders about going on a diet and getting more exercise. But Kallie Jo had turned out to be such a good replacement that he left her in charge. Under her watch business had improved, the profit margin had grown, and employee morale was never higher. Sure, Kallie Jo talked a lot, but she was always friendly, and unlike Chet, who seldom came out of his office except to berate his employees for anything and everything real or imagined, Kallie Jo was right there on the floor with them, helping to stock shelves, working the cash register, and cleaning up at the end of the day.

"Of course, it ain't all been easy," Kallie Jo was saying. "For example, with summer over with, I've been runnin' some clearance sales to get rid of inventory so's we don't have to warehouse it all winter long. Mr. Chet, he don't like reducin' the price on anything and he kind of took exception to that. The man does like a dollar, if you know what I mean, Sheriff. But I told him it cost more to haul all that stuff off the shelves and store it until next summer than it does to put it on sale and get it gone. He didn't like it, but he finally came around."

"Anyway," Weber interrupted, knowing that once Kallie Jo got on a roll it might take the rest of the morning for her to run down, "you were looking for Archer?"

"What? Oh yeah, Archer. Do you know I got to talkin' and plum forgot what I came in here for? Ain't that somethin'? You'd think I was gettin' all addle-brained like Aunt Irene if you didn't know better, wouldn't ya? 'Course, Aunt Irene ain't really my aunt, bless her heart. Not by blood, anyway. She was married to my Uncle Harmon, he was Daddy's younger brother. Daddy's actually got three younger brothers. Let's see, there's Ronald, and then there's Luther, and then Harmon. 'Cept Harmon ain't alive no more 'cause he got that there emphysema. Ain't it strange that the youngest of the brothers was the one that died first? 'Course, Granny Phillips said Harmon was sickly even when he was a little squirt, and he never did put on much weight. Not the rest of them boys though, no sir! My daddy, Buster, he stands about six foot two and he must weigh close to three hundred pounds. And Uncle Ronald and Uncle Luther, they's about the same size."

"Kallie Jo. Stop," Weber said holding out his hands as if he could push back the words coming from her. "You're way off on a tangent. I don't really need to know who was born first or how big they all are. You started to say...?"

Kallie Jo blinked in confusion for a moment, then her face brightened and she said, "Oh that's right, I did, didn't I? I do that sometimes, Sheriff . I'll start talkin' 'bout somethin' and pretty soon before you know it, I'm way off on a whole 'nother subject."

"Yeah, I've noticed," Weber said.

"Anyway, what I started to say was that Aunt Irene ain't really my aunt, like if she was Momma or Daddy's sister, since she was married to my Uncle Harmon and all. 'Course, even though he's gone, God rest his soul, she's still family to us. Yes sir," Kallie Jo said with a nod of her head, "once you's a Phillips, you're a Phillips forever."

Weber's head was beginning to ache and he wondered if he would ever be able to escape the conversation, but fortunately for him Mary came to his rescue.

"You were asking about Archer, Kallie Jo. He's over at the school on traffic duty. For a couple hours during the middle of the day we try to keep a car there to slow traffic down during lunchtime."

"Well now, that there is a good idea," Kallie Jo said, nodding her head vigorously. "And Archer's just the man for that job, what with the kids all lookin' up to him as one of them there role models and all. I was goin' to see if he wanted to go to lunch, but he's got work to do. But I may drive past him and blow him a kiss, if that's all right."

Weber tried to imagine how anyone would consider Archer a role model, but there was no way he was going to insert himself back into the conversation now that he had escaped. While Mary was assuring Kallie Jo that it would be fine for her to do a drive by, he slipped out of the office and made his way to the back of the parking lot, where the park model trailer Larry Parks used as the FBI's field office was located.

"Hey Bubba, did you recover from yesterday?"

Weber shook his head and shuddered. "Man, that was a hell of a way to start the week."

"Hell of a way to end a life, too," Parks said.

"I've seen some pretty ugly things in my time," Weber told him, "but that was absolutely the worst."

"When I was a kid back home in Oklahoma, there was a farmer down the road from us that had a heart attack," Parks told him. "When he went down one of his legs was inside the hog pen. He survived because his wife happened to be driving out to go to town and saw him. But those damn things took off his foot and part of his leg."

"Can we talk about something more pleasant?"

"Sure, Jimmy, I'm sorry. How about lunch?"

"You're just messing with me, aren't you Parks?"

"Nope," his friend said standing up and stretching. "But I'll tell you what, I heard that new espresso bar that opened up down the street serves vegetarian sandwiches. We can stop and pick you up something to go on our way over to the barbecue place."

Chapter 9

If Weber thought he had seen the last of Roseanne Duncan for that day, he was sadly mistaken. He and Parks were just finishing their lunch when his cell phone went off with the ring tone reserved for the Sheriff's Office.

"You can run, but you can't hide," Parks said as Weber wiped his fingers on a paper napkin and pushed the button to answer the call.

"Jimmy, I hate to interrupt your playtime with your friend, but you need to get back out to the Duncan place. Mona Bowers is calling from the Midway Store and she said there's a disturbance going on at the hog farm. Apparently Duncan's wife came in and started ordering Sonny to leave and he told her to go to hell or something, and now they're going at it."

"Isn't Dan still out there keeping the reporters from trespassing?"

"No, they all left and he's working a traffic accident on Meadowlark Street. Sarah Jenkins rear-ended David McCloud at the stop sign at Aztec Drive."

"Any injuries?"

"Not in the accident," Mary replied. "But from the way Mona sounded, there may be some out at the hog farm if you don't get out there fast."

Weber sighed and said, "I'm on my way."

The hog farm didn't smell any better the second day. If anything, it was worse on a full stomach. Mona Bowers was waiting at the end of the driveway in an old Toyota pickup that had probably been red at one time but whose paint was now faded to some sort of dull orange. She got out of the truck when Weber pulled up beside her.

"I'm sorry to bother you, Sheriff, but I'm afraid something terrible is going to happen!"

"What's going on?"

"Mrs. Duncan left earlier today, and she told Sonny when she left that she wanted him gone when she got back. He told her she was the one that needed to leave, and she said that she was going to see the judge and get some kind of order or something that meant Sonny had to go. Then when she came back she was on a rampage. I mean an absolute rampage! She jumped out of her car and started screaming at Sonny before her feet hit the ground. And he started yelling right back at her. I wish Leonard was here, but he had to make deliveries in Gallup today. Sheriff, you need to get in there and stop them before somebody gets hurt."

"Yes, ma'am," Weber told her.

He drove through the gate and up the driveway to find Roseanne and Sonny Duncan squared off in front of Sonny's mobile home. He was standing with his fists clenched while Roseanne had a tight grip on a shovel she held in both hands over her shoulder like a baseball player at home plate waiting for a pitch. Weber beeped his siren to get their attention, then got out of his Explorer.

"Put the shovel down, Mrs. Duncan. Do it right now!"

"If you won't get this squatter off my property, I'll do it myself."

"Squatter? I was born and raised here, you bitch. You're the one that don't belong!"

"Okay, everybody stop shouting," Weber said. "And Mrs. Duncan I'm not going to tell you again to drop that shovel."

"What are you going to do, shoot me?"

"No ma'am, but I will tase you," Weber told her. "And believe me, you're not going to enjoy it."

"Go ahead, I dare you. I bet that will make you feel real big and strong, won't it? That's probably all you're good for, beating up on women."

Weber pulled the Taser X2 from its holster on his belt. "I really don't want to do this, but you're not leaving me much choice."

"You had a choice, Sheriff," Roseanne shouted. "All you had to do was do your job like I told you to yesterday and we wouldn't be standing here today, would we? So you go right ahead and

Taser me or do whatever you want to do. Because I'll tell you right now, I plan on suing you and your department for malfeasance, and I'll be happy to add bodily injury to the suit."

While she was talking, the irate woman had not noticed Larry Parks leave the Explorer and walk around the rear end in a wide arc that brought him up behind her. He grabbed the shovel and jerked it out of her hands, pulling Roseanne off balance. Surprised, she stumbled and almost fell, but Weber grabbed her arm to keep her upright.

"Get your filthy hands off of me, you bastard!" She jerked free and slapped him in the face. "How dare you touch me!"

"Oh, I'm gonna touch you all right," Weber said. He holstered the Taser and grabbed her again. Roseanne tried to fight him off but she was no match for the sheriff. He spun her around and pinned her arms behind her. "You're under arrest. Stop resisting!"

Rosanne didn't hear him or didn't care, either way she continued to struggle. Parks dropped the shovel and helped him maneuver her over to the Explorer, where they pushed her face down across the hood and Weber handcuffed her. All the while Roseanne was shrieking like a wildcat, calling them names and warning them of the dire consequences of their actions.

"Jesus Christ, Rosanne, are you out of your freaking mind?"

"Don't you take the Lord's name in vain, Sonny Duncan. You are damned to hell!"

"Shut up," Weber said, no longer caring to be polite. "I don't get you, lady. You spout all this Bible stuff, but the way you're acting, I wonder what your preacher would say if he saw you right now."

"I don't answer to man, I answer to God."

"Yeah? Well I'm pretty sure he's not too happy with you right now, either."

"I want an attorney."

"That's your right," Weber told her. "Now let me read the rest of them to you." He gave the woman her Miranda warning, then put her in the back of the Explorer.

When he was done he turned to Sonny and said, "Okay, what happened?"

"You saw how she's been. She's a damned lunatic!"

"Yeah, I get that impression, too. Let's focus on what happened today."

"Last night when I was out tending to the hogs she had a bunch of people from her church up at the house. Three of the men came out and told me how sorry they were about my dad. Then they told me that it would probably be for the best if I left. I told him I wasn't going anywhere, and they said I really didn't have any choice, that's what Rosanne wanted. I let them know I didn't give a damn what she wanted. Then I asked them who was going to feed and take care of the hogs if I did leave. Since she ran José and Carmen off we've been shorthanded as it is, and now with my dad..." he choked up and had to stop for a moment. Sonny swallowed and rubbed the back of his dirty hand across his eyes. "Now with my dad gone, there's no way me and Leonard and Carl can keep up with things, let alone just the two of them. They told me I really needed to leave that up to God and start making my own plans for a life away from here. All I've ever wanted to do was be away from this stinking place, Sheriff, but I'm not gonna let her run me off!"

"All right, that was yesterday. What about today?"

"This morning she came out of the house and told me again that she wanted me gone by noon, and I told her to go to hell. She said she was going to town to get the judge to sign a court order that I had to go. Then she took off. When she got back she was screaming and hollering and started slapping me. Yelling about how terrible I was and how much my father hated me and wanted me gone. My own father! can you believe that?"

"You said she was slapping you?"

"Yeah, she slapped me half a dozen times. Carl can tell you, he saw it."

"Where is Carl?"

Sonny looked around and shrugged his shoulders. "I don't know. She probably scared him so much he ran away and hid. Like I told you before, Carl is a hard worker, but he ain't all there. When he gets scared he does that. Runs away and hides."

"What else happened?"

"Well, I ain't proud of it, Sheriff, but after she kept hitting me and I kept telling her to stop and she wouldn't, I finally shoved her away and she landed on her ass. If you want to arrest me for that, I don't care."

From what he had seen of Roseanne's actions, there was no way Weber was going to charge the man for defending himself.

"So you shoved her and she fell down, then what happened?"

"She got up and grabbed that shovel and was threatening to hit me with it. That's when you guys showed up."

"Okay, go sit on your porch or do whatever you need to get done," Weber said. "I'm going to talk to Mrs. Bowers and see if I can round up Carl."

Mona was standing in front of her truck, wringing her hands nervously.

"What's going to happen now, Sheriff?"

"To tell you the truth, I don't know yet," Weber admitted. "You said that when Mrs. Duncan came back from town she was mad and going off on Sonny. Is that right?"

"Yes sir. She started it, Sheriff. I mean, I guess they're both my boss, and I don't want to take sides, but Sonny was just working like he always does and she right away started yelling at him and hitting him and just acting like a crazy woman."

"You saw her hit Sonny?"

"Yeah. I mean, not like punching him with her fist, but she was slapping him."

"Did you see him push her down?"

Mona shook her head. "No sir. That must've happened when I drove down to the store to call for help. Oh, I wish Leonard was here. He would've known what to do. Maybe I shouldn't have gotten involved but..."

"You did the right thing," Weber assured her. "Do you know where Carl is?"

"Carl? No, I don't. He was there when this all started but I guess he ran away at some point. Carl is a real gentle soul, Sheriff. He's got, what do you call them these days? Challenges? He's a grown man, but he's still a child in many ways. We all look out for him. Well, all of us except for Mrs. Duncan. All she does is make fun of him and put him down. Carl don't deserve that."

"No ma'am, nobody does," Weber said. "Where do you suppose he ran off to?"

"Knowing Carl, he's either hiding in the closet in his bedroom or the barn, or else he's off in the woods somewhere."

"Thank you, Mona. Let me see if I can find him."

"How about if I go with you and we check his trailer first? Carl can be pretty skittish when he's scared."

"Thank you, I'd appreciate that," Weber said and followed her to Carl's mobile home.

Chapter 10

Carl's trailer was small, but very tidy. The living room and kitchen were in the front, separated by a half wall behind the sink. The living room held an old couch covered in a blanket, a coffee table and a cabinet that held a television set and a DVD player. There was a stack of Disney movies on the floor. A hallway led to a bathroom and the single bedroom in the rear.

"Carl? Carl honey, it's Mona. Are you in here?"

Weber followed her inside and she called his name again. Getting no answer, Mona walked down the hallway and peered inside the open bathroom door, then went into the bedroom. There was a single bed with a checkered quilt on top, a nightstand that held a small lamp and several comic books, a cheap wooden dresser, and a closet with sliding doors.

"Carl, it's okay, everything is going to be all right. You can come out now."

"Is the mean lady still there?"

"She's still here, but Sheriff Weber came and put her in his police car."

"I don't like her. She's mean. She calls me names and she hit Sonny."

"I know she did," Mona said. "That's why Sheriff Weber is here. He needs to talk to you about that."

"Is he going to take me to jail?"

"No, honey, he's not going to take you to jail. You didn't do anything wrong."

"The mean lady said I should be locked up in a cage."

"Well, don't you pay attention to what she says. She don't know nothing about that."

"But Duncan said she was the boss, too, and that I had to do what she says."

"I know that, but things have changed. Now, you come out and talk to us, okay?"

"Okay."

The sliding door moved sideways and Carl stepped out of the closet with his head hung.

"That's good," Mona said. "See? Everything's okay?"

"Hi, Carl," Weber said.

"Are you gonna lock the mean lady up?"

"I'm not sure yet. Can we sit here on your bed and you can tell me what happened today?"

Carl sat on the bed, keeping his head down.

"You don't have to hang your head," Mona told him. "You didn't do anything wrong, Carl."

He looked up at her and nodded. Weber sat next to him and said, "It's been a pretty rough couple of days, hasn't it?"

Carl nodded his head. "Yep. Them old hogs ate Duncan."

"I know they did," Weber said. "And that was just awful."

"Duncan was my friend. He always took good care of me."

"I'm sorry about your friend," Weber said.

"Sonny's my friend, too. But the mean lady says he has to go away."

"Well, we'll have to wait and see how that works out. But nobody's going anywhere right away."

"Except the mean lady? Is she going to jail?"

"I'm not sure yet," Weber told him. "Do you think she should go to jail?"

Carl nodded his head again. "Yep."

"Why do you think she should go to jail, Carl?"

"Because she was hitting Sonny."

"She was hitting him, huh? You saw that?"

Another head nod. "She was hitting him, and then Sonny knocked her down. Is he going to jail, too?"

"Why do you think Sonny should go to jail?"

"Because you're not supposed to hit girls."

"Well, that's true," the sheriff said. "Actually, you shouldn't hit anybody. But sometimes people get mad and they do things they shouldn't. And sometimes people do things like that because they have to make someone else stop being mean to them."

Carl looked at him and said, "That's why Sonny knocked her down, because she kept hitting him. It wasn't his fault. She's mean."

"When you say Sonny knocked her down, did he hit her with his hand or his fist?"

"No, he just shoved her and knocked her down. But he only done it because she was hitting him and she wouldn't stop. Is that what you meant when you said sometimes people hit somebody to make them stop being mean to them?"

"Yeah, that's what I meant. So if Sonny pushed Mrs. Duncan down, or even if he hit her to make her stop hitting him, that's okay. That's called self-defense. You're allowed to hit somebody in self-defense to make them stop hurting you."

"That's why he did it. I swear and cross my heart."

"All right. Then what happened after that, Carl?"

"I don't know. I ran away because I was scared. I read comic books about superheroes, but I ain't one. When I get scared I run away. Is that bad?"

"No," Weber told him. "Sometimes it's the best thing to do."

"I ain't scared of the hogs, even though they ate Duncan. And I ain't scared of the horses, either. But the mean lady scares me."

"Let me tell you a little secret," Weber said, putting his hand on the other man's shoulder. "Sometimes she scares me, too."

He left Mona with Carl and went back outside. Parks was standing on the ground at the bottom of Sonny's porch and Weber walked over to them.

"Is Carl okay?"

"Yeah. He was hiding in his closet."

"Doesn't surprise me," Sonny said shaking his head with a half smile. "Like I said, Carl ain't all there, but he's a good guy."

"How long has he been around here?"

"Just about as long as I can remember," Sonny said. "My dad found him sleeping behind a restaurant in Winslow years ago and brought him home. He wasn't much more than a kid. He said he had family in Flagstaff or someplace like that. But when Dad contacted them and said Carl needed help, they didn't want nothing to do with him. My old man was always taking in strays, and I guess he figured Carl was just one more stray that needed a home."

"So what are we gonna do here, Sonny? Do you want to file charges against Roseanne for assault? If you do, I'll take her in."

"I really don't want to do that, Sheriff. I mean, I can't stand the bitch, but for whatever reason, my dad loved her. Don't ask me why."

"You're within your rights to press charges."

"Can you just tell her to stay away from here?"

"Here's the problem," Weber said, "technically she's got as much right to be here as you do. Now, if you were living in the same house I could arrest her for domestic violence. But you don't. So I'm not sure exactly where the law stands on that, to be honest with you. Until a judge makes a ruling one way or another, or until your father's will is probated, there's really nothing to say who gets what, who has to stay, or who has to go."

Sonny nodded his head. "I understand. Can you at least tell her to leave me alone? I really don't want to send her to jail. I owe my dad more than that."

"Let me go have a talk with her and I'll see what I can do," Weber told him.

He and Parks walked back to the Explorer and Weber opened the rear door.

"Mrs. Duncan, Sonny says he doesn't want to press charges against you."

"Charges against me? For what? He's the one who's trespassing."

"Let's not start all that again," Weber said. "You assaulted him, and I've got witnesses that saw it."

"What witnesses? Mona Bowers? She and her husband are going to be gone, too. Who else? Carl? You're going to take the word of an imbecile?"

"Okay, enough with that crap. Is there someplace you can stay in Springerville for a day or two until you guys get Duncan's will sorted out?"

"I am not leaving my property. This is my home! George left it to me."

Weber sighed and closed his eyes for a moment, shaking his head.

"You are one of the most obstinate women I've ever met, do you know that?"

"Sheriff, do you really think I care what somebody like *you* thinks about me?"

"No, ma'am, I don't. And that's okay. All I'm asking is if there is someplace you can go so that you and Sonny won't be getting all sideways again until all of this gets sorted out?"

"Absolutely not! He's the one that needs to go."

"Okay, how about this? If I take the handcuffs off of you and send you into the house, do you promise to stay there and not come out and start any more trouble?"

"If you think I'm some helpless little woman that you can *send* to the house like that and I'll just mind my place, you are sadly mistaken, Sheriff. Who do you think you are, anyway?"

"Is that a yes or no, Mrs. Duncan?"

"It's a no! I already told you, if you won't get Sonny off this property, I'll do it myself. Even if I have to knock his brains out with a shovel and drag him out to the road."

"Fine, we'll do it your way," Weber said. "Get in, Parks."

He closed the door and got behind the wheel of the Explorer and started the engine. "Where are you taking me?"

"You're going to jail," Weber told her.

"For what? Sonny already said he doesn't want to press charges against me."

"Yes, ma'am. But I saw you threatening him with that shovel, and you assaulted me. So whether he wants to or not doesn't really matter, does it?"

"You can't be serious!"

"Trust me, lady, I'm as serious as a heart attack," Weber said, driving through the gate and turning the Explorer toward town.

Chapter 11

"You arrested that poor woman the day after her husband was killed in such a horrible manner? What kind of a man are you, Sheriff Weber?"

"The kind of man who doesn't appreciate being assaulted and won't stand by and let somebody get away with doing the same thing to someone else."

"This is inexcusable. Absolutely inexcusable!" Councilman Adam Hirsch slapped his hand down on the dais to make his point. "I move that the Town Council order Sheriff Weber to release Mrs. Duncan immediately. We will be lucky if she doesn't sue us for a million dollars after this outrage!"

"Hold on there, Adam," Councilman Kirby Templeton said. "First off, this Council doesn't have the authority to order the Sheriff to release somebody that he arrested for good cause. And second, while it's tragic that Duncan got killed the way he did, that doesn't give his widow a get out of jail free card to go around breaking the law."

"My God, Kirby, the woman's husband is dead!"

"I understand that. But like I said, that doesn't give Mrs. Duncan the right to go around breaking the law."

"You don't think Sheriff Weber could have shown any consideration at all for her situation?"

"Mr. Councilman, I gave Mrs. Duncan every opportunity to avoid going to jail," Weber said. "Even after she assaulted me and I had her handcuffed, I asked if she would give me her promise to go in her house and stop harassing and assaulting Sonny Duncan. She said no. In fact, she told me that if I didn't throw him off the property she would, and I'm quoting her here, *knock his brains out with a shovel and drag him off the property*. My job is to enforce the law and preserve the peace. It was obvious that leaving her there was not going to resolve the issue and that she was going to continue to assault Sonny."

"That's your opinion," Councilman Hirsch snapped. Adam Hirsch was a nerdy little man who had hated Weber since their high school days because a girl he had been interested in back then had shunned him and gone out with the future sheriff, instead.

Weber often suspected that his only purpose in seeking election to the Town Council was to give him the power to retaliate for that long ago slight.

"It doesn't sound like it's just Jimmy's opinion," Councilman Mel Walker said. "He just told us the woman said she was going to assault Duncan's son. "

"People say a lot of things when they're emotional," Hirsch argued. "That doesn't mean they're really going to do them."

"Let it go, Adam," Kirby said. "Neither you nor I were out there. And it's not our job to second guess Sheriff Weber's take on a situation when he was the man on the scene. If he felt this woman was going to continue to raise a ruckus and that the only way to prevent more trouble was to arrest her, that's good enough for me."

"It may be good enough for you, but it's not good enough for me," Councilman Hirsch insisted stubbornly. "Sheriff Weber isn't a psychiatrist, and he doesn't have a crystal ball, so how can he judge what somebody's going to do?"

"It's called experience," Mel Walker said with frustration at his fellow Councilman's obstinance. "Jimmy has spent a lot of time dealing with all kinds of difficult people in situations like this. A lot more than you or I have, Adam. That's what this town pays him to do."

"Well, if you ask me, we're not getting what we're paying for."

Mel started to respond when he was interrupted by a voice from the audience.

"May I interrupt?

"Judge Ryman, it's nice to see you with us tonight," Kirby said. "Please, do you have something to add to this conversation?"

"Yes, I do, Kirby," the judge said, standing up from his seat in the audience. "This morning Mrs. Duncan showed up at the courthouse demanding that I issue an eviction order against Sonny Duncan. I tried to explain to her then that until her husband's will is probated, I don't have the authority to issue such an order. When I told her that, she became very irrational. She was shouting and making all kinds of threats about what she was going to do. It got to the point where she was being so loud and acting in such an unstable manner that my court clerk had to call the Sheriff's Office and ask for help. When Sheriff Weber and Deputy Summers arrived she was just as out of control. The sheriff threatened to arrest her then. So while I understand that Mrs. Duncan has suffered a terrible loss, there is no question in my mind that Sheriff Weber did exactly what needed to be done."

"Still, Your Honor, don't you think..."

"That's enough, Adam," Kirby said. "We're not going to beat this dead horse all evening. We have other things on the agenda. Let's move on."

The junior Councilman scowled and folded his arms across his chest, making it clear that he was unhappy with what Kirby was saying, but he remained silent during the rest of the meeting.

The Town Council dealt with a few other routine matters, including whether or not they needed to impose a leash law, with half the people in the audience saying they were tired of stray dogs coming onto their property to harass their animals or do their business, and the other half saying dogs were dogs, and that's what they do, and that nobody ever needed a leash law before. It was those damn flatlanders moving up from the big cities who wanted all of these new rules and regulations about everything. The issue was hotly debated for well over an hour before the Council voted to have the town's attorney draft the ordinance, announcing it would go in effect immediately.

When the meeting ended, Weber caught the judge on his way out and shook his hand. "I appreciate you speaking up for me, Judge Ryman."

"I had a feeling that either Chet or Gretchen would try to make something out of you arresting Mrs. Duncan. I was surprised that Adam Hirsch beat them to the punch."

"Yeah, sometimes I feel like I'm wearing a target on my back when I go to these meetings," Weber said.

The judge smiled and nodded. "Just so you know, Jimmy, the majority of the Town Council and the people that live here in Big Lake appreciate you, and the job you and your deputies do. Keep it up, okay? How about you bring Mrs. Duncan by tomorrow morning, and we'll see if she's calmed down enough that we can cut her loose."

"Sounds like a plan," Weber said.

Chapter 12

"Geez, what's got into Chet and Gretchen that they just sat there and didn't back Adam up? That just upsets the balance of nature." Marsha Perry said half an hour later as they waited for their dinner at Mario's Pizzeria.

"I don't know about the mayor, but I believe *he's* what got into the councilwoman," Larry Park said, biting into a garlic bread knot and turning away before his girlfriend could snatch it out of his hand.

"Ewww. That's a picture I don't need in my head right before I eat," said Robyn Fuchette, Weber's deputy and fiancé.

Mayor Chet Wingate and Councilwoman Gretchen Smith-Abbott had spent years criticizing everything Weber did and trying to convince the Town Council to replace him. But in the last few months they had become more than political allies, they had started an affair that seemed to take up most of their time and energy. They were an unlikely pair - the mayor was a short, heavyset man, a bumbling egomaniac constantly disappointed by a world that never quite lived up to his expectations. Councilwoman Smith-Abbott was at least a foot taller than the mayor, a rail thin, severe woman who seem to have an unlimited supply of drab gray business suits that she wore on every occasion. Nobody Weber knew had ever seen her when her hair wasn't pulled into a tight bun on the back of her head. While some people in Big Lake shook their heads when they speculated about what went on with those two behind closed doors, the sheriff didn't really care. He figured that as long as they were paying attention to each other they weren't bothering him, which was just fine as far as he was concerned.

"What, girlfriend, you don't believe in romance?"

"Sure, I believe in romance," Robyn said. "But the idea of those two rutting around just makes my skin crawl."

"That's just because you're petite and pretty," Marsha said. "Fat people need love, too."

"You're not fat," Robyn told her.

"I wasn't talking about me. I'm just fluffy. I'm talking about this chowder head." She slapped Parks' hand as he reached for another bread knot.

"Me fat? I don't think so," he said. "I'll have you know I just passed my annual physical with flying colors."

"And the doctor didn't say anything about that spare tire starting to grow around your waist, right?"

"Come on, baby, those are just love handles."

"Yeah? Well you need to lay off the goodies if you want to keep putting your hands on *my* goodies! I'm not shacked up with you for your mind, mister!"

Weber had noticed that his friend had put on a few pounds, which amazed him. Parks had always seemed to have a voracious appetite, and while he could eat twice as much as Weber any day of the week, he never seemed to gain an ounce until recently.

"You know what I think? I think his body is reacting to some kind of negative reinforcement," Weber said.

"What do you mean?"

"Well, you're always nagging the man about not eating junk food and trying to stick him on some diet. He was doing fine until you started all that. I think when his body realized you were trying to change its ways, its reaction was to grab onto a few extra pounds and hang on to them."

"There you go, that's what it is," Parks said. "It's one of them passive-aggressive reactions, I think. Why, I bet if you would just sit there quietly and let me eat half a dozen donuts and wash them down with a chocolate milkshake every night, we'd both be better off. And thank you for bringing that up, Jimmy. I appreciate your support."

The two men fist bumped each other while Marsha and Robyn rolled their eyes. Before anything else could be said, Salvatore Gattuccio brought their pizza to their table. "Here you go, my friends, fresh out of the oven. Enjoy."

"Thank you. Sal," Weber said. "We always do."

The restaurant's owner was a huge, jovial man who had never met a stranger. Whether you were a regular customer or it was your first visit to the shop, you could expect a warm greeting that made you feel like you were among friends the moment you stepped through the door.

"That does my heart good, Sheriff Jimmy. I like to see you smile when you eat my food. And these two," Sal said, patting Robyn and Marcia affectionately on their shoulders, "such beautiful ladies. You two are lucky men to be blessed with them."

"Why, thank you, Sal! We keep telling them the same thing, but it always helps if they hear it from somebody else, too."

"Oh, Miss Marsha, don't you worry about that. These two," he said waving his finger at Weber and Parks, "they know it. Trust me, they know it."

"Speaking of lucky men and beautiful ladies, you and Christine seem to be getting along real well," Robyn said. "Didn't I see you two sitting at a picnic table in the park holding hands the other day?"

"Oh yes," Sal said with a broad smile, patting his heart with his hand. "I don't know what she sees in me, but I am grateful for whatever it is. I never thought a man like me could find love. Especially with such a wonderful woman as Miss Christine."

To the delight of all their friends, the pizza maker and Christine Ridgeway, the director of Safe Haven, Big Lake's shelter for abused and battered women, had recently become an item. Both were big people physically, with even bigger hearts, who gave of themselves to make life better for others in any way they could. While Christine always opened the doors of the shelter and her arms to any woman in need, there was not a charity event, a school student council meeting, or a gathering of anybody to do something for the community where Sal didn't supply free food. Nobody ever asked him to do it, and when he was thanked for his generosity, Sal always said it was his way of giving something back to the community that supported the pizzeria since the day his parents had opened it when he was just a little boy.

"Don't you sell yourself short," Robyn admonished him. "You're a pretty special guy yourself, Sal. I think you two make a perfect match."

He beamed at the compliment, then turned as the door opened and a couple came in. "Excuse me, my friends. Enjoy your meal."

Turning to the newcomers, Sal said, "Welcome! Please, have a seat wherever you choose. I'm so glad you came to my little shop."

"Those two do make a cute couple," Marsha said when Sal was out of hearing range. "They're like a couple of high school kids, holding hands and gushing at each other."

"Okay now, explain something to me," Parks said as he put two slices of pizza on his plate. "You two think the mayor and the councilwoman doing the nasty is disgusting, but you're both all goo goo-eyed over Sal and Christine. Now don't get me wrong, I'm happy they got together. But am I seeing a double standard at work here?"

"There's a difference," Marsha replied. "We *like* Sal and Christine, and nobody likes Chet Wingate or Gretchen."

"So there is a double standard? Just so I'm clear on that."

"Hey, I don't care who's bopping who," Weber said. "I'm thrilled for Sal and Christine, and as far as Chet and Gretchen go, as long as they're screwing each other and not screwing with me, more power to them."

"Speaking of unlikable people, what's going to happen with that lady you've got locked up?"

"Trust me, that ain't no lady," Parks said. "I was out there at that farm today with Jimmy. She may quote Bible verses and talk a good story, but that is one twisted female."

"Yes, she is," Weber said. "And to answer your question, Marsha, I'm going to let her spend the night in jail, then take her over to see the judge tomorrow. Maybe it will cool her down a little bit."

If the sheriff believed that was true, events would soon prove him wrong.

Chapter 13

A night in jail had not been kind to Rosanne Duncan. While Weber had allowed her some time to make herself ready for court, providing her with a toothbrush and toothpaste, along with a hairbrush, the well-coiffed woman he had met at the hog farm the day of her husband's death now looked tired and washed out in the rumpled clothing she had worn the day before and slept in overnight. But she was quick to show that her attitude certainly had not improved.

"Mrs. Duncan, I'm very sorry to see you in my courtroom this morning," Judge Ryman said when the sheriff brought the woman before him at 9 o'clock that next morning. "You have been through some traumatic events, and I know that can make anybody react out of character. I hope that you have had some time to reflect on your actions and that you are in a better frame of mind today."

"*My* actions? All I have done is assert my rights to my property," Roseanne said. "You're the one who needs to rethink *his* actions! You and Sheriff Weber both! If you two would have done what I told you to do and thrown Sonny off of my property, none of this would have happened in the first place."

The judge put his hand over his face and massaged his forehead with his fingers before looking back at the defendant with dismay.

"You really don't get it, do you, Mrs. Duncan? You don't dictate the law and mold it to fit your wants and demands. That's not the way it works."

"No, you're the one who doesn't get it," the woman said vehemently. "I know my rights!"

"Really? And just what law school did you graduate from, Mrs. Duncan? Because you seem to know a lot more about the law than I do."

The door of the courtroom opened and a tall, gaunt man dressed in dark slacks, a blue sport jacket, shirt and tie entered.

"Excuse me, Your Honor. My name is Dean Wicklund and I have been retained by Mrs. Duncan's church to represent her in this hearing."

"I see. And are you a member of the bar, Mr. Wicklund?"

"Yes, Your Honor. I have a practice in Springerville." He pulled a business card and his Arizona Bar identification card from his jacket pocket and held them out. "May I approach the bench?"

"We don't stand too much on formality around here, sir," the judge said, nodding and waving him forward. He looked at the card the man had given him and said, "Very well. Would you like a few minutes to consult with your client?"

"Thank you, I would."

"Let's take a fifteen minute recess," Judge Ryman said.

"Wait a minute," Roseanne said. "Why do we need a recess? You don't have to drag this out any longer than it has to. All you have to do is dismiss these bogus charges and do what I told you and evict Sonny from the property and we'll be done with it."

The judge sighed with obvious exasperation. "Mrs. Duncan, first of all, you are charged with assaulting two people, one of them a police officer. I hardly consider that a *bogus* charge. And as for the situation with your stepson, I don't know how many times I have to tell you that it's a civil matter and the only way that it's going to be resolved is by probating your late husband's will."

"Nonsense! I know what this is. It's the good old boy network taking care of each other. Duncan was one of your own, and so is Sonny. And you two see me as the outsider. But I'm telling you right now..."

The judge raised both hands and waved them to cut her off. Mr. Wicklund, let's make it a thirty minute recess. I think you're going to need it."

~***~

Rosanne did not seem any more contrite when the court reconvened in half an hour, but she did remain quiet and let her attorney speak for her.

"Your Honor, we all know that Mrs. Duncan has been through a rough time, and she's under a lot of emotional stress. While I can't ask you to ignore the mistakes she has made, I would hope that you would take her mental state under consideration as we proceed in this matter."

"Understood," the judge replied. "Nobody here wants to cause your client any further distress, sir. But you and she must understand that she needs to get some control of herself."

"Yes, Your Honor."

The judge looked at Weber and said, "Sheriff, do you have anything to say at this point?"

"No sir," Weber said shaking his head. "We all want what's best for everybody involved, and I do understand that this is a difficult situation. As I told Mrs. Duncan the other day, my job is to keep the peace."

The judge studied the defendant for a long moment, then said, "Mrs. Duncan, if I give you a break here, do you think there is some way that you can get some counseling or maybe talk to your minister to help you get a grip on your emotions and your actions?"

"Your Honor, I'm a member of the congregation at New Light Christian Church," Wicklund said, "and we are all there to support Mrs. Duncan in any way we can, emotionally and spiritually."

"Okay, here's what I'm going to do," Judge Ryman said, making a note on a yellow legal pad as he spoke. "I'm going to continue these charges for fourteen days. During that time, Mrs. Duncan, you are to refrain from having any confrontations with Sonny Duncan. No outbursts, no threats, and definitely no physical contact. I strongly advise you to spend that time talking to your attorney and finding out exactly what is specified in your late husband's will so the difficulties between you and Sonny can be resolved. But I'm warning you, Mrs. Duncan," he said, raising a cautionary finger, "if I hear any more reports about you causing trouble out there at the farm, if you come into my office creating another scene like you did the other day, if you do anything at all like that, you are going to be back here. And I won't be quite so generous next time around. Do we understand each other?"

"Yes, sir, Your Honor, we understand," Wicklund said.

The judge shook his head. "I want to hear it from your client, Mr. Wicklund. Do you understand the conditions of your release, Mrs. Duncan?"

"Yes, I understand," she replied through clenched teeth. "Believe me, I understand completely."

Judge Ryman studied her for a long moment and it was obvious that he didn't believe the matter was settled in Rosanne Duncan's mind yet. But nonetheless, he rapped his gavel and said, "We're done here."

~***~

"Do you think she learned her lesson?"

Weber and Parks were standing in the parking lot of the courthouse watching as Dean Wicklund and Roseanne drove away in the attorney's white Lincoln Navigator.

Weber shook his head."Oh, hell no. I get where the judge is coming from and all that. I didn't want to see her locked up either. But that woman is not going to back off, come hell or high water."

~***~

Cupid's arrow may have injected Mayor Chet Wingate with some kind of love potion that had improved his demeanor for a while, but judging from his first words to Weber when he returned to the Sheriff's Office, it had worn off.

"Where have you been, Sheriff Weber?"

"I was in court taking care of the issue with Mrs. Duncan."

"So you're still harassing that poor woman over nothing, while we have real crimes going on here in Big Lake!"

"She's been released on her own recognizance," Weber said. "As for *real* crime, what are you talking about, Chet?"

"I'm talking about grand theft auto, you idiot. That's what I'm talking about!"

"Now, are we talking about that videogame that the kids play on their computers or Nintendo's or whatever the hell they do, or are we talking about the real thing?"

"The real thing, of course. How can the citizens of Big Lake rest assured that you and your department are doing your job when their own mayor has been the victim of grand theft auto?"

"Didn't I just see your Escalade out in the parking lot?"

"I'm not talking about my Cadillac, I'm talking about my cart!"

"Your cart, Chet? Do you mean that dumb little thing you drive all over town on?"

"Yes, my handicap cart. Somebody has stolen it!"

A while back, the mayor had suffered a couple of cardiac incidents and decided he was an invalid despite his doctor telling him that as long as he exercised regularly, maintained a healthy diet, and refrained from too much stress, he had a long and healthy life ahead of him. Chet Wingate did not want to hear that and instead had outfitted himself with an electric powered mobility cart that he drove around Big Lake, scattering pedestrians from the sidewalk and forcing automobiles to make panic stops as he darted in and out of traffic, beeping his horn all the way. Weber had warned the mayor that he was going to hurt somebody or get himself hurt with his recklessness, but had drawn the line when Chet suggested maybe he should mount police lights and a siren on the cart to get people's attention.

"Okay, that's a crime, but it's not exactly grand theft auto, Chet."

"Of course it is!"

"No, it's not. It's not a licensed automobile."

"I don't care if it's licensed or not, I ride it everywhere!"

"I know you do, Chet. And you shouldn't be riding it. I've told you that as the Sheriff, and your doctor has told you that as your physician. It's not doing anything to help your health, and sooner or later you're going to get run over. Or else somebody's gonna smack you upside the head and knock you off of it when you try to run them down on the sidewalk."

"I want action, Sheriff Weber, and I want it now!"

"From what I hear, you're getting some action, Chet. Unless things have gone south between you and Gretchen."

"How dare you? Keep your filthy mouth shut. I come in here to report a crime and that's the way you're going to act?"

"My apologies, Chet. I was out of line with that one. Look, let's take a report and see what we can figure out about your cart, okay? Jordan? Got a minute?"

The young deputy had not been on the job long, but he had enough time in to know that dealing with the mayor was never a pleasant experience. But he just nodded his head and said, "Sure, come over here and have a seat, Mr. Mayor. Let's see if we can't figure out where that cart of yours has gone off to."

"It hasn't *gone off* on its own, Deputy. Somebody has stolen it. I want it found, and I want whoever did this brought to justice." The mayor turned to Weber and asked, "Don't you have somebody with some experience that can investigate an important case like this, Sheriff? I hardly think this is something a rookie can handle."

"Hey, everybody has to start somewhere. But don't you worry, Chet, Jordan here may be young and a little wet behind the ears still, but if anybody can find that missing cart of yours, he's the man for the job."

Chapter 14

At Mary Caitlin's insistence Weber managed to work his way through about half of the latest stack of paperwork she had piled on his desk. Weber was a hands-on guy and he loved being out in the field dealing with the public. But he loathed the administrative side of the job and tried to avoid dealing with reports, requisitions, employee evaluations, and the rest of the red tape that always overwhelmed him. It always seemed to him that the more time spent dealing with all of the paperwork only encouraged it to replicate itself; that when he finished whatever form needed his attention, it resulted in two more showing up to replace it. More than once he had considered having another door installed in his office that led directly outside so that he could escape without Mary catching him and forcing him back to his desk to sign something else.

But this day he got a break when dispatcher Kate Copeland buzzed him on the intercom and asked, "Sheriff, do you have a minute?"

"If it will keep me from getting writer's cramp signing anymore of this stuff, I've got all day. What do you need, Kate?"

"Roberta Jensen is on the telephone and said she needs to talk to you. Line three."

"Thanks," Weber said, then picked up the telephone on his desk and push the blinking light. "Miss Jensen, Sheriff Weber here. How can I help you?"

"I know you're busy and I hate to bother you, Sheriff, but I have a situation and I was wondering if you might have some time to stop by my office."

"What kind of situation, ma'am?"

"It's not an emergency or anything like that. But I'd feel more comfortable talking to you about it in person if you could find the time."

Weber looked at the paperwork he still had to complete that day and nodded his head. Anything was better than being stuck behind his desk. "Sure, I could come over right now if that's okay."

"That would be fine. I'll see you soon."

~***~

Several generations of Roberta Jensen's family had lived in Big Lake, and though she and Weber were close in age, he did not know her well. A childhood accident on her family's small farm had blinded her and she had been sent away to the Arizona State School for the Deaf and the Blind in Tucson for her basic education and to learn the skills someone with her physical challenges needed to live independently. Not only had she learned to cope, she had thrived, going on to graduate at the top of her class from the University of Arizona's Law School and establishing a successful family law practice in Tucson. Five years earlier she had grown tired of life in the big city and returned to her roots, opening an office in the home she bought two blocks from Main Street in Big Lake.

When Weber rang her doorbell he heard someone approaching from the other side, and a moment later it was opened by a woman with long dark hair that was naturally curly and a friendly smile. "Hello Miss Jensen, it's Sheriff Weber."

"Please, come in, Sheriff. Thanks for making time for me on such short notice."

"Anytime I can get out of the office and away from my desk, I'm happy to do it."

He followed her down a short hall with a living room on one side and an office on the other. The attorney took a seat behind her desk and motioned for him to sit in a chair opposite her. Weber looked around and realized that he wasn't the only one who had to endure paperwork. There were unruly piles of it on her desk, on the credenza beside her, and on a second, smaller desk set off to the side with a steno chair in front of it. He wondered how an unsighted person could deal with so much paperwork, but Miss Jensen seemed to read his mind and answered the unasked question.

"Diana, my paralegal, just had a baby and is off for a few days."

Weber nodded and realized she couldn't see him and said "I see." Then, thinking that might seem inappropriate, he said, "What

I meant was... um...... I'm sorry, Miss Jensen what I meant to say was..."

The woman chuckled as he stumbled over his words and said, "Relax. You're going to break your tongue trying to sound politically correct."

"I'm sorry, I haven't dealt with many blind people and I'm not sure what the protocol is," he admitted.

"We're just like anybody else. Sighted people go to movies, watch TV, listen to the radio, and so do those of us who are blind. I don't expect someone to learn a whole new vocabulary just to talk to me. All I ask is that people don't move things around on me, and please, whatever you do, if you have to use the bathroom while you're here, put the seat back down. No woman likes it when you don't, but it really matters when you're blind."

Weber couldn't help but laugh. He decided this was somebody he could enjoy having as a friend.

"I'll be sure to remember that, Miss Jensen."

"Please, Sheriff, call me Roberta."

"Okay, as long as you call me Jimmy."

"It's a deal," she told him.

"So what's on your mind today, Roberta?"

"George Duncan. I'm afraid his death leaves me with an uncomfortable situation."

"Duncan?"

"He was my client. He came to see me last week about a will."

"It was my understanding that Neil Deferris over in Springerville was his attorney."

"Yes, for his business affairs. But he contacted me right after he and Rosanne got married. He said he needed me to handle some personal matters for him that were not related to the business end of things."

"Okay."

"Normally, this isn't something I would share with you, what with attorney-client privilege and all that," Roberta said. "But it's not a normal situation, given the way he died, and what he told me when he was here."

Weber leaned forward in his chair, his senses alert. "What do you mean?"

Roberta's face grew serious and she said, "When I first started dealing with him he always seemed to be pretty much a happy-go-lucky kind of person. But lately he seemed to change."

"What do you mean?"

"He just seemed rather tense when he came in. I still remember one of the first times he was here. When I asked him how he was doing, Duncan laughed and said something about as long as the hogs were eating and pork was selling, he was doing fine. But the last couple of times he was in, he said things were tense on the home front."

"Did he give you any idea what he meant by that?"

"Not really. He just said something about family drama."

"Okay, and when he came in this last time something was different about him?"

Roberta nodded her head. "Obviously I can't read facial expressions and body language, but I'm pretty intuitive about people, Jimmy. Their tone of voice, the sound of the way they move... for want of a better word, I would say they put out a vibe that I can pick up on. I don't mean in a psychic way, and maybe as a sighted person, that doesn't make any sense to you. But that's how I get a feel for people. And I'm usually right."

Weber couldn't deny that she had quickly picked up on his own initial discomfort when he arrived. His years as a lawman had given him the ability to often sense how somebody was going to act when he arrived on the scene of an argument over a traffic accident or a domestic disturbance or something else out of the ordinary scope of everyday life for most people. Then again, those same years had taught him that you never really knew what anybody was going to do in any given situation.

"I believe you. So what was up with Duncan?"

"He called on Friday, the very first thing in the morning and said he was in town and asked if he could come see me right then. I could tell from his voice that something was wrong. I had another appointment scheduled, but I said sure, as long as we could make it quick. Like I said before, when he first started coming to see me he always seemed relaxed and made small talk. But not this time around. I could tell something was wrong the minute he walked in."

"Did he say what it was?"

She nodded her head. "Duncan said things were getting real ugly out at the farm and he told me he was afraid someone was going to get killed out there before it was all over with."

"Did you ask him what he meant by that?"

"Of course I did. He said that things between his wife and his son had gone downhill from the time he brought Rosanne out to the farm. He said she was always criticizing his son and calling him worthless and saying she wanted him out of there. He said that there were several times when his wife and Sonny had gotten into bad fights."

"When you say fights, do you mean physical confrontations?"

"It sounded like that. The way he talked, Rosanne had pushed Sonny and slapped him more than once. He said the night before he came to see me it had gotten real bad and he had to step in between the two of them to break it up. That's when he said he was afraid somebody was going to get killed out there."

"Did Duncan say if Sonny ever retaliated? Ever hit her back or anything like that?"

Roberta shook her head. "No, the way he talked it was mostly Rosanne getting mad and going on the attack."

"Did he give you any idea why she had it in for Sonny like that?"

"Not really. He did say that he didn't really understand it because she hated living at the farm and that she was constantly wanting him to buy a place in town. He said at first he didn't want to do that, but he decided that if it would keep peace between her and Sonny he'd do it. But then right away, that wasn't enough either. She wanted Sonny gone completely. He said she didn't think he was capable of running the place on his own. That all he would do is bankrupt the business with his drinking and carrying on."

"It sounds like he was damned if he did and damned if he didn't when it came to making her happy," Weber said.

"That's the impression I got," Roberta agreed.

"You said something about a will? Because I'll tell you something, the quicker that thing comes to light and we can determine what Duncan wanted done, the better it's going to be for everybody."

"You'd think so, wouldn't you?"

"What do you mean?" Weber asked warily.

"When he came to see me last week, Duncan said he had been up all night long trying to figure out what the best thing to do was. He said he loved his wife, as difficult as she could be, but that he loved his son, too, and he wanted to do the right thing by him. He said the problem was, he just didn't know what the right thing was. So he had written these up."

She reached for a manila folder on her desk like she could see it and handed it to Weber.

"What do we have here?"

"George Duncan's wills."

"Wills? As in more than one?"

"That's right. And that's why I told you his death leaves me with an uncomfortable situation. As I said, my paralegal has been off having a baby, so they have not been transcribed into my computer so I could read them with JAWS, my screen reader program." As if she could read his mind, the attorney said, "I guess it probably sounds strange to you, a blind person reading. But that's how it's done. I actually read quite a bit. I'm a big fan of audiobooks when I'm not working."

"I learn something new every day," Weber admitted.

"I think we all should learn something new every day. Don't you, Jimmy?"

He nodded, then realized the gesture wasn't received and said, "Yeah, that's a good point. So is it okay if I look at these?"

"That's why I called you."

He opened the folder to find several handwritten pages and began to read. When he was done, he looked up and said, "And just when I thought this case couldn't get any more complicated!"

Chapter 15

"You're kidding me? Duncan had *three* wills?"

"Yep. I read them myself," Weber said as he poured himself a cup of coffee and carried it into his office, where he sat down at his desk.

"And each one is different?"

"That's right. One gives everything to Sonny. One gives everything to Rosanne. And the third one divides everything right down the middle, with each of them getting half."

"Then which one is the valid one? I mean, the way I've always understood it, the last will is the one that carries water," Robyn said.

"Me, too," Weber told her. "But here's the thing. He told Miss Jensen he wrote all three of them the same night and they are all dated for the same night. So there's no way to know which one was the last one."

"So now what happens?"

"I don't know, Robyn. I'm going to go talk to Judge Ryman and see what he has to say about it. I was hoping Duncan's will would have put an end to all the fighting between Sonny and Rosanne, but this is just going to make things even more complicated."

"This is just crazy," Mary Caitlin said. "I've known Duncan all my life and he always seemed like he was a pretty sharp fellow. And it seems like he had been trying to keep things on an even keel in his family. So why would he do something like this?"

"You'd have to ask him that," Weber replied. "And I don't think he's in any condition to be telling us anything."

When the sheriff said those words, little did he know that the dead man *did* have more to say.

~***~

Judge Ryman carefully read the copies of the three wills Weber had brought him, and then he read them a second time. When he was done he put them back in the folder on his desk, took off his reading glasses, and was silent for a long moment. Then he looked up at the sheriff and said, "If there's one thing I can always count on with you, Jimmy, it's that you do make life interesting."

"Don't kill the messenger, Judge. I don't like this any better than you do."

The judge put his hands on top of his balding head and slowly drew them down across his forehead and his eyes. "I'm glad I have to recuse myself from the probate case because of my earlier contact with Mrs. Duncan, because this is a can of worms I don't want to be involved in."

"So what happens now? Which one of these is legal? With three of them handwritten on the same night, are any of them legal?"

"Off the top of my head, I don't think they are," the judge replied. "As I understand the law, a handwritten will, which is called a holographic will in legalese, must be signed by two people who either witnessed the person writing the will sign it, or else received that person's acknowledgment that it is his or her signature or acknowledgment of the will. In other words, two people would have had to sign that they saw Duncan signing the will, or else he would have had to tell two people that he did so and they would have to attest that. Maybe he intended to tell Miss Jensen and somebody in her office that it was his signature and had them sign as witnesses. But that never happened."

"So they're not valid because of that?"

"That's the first problem we have with them. But even if they were witnessed, there's no timestamp or anything to determine which one was written last. I'm not a probate judge, Jimmy, but in my opinion all these things do is muddy the water even worse than it was to start with. Because as of now, unless somebody comes up with a valid will, Duncan died intestate."

"Why in the world would he do this? What's the point of writing three different wills on the same night that all invalidate each other, even if they were witnessed and legal and all of that?"

"Your guess is as good as mine," the judge said.

"What are we supposed to do with this information?"

"What does Miss Jensen have to say about it?"

"She was just as perplexed as I am."

"Perplexed? Have you been trying to expand your vocabulary again, Jimmy?"

"Hey, I get around!"

"I'm sure you do. Anyway, what was her take on all of this?"

"Like I said, she doesn't understand why he would have done it, either."

"She didn't ask him when he brought these to her?"

"No, Duncan came in without an appointment and she had somebody else on the schedule, so it was just a quick visit. Her paralegal normally reads things to her, but she was out having a baby. All she knows is he told her there were three wills there and he wanted her to type them all up for him."

"She knew there were three wills?"

"Yeah. Like I said, he showed up unannounced and her other appointment came in right behind him. So there wasn't really much time to talk it over with him. He said he would get back together with her on Monday to explain everything. But we know what happened then."

"Didn't Mrs. Duncan say something about her husband's attorney being out of town or something and she couldn't locate his will? I'm assuming she doesn't know about him working with Miss Jensen or anything about these wills?"

"Apparently not," Weber said. "Duncan had an attorney named Deferris over in Springerville, but he came to Miss Jensen not long after he got married to Rosanne and said he needed her to handle some things for him."

"I know Neil Deferris," the judge replied. "He pretty much concentrates on business law, corporate filings, those kinds of things. So I'm not surprised he would refer Duncan to a general practice attorney for wills and such. Have you by any chance spoken to Neil yet?"

"No, Weber said, shaking his head. "I called his office and his secretary said he took his two grandsons on a rafting trip down the Colorado River through the Grand Canyon. And from there they were going over to Sedona to do some camping in the red rock country. He's supposed to be back early next week."

"Okay. You need to try to talk to him as soon as he gets back and see if he has anything he can add to this. Like I said, I don't think these things are valid. So unless there's a signed and dated and witnessed will out there somewhere, Duncan was intestate and things are still a mess."

"There's more to it than that," Weber said.

The judge looked at him and raised his eyebrows in question. The sheriff told him what Roberta had said about Duncan's fears that somebody was going to get killed out at the hog farm. When he was done, Judge Ryman shook his head and repeated, "Yes, you do make life interesting. Do you think there was more to Duncan's death than a simple accident?"

"I don't know." Weber shrugged his shoulders. "As a cop, I'm naturally suspicious. But from what Miss Jensen told me, it sounded more like he was afraid that either Sonny or Rosanne would wind up dead. And from the sounds of things, I would have bet on Sonny being the one wearing a toe tag if it went that far."

"What if Duncan showed his wife these wills?"

"Who knows? Let's say she saw the one giving everything to her. If she was greedy enough, would she take him out so she could own it all? Things like that have been known to happen."

The judge nodded in agreement. "Or, given what we've seen of her temperament, is it possible it went the other way?"

"What do you mean?"

"What if he showed her the will giving Sonny everything? Could she have done something to him in a fit of rage?"

"I don't think so," Weber said shaking his head. "First of all, that will gives everything to Sonny. As volatile as she is, I don't think she would do something to Duncan until she figured out some way to convince him to change the will. And all this is speculation until we hear from the Medical Examiner's Office about the autopsy anyway. Duncan was a big man and Rosanne isn't all that big. I don't know how she could physically manage whatever happened to him."

"You're probably right, but what's your gut telling you, Jimmy?"

"To be honest, Judge, ever since we pulled up out there at the hog farm and I saw what was left of Duncan, my gut's been telling me I need to find a new line of work."

Chapter 16

One of the great things about being a small town sheriff in the community where he had grown up was that Weber knew just about everybody. Or at least he had at one time, before the developers had moved in a few years ago and started building condos and vacation cabins everywhere. Now he was lucky if he recognized half the faces he saw on the sidewalk. Some saw the boom as a good thing, bringing lots of money into town, which had resulted in new businesses opening up and an increase in the tax base.

But there were a lot of old-timers who longed for the way things used to be, when the pace of life was slower. Back when you knew everybody on a first name basis and nobody ever thought about locking their doors at night. There was no question that things had changed with the influx of newcomers. Traffic was heavier, especially on the busy summer weekends, and crime had increased to the point where vacant cabins were a prime target for burglars in the off-season. Weber and his deputies spent a lot of time dealing with everything from nuisance animal calls to narcotics cases, to assaults at the local taverns caused by conflicts between the weekenders who seemed to have an attitude of superiority over the local yokels and the full-time resident good old boys who resented them.

Weber and Deputy Dolan Reed had just returned from breaking up a disturbance at the Redeye Saloon that had started when two young men from Tempe had been overheard wondering out loud what one of the cute waitresses was or was not wearing under her short calico skirt. The person who heard their remarks happened to be Jerry Gardner, a husky ranch hand, and the waitress who was the topic of their conversation was his younger sister Kimberly. Jerry was at the new western-themed saloon to give her a ride home at the end of her shift and he took exception to the way they were talking about her. He took even more exception when one of them had lifted the back of his sister's skirt as she passed by to settle the bet once and for all.

Kimberly had only been a waitress for two weeks, but she was a fast learner and it didn't take her long to figure out that the skimpy costumes her employer required the waitresses to wear were as big a draw as the cold beer she served. And truth be told, she kind of enjoyed the admiring look she got and wasn't above some mild flirting, as long as everyone understood that it was just business. But those two had taken it too far, and once Jerry got his dander up, he wasn't going to back down easily in spite of her efforts to calm him down.

As for the two out-of-towners, they figured there was strength in numbers, and all of those hours spent working out in the gym back home had left them with hard abs and a lot of misplaced confidence. As it turned out, their superior numbers and their abs were no match for a country boy who spent his time pitching hay bales onto the back of a flatbed truck and wrestling stubborn steers to the ground at branding time. By the time Weber and Dolan had arrived on the scene it was all over except for picking up the bruised and bloodied duo whose mouths had written checks their brawny muscles couldn't cash and sending them packing.

Then they had to break up the heated argument between Jerry and Reggie Sosin, the bar's owner. Reggie wanted Jerry arrested for disturbing the peace, and had told Kimberly she was fired. Her big brother told Weber if he needed to take him to jail that was fine, but warned Reggie that if he took his anger out on his kid sister he better think twice. After all, Reggie was the one who insisted his waitresses dress that way in the first place!

It had taken a while to get everybody to stop shouting, and while Reggie had not been willing to back down in his argument with Jerry, he had a change of heart when Weber took him aside and explained that reconsidering would be in his best interest. Sure, the sheriff had looked the other way a time or two when the beer delivery truck had blocked the alley behind the business, and as long as they hadn't gotten behind the wheels of their cars, he had not hassled the occasional patron he saw stumbling outside the place with too much to drink. But the law was the law, and if his deputies had to write some tickets to keep that alleyway open for traffic, or start coming into the saloon on a regular basis to make sure the state liquor laws were being obeyed, the sheriff would certainly make sure they did their jobs. Once he understood the situation clearly, Reggie admitted that he had probably overreacted just as much as Jerry had, and the two men shook hands grudgingly while Kimberly counted her tips and promised to be on time for her shift the next day.

Weber and Dolan were still commenting on how those two city boys had gotten a lesson in manners when Mary Caitlin answered the telephone and told him that someone from the Medical Examiner's office in Tucson needed to talk to him.

"I have to tell you, Sheriff Weber, this latest case you sent us caused quite a stir in our office," Doctor Hurtado said when Weber took the call.

"Why's that?"

"We deal with all kinds of deaths here, as I'm sure you can imagine. You name it and we've seen it. Homicides, suicides, traffic accidents, work-related fatalities, folks who got lost in the desert and didn't make it back out. But I don't think anyone here had ever dealt with a case where someone was devoured by hogs before. I know it sounds ghastly from most people's point of view, but from our perspective it was a once in a lifetime case. I don't think we've had so many personnel taking part or watching an autopsy in the history of this office."

"Well, if I go the rest of my life without seeing something like that again, it won't be too soon," Weber said.

"I understand, and I certainly wasn't making light of the way Mr. Duncan died. But from a professional standpoint... let's just say this isn't a case any of our people are going to forget anytime soon."

"I wish I could forget," Weber said. He, too, had seen a lot of ugly things in his time, but Duncan's death had been the worst of the worst. "So what can you tell me about it?"

"I will email you the full report first thing in the morning, but I wanted to go over a couple of things with you before I left for the day."

"I'm listening," Weber said.

There was the sound of paper shuffling, and then Dr. Hurtado said, "Obviously, determining a cause of death for Mr. Duncan wasn't easy, considering the amount of trauma his body suffered both antemortem and postmortem. Any number of his injuries could have killed him."

"But were you able to determine just one?"

"Yes, I have, Sheriff. I'm listing the cause of death accidental due to massive blood loss. In layman's terms, George Duncan bled to death as a result of being gored by a bull."

"Do you think he was alive when the hogs got to him?"

"Based on the photographs and drawings you sent to us, to be honest I'm surprised he managed to get from where the bull attacked him all the way to the hog pen. Most men I know could not have made it half that distance after sustaining the injuries he received."

"He was a tough old guy, no question about that," Weber said, reminded of his own father and countless other small farmers and ranchers he had known growing up.

"No doubt about that, and we'll get into that in a moment. But in answer to your question, I really can't say if he was alive or not by the time the hogs started in on him. I certainly hope not."

Weber shuddered. "Yeah, I hope not, too. I can't even imagine what that must have been like. I don't *want* to imagine it!"

"If it's any comfort to you, Sheriff, if he was alive, I think he was beyond having the capability to know what was happening to him."

Weber didn't know if there was any comfort in that or not.

"Anyway, the autopsy shows that he had a large penetrating injury to the front of his torso that shattered his sternum and destroyed the thymus."

"I wasn't the best student in high school, and biology wasn't my favorite subject anyway, so I'm not very well versed on anatomy," Weber admitted. "I never heard of that."

"A lot of people haven't," the doctor said. "It's a small butterfly-shaped organ that is located between the heart and the sternum. Basically, the thymus is part of the immune system. It produces T cells, which are a type of white blood cell."

"And that's what led to all the bleeding?"

"No, the victim's right lung was also punctured, pretty much destroyed, actually. And there were deep lacerations to the thoracic diaphragm."

"Again, you're talking above my pay grade," Weber said.

"The thoracic diaphragm is a sheet of muscle that's located at the bottom of the rib cage. It separates the chest cavity from the abdominal cavity. I think injuries to it were made secondary to the initial penetration by the bull's horn. Probably when it was shaking its head to dislodge Mr. Duncan. All of that added up to massive blood loss. You put all those injuries together and there's no question that it was a fatal wound."

"Duncan's son and one of his workers at the hog farm both said that they warned him over and over about getting too close to that bull, but he seemed to think they were buddies. Apparently the bull didn't get that message."

"No, it doesn't look like he did. I'm a city boy, so you probably know more about bulls than I do, Sheriff Weber. But what I do know is that I sure wouldn't trust one enough to get that close to it. But there's something else I discovered during the course of the autopsy that I think you might find interesting."

"What's that?"

"We talked about what a wonder it was that Mr. Duncan was able to make it all the way to the hog pen from where he was gored. What did you say it was? Twenty yards or something like that?"

"We measured it. 22 yards. Like you said, it's amazing he made it that far, as torn up as he was after that damn bull got finished with him. But again, he was a tough old guy."

"There's no question about that," Dr. Hurtado agreed. "But he may not have done it all by himself."

"What do you mean?" Weber asked.

"I think he may have had help."

Chapter 17

Weber knew enough about computers to receive and answer email, and he could plot a route with a computer mapping program when he was planning a road trip, but when it got much further than that he had to call in the experts. One of those experts was Dan Wright, who turned on the sheriff's computer and logged onto the Medical Examiner's secure website using the password Dr. Hurtado gave him. Then he navigated his way to a file folder and clicked to open it, revealing thumbnail pictures of Duncan's autopsy.

"If you will click on photo 27 and open it, there's something I want to show you," Dr. Hurtado said through the speakerphone.

Dan clicked on the thumbnail and the color photo opened up.

"What you're looking at is Mr. Duncan's upper torso, just under his left arm," the medical examiner said. "Do you see that area circled in red?"

"Yeah, we see it," Weber said.

"Okay, now click on the next photo, number 28."

Dan did so and a close up of the indicated area of the arm came onto the screen.

"Do you see those three small lacerations in the skin?"

"That's what we're seeing," Weber said.

"In examining Mr. Duncan's body, besides the obvious trauma that he suffered at and after his death, we noticed numerous scratches and small wounds and scars that all happened sometime before he died. I'm talking days, or even weeks before. And that's not surprising for a man who did hard physical labor outdoors."

"No, it's not," Weber said, looking at his own left hand, which still bore a noticeable scar just above the base of his thumb. It was a reminder of the time he had mistakenly got it caught between his lariat and the saddle horn when roping a cow back when he was in high school. He was lucky; he had seen two or three old cowboys who were missing thumbs from such carelessness. The sheriff's body carried a couple of other reminders of his days spent on the ranch, and he remembered his father's hands and arms always being banged up back when he was still alive. "There are a thousand ways to get injured when somebody does that kind of work," he said.

"Agreed," Dr. Hurtado replied. "But these little marks I'm talking about here, I thought they looked like something different. I just couldn't put my finger on what it was. Then we looked at the clothing Mr. Duncan was wearing when he came in. Please click on photo number 29."

Dan did and Weber looked at a small crescent-shaped red object and asked, "What is this?"

"I wasn't sure at first myself," Dr. Hurtado replied. "But Jenna McCallum, one of our assistants here, recognized it right away. It's part of an acrylic fingernail. It was lodged inside the fabric of Mr. Duncan's flannel shirt, right where the innermost of those three small wounds are. Then I realized immediately what I had been looking at. Those three little marks on Mr. Duncan's body are consistent with what we see in wounds when a woman digs her fingernails into somebody."

"What does this mean? How did they get there?"

"Your guess is as good as mine, Sheriff. This is pure speculation on my part, but is it possible that somebody had hold of Mr. Duncan at some point and was helping him stay upright?"

"Like after he was injured? That could explain how he got so far away from where the bull gored him in the first place."

"Maybe. But as I said, this is pure speculation on my part. There could be a dozen other explanations."

"Such as?"

"Who's to say, Sheriff? Maybe as he was going out the door that morning somebody embraced him in a moment of passion. Or anger. We don't know. The first thing to determine is who was wearing the fingernail this piece broke off from."

"Did you find anything else? Any other pieces of the fingernail?"

"No, not of the fingernail itself. But on closer examination of the three little lacerations I showed you in photo 28, I was able to find microscopic pieces of the same material in two of them."

Weber's mind was racing as he tried to picture what might have happened out at the hog farm in Duncan's last moments of life and how he had received those small wounds to his upper torso. He didn't like any of the possibilities that he came up with. But he was becoming convinced that Duncan's death might have been more than just a tragic accident.

~***~

"I don't know, Jimmy," Dolan Reed said. "What did Duncan weigh? Over 250 pounds, I'm sure. I don't think his wife weighs much more than half that soaking wet. Would she be able to help him move very far in the condition he was in after that bull got done with him?"

"We've all heard of people doing some pretty amazing things when the adrenaline kicks in," Chad Summers replied. "Lifting cars off of somebody when a jack slipped and things like that. I guess it's possible."

"Yeah, do you remember when Phil Baker rolled his pickup truck out there on the mountain a couple three years ago? That boy of his, Terry, he was like twelve or thirteen years old, but he managed to pull his dad out from where he was stuck under the truck. That kid looked like a strong wind would blow him over, but he got his daddy out from under there and then he hiked down off that mountain and got help for him."

"That's what I'm talking about, Buz. I think it's entirely possible."

"But if she was helping him, why did she stop? And why didn't she call for help? According to her story, she didn't know what had happened to her husband until she heard all the commotion after Sonny and the hired hand found him."

"Good question, Robyn. *If* that's what happened at all. Doctor Hurtado said more than once that this is just pure speculation. We just don't know. Jordan, do you remember if Mrs. Duncan was wearing any kind of artificial fingernails when you were there in the house with her? I don't recall, myself."

The young deputy shook his head. "I'm sorry Sheriff, I don't. I just remember she didn't seem like somebody who was all that upset that her husband had died in such a terrible way."

"What about the other lady that was out there? Mona Bowers?"

Weber shook his head. "No, she's not the kind of woman to go in for that sort of thing. I do remember seeing her hands when she poured me coffee, because they reminded me of my mother's. Red and rough from work."

"Well, I damn sure don't see Sonny Duncan or either of those hired hands of theirs wearing fake fingernails," Buz said.

"Maybe we're barking up the wrong tree with all of this," Deputy "Coop" Cooper said. "I'm just playing devil's advocate here, Jimmy. From what we know of Roseanne Duncan, she's not a very nice woman at all. But does that mean she had anything to do with her husband's death?"

"No, it doesn't. You could be right, Coop, and we're just jumping to conclusions or looking for something that isn't there. But when we consider what Miss Jensen told me about Duncan saying he was afraid somebody was going to get killed out there at the farm, I do think we need to at least look into this further, don't you?"

"Oh, I agree completely with what you're saying. I'm just trying to look at it from all angles, boss."

Before retiring from the Army and joining the Big Lake Sheriff's Department, Coop had a career as a military policeman and served as an investigator with the Army's Criminal Investigation Division. He brought a lifetime of experience to the Sheriff's Department and Weber trusted his judgment and valued his opinion.

"So where do we go from here?"

"I really want to talk to that other attorney of Duncan's, this Neil Deferris, as soon as he gets back from his trip. I'm wondering what he can tell us about Duncan's situation. In the meantime, we need to know more about Rosanne Duncan. Dan, I want you to run a complete background check on her, from the day she was born until now. And while you're at it, on Sonny Duncan, Leonard and Mona Bowers, and Carl Turner, too."

"I'm on it," Dan Wright said. "What about that couple that worked out there that Mrs. Duncan run off? What were their names?"

"José and Carmen Barela. Yeah, as long as you're at it, them, too. And Robyn, tomorrow can you nose around at the beauty shops here in town and over in Springerville and Eagar and see if you can find out if Roseanne Duncan went to any of them, and if so, if she wears those fake fingernails?"

"You're giving me that job because I'm a girl, right?"

"Hey, if you'd rather, you can ride back out to the hog farm with me to talk to Sonny and the hired help."

"No, thank you," Robyn said, shaking her head. "I washed the clothes you wore out there twice, and they still stink."

"Damn, girl, the wedding isn't until June and Jimmy's already got you washing his britches for him? He's training you right!"

Robyn stuck her tongue out at Parks and said, "Shut up. You're not even officially on this case."

"Oh, I wasn't picking on you," the FBI agent said. "I just want to know how he does it. I could use some help with Marsha."

"You need some help, all right," Robyn shot back with a smirk. "At least that's what she tells me when we're having girl talk."

"What does that mean?"

"Damn, *boy*, you've been with her this long and you *still* have to ask?"

"Now I'm going to spend the rest of the day wondering what I did wrong this time," Parks pouted.

Dolan slapped him on the back and said, "Don't even try to figure it out, buddy. Trust me, I've been married long enough to know that even if you did, by the time you corrected it there would still be a long list of other sins you've got to atone for. All you can do is the best you can do, and hope they don't smother you with a pillow in your sleep."

Chapter 18

The days were growing shorter and it was almost dark when Weber and Coop got to the hog farm. They found Sonny Duncan, shovel in hand, ankle-deep in the muck of one of the pens. He was wearing knee high rubber boots, jeans and a T-shirt, and was sweating in spite of the chilly air.

"She came back with that attorney of hers and her preacher and packed some stuff and left," he said when Weber asked if Rosanne was there. "But she made sure to tell me that she was only staying in town until my dad's will was done, and then I was out of here once and for all. I wanted to tell her she had another think coming if she thought my dad was going to cut me out in favor of her, but I didn't. I'm just trying to get along out here, Sheriff. That's all I can do right now."

Weber had not donned one of the paper masks that he and his deputies had used on their first trip to the hog farm, and now he regretted it. He wasn't sure which was better, breathing through his mouth or his nose. Neither way helped. He wondered again how Sonny and Duncan and the rest of them could have stood living there full-time.

"We've got a few more questions for you, if you can take a break."

Sonny nodded, nudged one of the pigs out of the way, and climbed out of the pen. He leaned the shovel against the wall of a wooden shed, sat down on a bench and used the heel of one foot to nudge the rubber boot off the opposite foot, revealing a tennis shoe underneath, and repeated the process with the other boot.

"What do you need?"

"Can we go over to your trailer and talk?"

"Sure," Sonny said leading the way. Weber wasn't sure how much of the hog smell was shielded by being inside the mobile home, but at least it was warmer. Sonny waved them to chairs at the kitchen table and sat down.

"Sonny, do you know who your father's attorney was?"

"Yeah, Neil Deferris over in Springerville."

"As I understand it, Mr. Deferris pretty much handles business law. Is that right?"

Sonny shrugged his shoulders. "I guess so, I never got involved in any of that stuff. That was my old man's thing. Although, to him a handshake was better than a contract any day of the week. You know that if you ever had anything to do with him."

"I never did business with him, but from everything I have ever known about him, I'm sure you're right."

"He hooked up with Mr. Deferris years ago, because as the business started expanding it was too much for him to keep track of the different agreements he had with customers. And we got burned by more than a couple of restaurants who went belly up and never paid us. I never cared enough about the business to get involved in all that. Like I said, I never was too fond of this place to start with."

Weber didn't want to reveal his cards by mentioning Duncan's association with Roberta Jensen, so he just asked, "Do you think this Deferris fellow would have drawn up your father's will, or did he have somebody else handle things like that?"

Sonny shrugged his shoulders again. "I have no idea, Sheriff. I don't even know if my old man had a will. If he did, he never mentioned it to me."

"Okay. Let me ask you something else. I know things aren't good between you and Rosanne, but was it like that right from the start? Or did something change somewhere along the way?"

"What does this have to do with my dad being dead?"

"Nothing, really. You have to understand, Sonny, it's not like he keeled over from a heart attack or something like that. When somebody dies like your dad did, we have to make sure we cover all the bases."

The other man's eyes narrowed and he looked at Weber carefully. "Do you think that bitch had anything to do with what happened to my dad?"

"No," Weber said, shaking his head and backpedaling. "I didn't mean to imply that at all. It's pretty evident that bull of his gored him, and as for the rest of it, with what happened with the hogs and all, it's tragic. But I talked to the medical examiner who did your fathers autopsy, and there's no question that the injuries he suffered from the bull are what killed him."

"That frigging Montezuma! I told my dad to get rid of that son of a bitch over and over, but he'd just laugh and say they were buddies."

"I remember you telling me that."

"I tried to at least talk him into having Duane Matlock dehorn him. Even he told my dad it needed to be done. He always took anything the vet said as gospel when it came to the livestock, except for that. He said if you cut a bull's horns and balls off, all you had left was a cow with a pecker, and this wasn't no dairy farm."

"Getting back to the situation between you and Rosanne, like I asked, were things bad between you two right from the get-go?"

"To be honest, I didn't like her the first time I saw her. I was kinda blown away when my dad told me he had met somebody in the first place. He'd been alone for so long. But I wanted him to be happy, and he damn sure deserved to be. So I didn't say anything when he first brought her around."

"And how was she, at first?"

"Oh, she was so sickly sweet it was disgusting. She was hanging on his arm and calling him Georgie. *Georgie.* Can you believe that? Nobody ever called my old man that. Shoot, most folks didn't even call him George, just Duncan."

"That's all any of us knew him by," Weber said. "In fact, to be honest I didn't even know that wasn't his first name until all this happened. And I'd known him as long as I can remember."

"Right. So you know how weird that was. Anyway, like I said, she was kind of hanging on him and my old man was eating it up. But I figured if she put a smile on his face, it wasn't any of my business how it got there."

"And how was she toward you back then?"

"Oh, she tried to play the game. But it didn't take me long to see right through her."

"How so?"

"She was just all fake and plastic," Sonny said. "Like when we first met. I could see in her eyes that she didn't like me before she even knew me. Trust me, Sheriff, I've had enough women look down their noses at me to know when it's happening. But she tried to cover it up at first, telling me I was just as handsome as my old man and bullshit like that. But I could read right through her and I wasn't falling for it. But I tried not to let on, for my dad's sake."

"You said at first she was coming across, how did you say it, *sickly sweet*? What do you think changed things between you and her?"

"They got married, that's what changed things! The ink wasn't even dry on the marriage license before she started showing her true colors. Like the way she acted when she met Leonard and Mona, and the Barelas. You could tell she thought they were way beneath her. And I told you what she did when Carl hugged her, pushing him away and jumping down his throat like that. But they were married by then and my dad seemed blind to the way she was."

"Do you know much about where she came from, before she met Duncan?"

"What do you mean?"

"I don't know, like, was she married before? What did she do for a living? Any background?"

"What are you onto, Sheriff? Why all these questions about Rosanne if the autopsy says that the bull killed my dad?"

"Like I said, Sonny, we just want to make sure we cover all the bases."

"If that bitch did anything to my dad..."

"Now don't be going off half-cocked," Weber cautioned him. "Like I said, he died from the injuries he received when the bull attacked him. There's no question about that."

"Okay, then why do you keep asking questions about her?"

"You can't deny she's been acting really strange," Coop said. "We're just trying to get a handle on her."

"The thing you guys don't get is that she isn't acting strange," Sonny replied.

"What do you mean?"

"I mean, she's been acting just like she always did. Like a crazy bitch who wants her way every second of every day. Nothing's changed just because my dad is dead."

"Okay, it's getting late and you've had a long day. Let us get out of your hair."

Weber and Coop stood up, and Sonny asked, "Now that the autopsy's done, what next? Will they be sending him back up here for the funeral? I was a kid when my mom died and I don't even know what's involved or what I have to do, or anything about how to get it done."

"I'd suggest you call one of the mortuaries in Show Low or Springerville and let them handle that end of things," Weber said. "As much as I hate to say it, you and Rosanne are going to have to coordinate on all that, her being his wife."

"Yeah, I guess so. I'm not looking forward to that, but I'll do what needs to be done."

Sonny walked them to the door, and before they left, Weber asked, "Speaking of which, you said Rosanne was staying in town. Do you know where?"

"No idea, Sheriff. I was just glad she was leaving. I know that she stopped and talked to Mona on her way out. Maybe she can tell you something."

"Thanks, Sonny. We appreciate your time."

Sonny stood in the doorway of his trailer and watched them walk back to Weber's Explorer, then closed the door.

"So, did we learn anything from that?"

"I don't know, Coop. What do you think?"

"I think it's a good thing you told him a couple of times that his father died from what the bull did to him. Because I think if that boy even suspected his stepmother had a hand in the old man's death, it wouldn't end up pretty."

Chapter 19

Mona Bowers answered Weber's knock on her door and led them into the living room of the mobile home she shared with her husband. The TV was turned to a news channel and Weber could smell chicken frying from the kitchen.

"Hello, Sheriff Weber. What can I do for you?"

"Just a few more questions if you have time, Mrs. Bowers. I don't want to interrupt your cooking."

"No problem," she assured him. "Do you mind talking in the kitchen?"

"Not at all," Weber told her. He knew country folks do a lot of their visiting in the kitchen and was used to it. And the aroma from the frying pan was a lot more pleasant than what they had left behind outside.

She turned the flame down a little and asked if they wanted coffee, then poured two thick mugs full without waiting for an answer. "I'm afraid Leonard's not back from his delivery run yet, but hopefully he will be here before too long. We're really shorthanded and he's been putting in a lot of hours since we lost Duncan."

"I understand," Weber said. "Are you going to get some more help out here anytime soon?"

A worried look crossed her face and she shook her head as she shrugged her shoulders. "I really don't know what's going to happen, Sheriff. Things are so up in the air that I don't know from one day to the next if we even have jobs anymore. I mean, Sonny's never made any secret of the fact that he hates this place and wants nothing to do with it, and Mrs. Duncan... well, I won't even go there."

"Hopefully it'll work out before too much longer," Weber told her, not envying her and her husband's position, caught in the power struggle between Duncan's son and his widow.

"You said you had some questions?"

"Yes, ma'am. We just talked to Sonny and he said that Mrs. Duncan was staying in town someplace."

"That's right. She was here with her minister and some other man and packed a suitcase. As they were leaving she saw me and stopped to tell me she would be staying in Springerville until things were settled, and to keep an eye on Sonny and let her know if he was up to any funny business."

"Funny business?"

"Yeah, whatever that means. I wanted to tell her I'd didn't want to be stuck in the middle of whatever was going on between the two of them, but I thought better of it. But I have to tell you, if it comes down to it, me and Leonard's loyalties are with Sonny all the way."

"I understand that," Weber said. "You said she wanted you to let her know what Sonny was doing. Did she give you a phone number or anything, to get hold of her?"

"She did. Hold on just a second." Mona went to the refrigerator and lifted a magnet to remove one of Dean Wicklund's business cards. She handed it to Weber and said, "She wrote her cell phone number on the back."

He copied the number into his notepad, along with Wicklund's office number, and handed the card back to her. "Did she say where she was going to be staying?"

Mona shook her head. "No, she didn't."

"Do you happen to know where she lived before she and Duncan got together?"

"Not really. Someplace in Springerville, as I recall."

"When she moved out here, did your husband and Duncan or anybody move a bunch of furniture or anything from her old place?"

"No, she just had four or five suitcases full of stuff. I remember Leonard saying that for a woman her age, she sure traveled light."

"I know you guys didn't have much of a relationship, but did she ever say anything about where she came from or anything like that?"

"No, we weren't exactly confidants. She pretty much kept to herself except when she was yelling at somebody about something. I tried to make her feel welcome and to get to know her, for Duncan's sake if nothing else. Two or three times after she first got here I went up to the house to visit with her or see if there was anything I could do to help her get settled in. Just trying to be neighborly, if you know what I mean. And she let me know she didn't need anything from me and she didn't want me coming around like that."

"How about Duncan? Did he ever say anything about her past that you can recall?"

"No, sir," Mona replied, using a pair of tongs to turn the chicken in the frying pan. "He was so smitten with her right from the start that if she had told him she came from Mars or Venus I don't think it would have mattered to him."

"One other question, and then we'll get out of your way," Weber said. "Did you ever notice Mrs. Duncan wearing much in the way of makeup or lipstick, or artificial nails? Any of that kind of thing?"

Mona snorted and shook her head. "No. I'm pretty sure she would have considered anything like that immoral. In fact, Carmen liked to put on some makeup and make herself look nice, and I remember Mrs. Duncan telling her that she looked like a painted whore. Well, harlot is the word she used, but it means the same thing. Said it right to her face."

"Carmen? Carmen Barela, right?"

"Yes. I couldn't believe anybody would say something like that to somebody else. Especially someone as sweet as Carmen. It's not like she had it painted on like a circus clown like you see some of the young girls do. It was only some mascara and lipstick. But that's Mrs. Duncan for you. Nobody measures up to her standards, and she doesn't hesitate to let them know it."

"How did Carmen react to that?"

"Oh, it hurt her. It hurt her bad. I could see it in her face. The poor girl was humiliated."

"What did she do?"

"Nothing. Nothing at all. Carmen and José are wonderful people, and like I told you before, we were all just one big family here before Mrs. Duncan showed up. But, I'm not sure how to say this right, but Carmen and José, they knew their place, if you know what I mean."

"I'm not sure I do," Weber replied, though he did.

"Them being Mexican and hired help and all, they weren't the type to question or talk back to the boss man. Or the boss lady, as far as that goes. Now don't get me wrong Sheriff," Mona said waving her hand, "I don't mean that Duncan or anybody else out here ever treated them any less at all. Not one bit. I meant it when I said we were all family. Well, we were before Duncan married that woman. But like I said, Carmen and José always kind of deferred to others. Does what I'm trying to say make any sense to you?"

"Yes, it does," Weber assured her. Over the years his parents had employed two or three different Hispanic ranch hands and they had lived on the property with their families, just like the Barelas had at the hog farm. And just like Duncan and the Bowers, they had not seen color or cared about race, but there was a cultural difference that was never stated but always understood.

"We'll get out of your way," he said draining his coffee cup. "We appreciate your time, Mona. And we appreciate the coffee."

She walked them to the door, and just before she left, she said, "I wish we could turn back the hands of time, Sheriff. Just turn them back to before that woman came here, before Duncan got himself killed, before everything changed."

"I understand, ma'am. Please give our regards to your husband."

Chapter 20

The autopsy report was waiting for Weber when he got to the office Thursday morning, and held no surprises. It confirmed what Doctor Hurtado had told him on the telephone the previous day - George Duncan had died from massive blood loss as a result of being gored by a bull, and his lower extremities and most of his left hand had been devoured by his hogs. That had most probably happened after his death. The report also included the notation about the three small lacerations on the dead man's upper arm and the discovery of the fragment of acrylic fingernail that the medical examiner had talked to him about the day before.

Coop and Larry Parks read the autopsy report after Weber was finished with it, and the FBI agent said, "I guess the only good thing about all of this is that it doesn't look like he was alive when the hogs got to him."

"There is that," Weber said. "What do you think about this thing with a piece of broken fingernail and those marks on his arm?"

"I think it's like this Dr. Hurtado said, it could be a lot of things. Maybe Duncan and his wife got frisky that morning before he went outside to do his thing."

"I don't know, Parks. You've met the woman. Can you picture her ever being frisky?"

"Hey, you never know what happens behind closed doors. And sometimes those church ladies can be pretty freaky when they let their hair down."

"Maybe, but I just don't see it in this case."

"Do you really think it was like the ME suggested? That somebody was out there helping him at some point after the bull attacked him? And was that somebody Mrs. Duncan?"

"I don't know, Coop," Weber admitted. "According to her statement, no. And if she *was* out there, why did she help him and then just stop and go back inside the house and act like it never happened? Why didn't she scream for help, or go get Sonny or somebody to help?"

"Since nobody else wants to be the one to ask it, I guess I will," Parks said. "Do you think Roseanne Duncan had anything to do with her husband ending up in the hog pen in the first place?"

"That's a horrible thought, but I have to admit it's crossed my mind," Weber replied.

"It's possible, but I don't know if it's plausible," Coop said. "What did Dolan say yesterday, that Duncan weighed at least 250 pounds, and his wife is a lot smaller? Could she have hoisted him up and over the rails into the hog pen? Even with that adrenaline rush Buz was talking about, I just don't see that happening, to be honest with you."

"It's a stretch," Weber admitted. "But I still think we need to consider it."

"Can I put one more thing out there to muddy the water even more?"

"Sure, why not? What are you thinking?"

"From everything we've heard, this José and Carmen Barela were salt of the earth type people. But is it possible that there's a connection there to all of this?"

"I'm not following you, Coop. What are you suggesting?"

"I'm not suggesting as much just thinking out loud, Jimmy. According to Mona Bowers, Carmen Barela liked to wear makeup and things like that. And maybe she wore those fake nails."

"Yeah. But from what we know, they moved up around Holbrook someplace after they left the hog farm."

"Right, but could they have gone back. Or at least her?"

"For what reason?"

"I don't know. Maybe things weren't working out where they are now and she, or they, tried to talk Duncan into taking them back?"

"From what Sonny told us, it was more like Duncan trying to talk them into staying after Roseanne accused Carmen and her husband of having something going on."

"Okay, maybe one or both of them went back because they were upset about the way things ended? Maybe they thought they were owed more than they got at the end. I'm just spit-balling ideas here, Jimmy."

"Anything's possible. But from what I know about Duncan, I don't think he would ever short anybody when it came to money."

"No, I don't think so either, from what I've heard about the man. I'm talking more about the fact that they worked hard out there and maybe felt like they got the short end of the stick with him caving in to his wife and all that."

"I guess it could happen. Maybe we need to take a ride up to Holbrook and talk to them. Let's see if Dan's been able to come up with anything on them that we need to know about."

~***~

"Just like Sonny and the Bowers said, they're good people," Dan Wright said when Weber asked him about the background checks on José and Carmen Barela. "Neither one has any kind of a record for anything at all. Not even a ticket."

"How about the others?"

"Leonard Bowers actually has had two traffic violations in the past four years. One was an equipment stop for a bad taillight over in Gallup, New Mexico four years ago next month. He got a fix-it ticket, no fine or court appearance required. The other was a ticket for doing 62 in a 55 in Apache County two years ago. He paid a $135 fine by mail and that was it. Nothing at all on his wife."

"What about Roseanne and Sonny Duncan?"

"I'm not finding a lot on her and nothing that raises any red flags. Before moving to Springerville she lived down in Benson, Arizona for three years, and before that in Deming, New Mexico. She was married once before and her first husband passed away seven years ago. She had one traffic ticket a year ago, for failure to yield to an emergency vehicle, but that's it. Nothing that stands out."

"How about Sonny?"

"That's another matter, Jimmy. He has a history, and it's not all good."

"Okay, fill me in."

"He had a DUI last year over in Springerville. He paid a fine and his license was suspended for 30 days. And a couple of speeding tickets, nothing crazy."

"That's it?"

"No," Dan said, shaking his head and pointing a finger at an entry on his computer monitor. "There's more. Look at this."

Coop and Weber looked at the entry and Coop whistled. "That could change things."

"Yeah," Weber said. "Nobody told us about Sonny's domestic violence arrest."

~***~

"Yeah, I did something stupid and I'm ashamed it ever happened. But I paid the price for it, and then some. But what's that got to do with what happened to my dad?"

"Why didn't you tell us about this before, Sonny?"

"Like I said, it's not something I'm proud of, okay? Believe me, if I could take back what happened that night I would. I'm not making any excuses for it. But I don't see what that has to do with what happened to my dad. There's something you're not telling me, Sheriff."

"Why don't you tell us what happened?"

"By now I'm sure you know. So what's the point?"

"We'd like to hear it from you."

"Look, I screwed up. I never thought I would find a woman that wanted anything to do with me. And it turns out I was right. Claudia couldn't stand living out here right from the start. And can you blame her? You'd think after spending my life here I'd be used to the smell of those damn hogs. And maybe I am, a little bit. But the first time I brought her out here she almost puked. She tried to stick it out for a while, but she couldn't handle it. I understood that and I told her we'd get a place in town. And we did. A little one-bedroom apartment in Eagar."

"And that didn't help things?"

"You grew up on a ranch, Sheriff. You know how it is. This isn't a 9-to-5 job. I had to leave early every morning, most of the time while she was still asleep. And a lot of nights it was real late

117

when I got home. She couldn't stand being alone, she couldn't stand the way I smelled when I came home, and before long she couldn't stand me. So she started going out. And that led to staying out all night. And that led to her bringing a guy home with her. I was supposed to be here all night because we had a bunch of sows farrowing. But things went faster than we thought, and my old man sent me home an hour or so after midnight. So I came home and found her and this guy in bed together."

"That had to suck," Weber said.

"Yeah, it did. But that's still no excuse for the way I handled it."

"What did you do, Sonny?"

"What would you have done? I lost it. I started beating the guy's ass. Claudia was trying to stop me and got in the middle of it. I didn't mean to, I really didn't. I was swinging at him and she got between us and I smacked her right upside the head with my fist. As soon as I realized what I'd done I forgot about him and tried to help her."

"What about the man she was with?"

"He was out of there. Took off bare ass naked! The next thing I knew the cops were there and I got arrested. Claudia took out a restraining order against me and filed for divorce. Like I said, I'm not proud of it, but it happened."

Weber and Coop had both broken up enough domestic disturbances to know that there are always two sides to every story. Sonny seemed to be honest and upfront with them about what had happened between him and his ex-wife and took responsibility for his actions, but Weber wanted to see what she had to say about it, too.

"Do you know where your ex-wife lives these days?"

"Last I heard, she was still in Eagar. I think somebody said she was working at the pizza place in the shopping center there. But I haven't seen her in a long time."

"Okay, thanks for your time," Weber said, "We'll let you get back to work."

"I still don't see what any of this has to do with my dad. You can't believe I would ever do anything to hurt him, no matter what happened between me and Claudia."

"No, I don't believe that. Not for a second," Weber assured him.

"Then why do you have to drag all of this up again? What's it going to accomplish?"

"It's just routine," Coop said.

But both the lawman knew Sonny Duncan wasn't buying their story. There was nothing routine about the way his father had died, or the way this case was shaping up.

Chapter 21

Sonny's ex-wife had taken her maiden name back after the divorce, and the manager at the pizza parlor told him she had quit for another job at a restaurant a few blocks away that offered longer hours. They found her working at the counter there.

"I was so sorry to hear about what happened to Duncan," Claudia said. "I wanted to call Sonny and tell him that. But the way things ended between us, I think I'm probably the last person in the world he would want to talk to."

She was a large-framed woman who carried a few extra pounds well, and while no one would ever mistake her for a beauty queen, she was attractive and very open about her relationship with Sonny when Weber asked.

"I put all the blame on myself," Claudia said, pushing her ash blond hair back from her face. "What can I say? I was young and stupid, and I've regretted it ever since. Sonny deserved a lot more than the way I treated him. He really is a good guy. And his dad was one of the nicest people I've ever known in my life. I loved him. Everybody loved Duncan."

"Sometimes things just happen that way."

"I wish it hadn't," she said. "And that guy I was messing around with? I never saw him after that night. He was out the door and gone and didn't care what happened to me. But Sonny? It just devastated him. I mean, he whacked me a good one and my head was really spinning. But I still remember him on his knees holding me and crying and telling me how sorry he was. Then the cops were all over the place and they were dragging him away and..." she shook her head. "You have no idea how much I wish I could go back and change all of that."

"You got a restraining order against Sonny after that happened. Were you afraid he was going to come back and hurt you again?"

"No," Claudia said, shaking her head adamantly. "I didn't think that for a minute. But my mom and dad, they made me do it. They said there was no reason in the world for a man to hit a woman, no matter what she did. I knew I'd done wrong, and I guess looking back, once they were over the anger about it, they did, too. We've never talked about it since then. But back then, I just went along with what they said."

"Let me ask you something, Claudia. How did Sonny and his father get along?"

"I don't know," she said shrugging her shoulders. "Okay, I guess."

"You guess?"

"Yeah. Well, I mean, usually they got along fine. 'Course they argued sometimes, but it wasn't nothing."

"Do you know what they argued about?"

"Sonny hated the hog farm, and he hated working out there. And I'm sure my bitching at him didn't help matters any. Sometimes he would just get all pissed off and start complaining and one thing would lead to another."

"If he hated it so much, why did he stay?"

"Why? I'll tell you why. Because as much as Sonny hated that place and hated those hogs, and hated everything about it, he loved his daddy. There ain't no question about that. He was always talking about leaving and getting a different job someplace, but he was never going to do it because he didn't want to disappoint Duncan. That's why he stayed."

The restaurant's manager, a short man with thinning hair and thick glasses, came by and said, "You're not getting paid to stand here and visit with people all day, Claudia. Table three needs their check."

"Okay, I'm sorry, Charlie. I'll get right on it."

"See that you do."

He walked away and Claudia said, "I'm sorry, guys. I can't afford to lose this job. It don't pay much and the tips aren't all that great, but there aren't many opportunities around here."

"No problem," Weber told her. "Thank you for your time, Claudia."

"I hope it helped. Like I said, Sonny's a good guy and I wish I had been a better wife to him and that none of this ever happened. Will you do me a favor, Sheriff? Will you tell him I'm really sorry about what happened to his daddy?"

"I'll do that, I promise," Weber assured her.

"Claudia! Last warning. Get to work or get out!"

She gave them an apologetic look and hustled over to a table to deliver the bill.

As he buckled his seatbelt when they were back in the Explorer, Coop asked, "What do you think?"

"I don't see any reason why she would lie to us, do you?"

"No."

"What do you think?"

"I think those are two people who could have made it work out between them if things had been different. It's pretty obvious they both regret what happened, and that they still have at least some feelings for each other."

"Are you getting sentimental on me in your old age, Coop?"

"Naa, Jimmy. But sometimes you look at people and your hear their story and you can't help but wonder what if?"

"Yeah, that's true. Sometimes life doesn't turn out like we thought it was going to, or the way we thought it should."

They drove to the law office Neil Deferris had in a small six office complex. The friendly young woman at the reception desk told them that her boss was not officially going to be back to work until the following Monday, but that he would be back in town Friday night, because the next day was his wife's birthday.

"We really need to talk to him as soon as we can," Weber told her, giving her his card. "My office and cell number are both on there. If you talk to him, can you ask him to give me a call at his earliest convenience?"

"I sure will," she promised. "I was so sorry to hear about Duncan. He was such a nice man."

"Yes, he was," Weber said. "It was tragic."

"He didn't deserve to die that way," said the receptionist, whose name was Marcy and who wore large silver hoops in her ears.

"No, he didn't. Did you know Mr. Duncan very well?"

"Not well. I mean, just from him coming in to talk to Mr. Deferris. But he was always very polite and very friendly to me. Not at all like..."

She seemed to realize she may have said too much and didn't finish.

"Not at all like what?"

Marcy looked around to make sure they were alone, and though they were the only people in the office, she still lowered her voice when she said, "I really shouldn't say anything, and please don't repeat this. But Mr. Duncan's wife... well, let's just say she's not a very nice person."

"What do you mean by that?"

"She's just really rude and demanding. And sometime she's even kind of scary."

"Scary?"

"Yeah. When she was in here the other day I was afraid she was going to do something crazy."

"What happened?"

"She came in here demanding to see Mr. Deferris, and when I told her he was out of town she went ballistic on me. She wanted me to call him. I tried to explain to her that he was on a rafting trip with his grandsons and there was no way he was going to be able to get a phone call at the bottom of the Grand Canyon. But she wouldn't accept that and just told me to do it. So I called, knowing it was a waste of time. When I told her it just went to voicemail, she demanded that I call again, and then she took the phone and started screaming into it like if she yelled loud enough he would hear her and answer."

"When was this?"

"That was on Tuesday. By the time I got in here in the morning she had already called and left three messages wanting to know about her husband's will. Then when she came in and found out Mr. Deferris wasn't here she wanted me to give it to her."

"And you didn't?"

"No, Sheriff. We don't have it here. All Mr. Deferris does is business law. Filing incorporation papers for companies, partnership agreements, assigning debt collection, things like that."

"So does your boss farm that kind of work out, or what?"

"Usually he just refers people to somebody here in town. Either Kate Whitney or Michael and Stefanie Masterson. They're a husband-and-wife team. Any of those three are excellent general practice attorneys."

"Do you know if he referred Mr. Duncan to any of them?"

"I'm sorry, I really don't."

"Do you know an attorney named Dean Wicklund?"

"I know who he is," Marcy said. "I think I've dropped off papers at his office a couple of times. That's about it."

"How about Roberta Jensen?"

"Is that the blind attorney lady over in Big Lake?"

"Yes, that's her."

"I don't really know her, except for talking to her on the telephone a few times," Marcy told him. "She seems really nice, and she really seems to know her stuff. I know that Mr. Deferris is impressed with her. He met her at a couple of different functions and was telling me all about her. He said he barely squeaked through law school, which I'm sure isn't true because he's really smart, but he said he couldn't have imagined even trying to do it if he was blind. And she graduated magna cum laude, too!"

"You said that Mrs. Duncan came in here causing a disturbance, wanting access to her husband's will. Anything else?"

"Yeah, she wanted me to do something to make Sonny Duncan leave the farm. To be honest, I couldn't believe it. I mean, her husband had just died the day before and she was already wanting to know about the will and wanting Sonny out of there? It just seemed wrong to me."

Weber wanted to say that it seemed wrong to him, too, but he didn't. Instead, he asked, "What happened after you couldn't get in contact with Mr. Deferris and told her that you didn't have her husband's will here?"

"She was screaming and hollering, calling me a liar and threatening to tear the office apart herself and find it. I'll be honest with you, I got scared and told her she had to leave. When she wouldn't, I picked up the phone to call the police."

"What happened then?"

"She came around my desk here and grabbed the phone out of my hand and slammed it back down. I thought she was going to take a swing at me or something. But instead she just got right in my face and told me that if I knew what was good for me, if I wanted to keep my job, I'd better get in touch with Mr. Deferris, even if I had to get in my car and drive to the bottom of the Grand Canyon to find him. At that point I wasn't even going to try to tell her you can't drive to the bottom of the Grand Canyon. I just wanted her to go, so I kept nodding my head. And then she left. But before she did, she turned around and looked at me and told me that I had better do what she told me to, because I had no idea at all who I was messing with. After she left I just sat here shaking so bad. I was so afraid she would come back that I locked the door, and I kept it locked the rest of the day."

"Did you call and tell the police about what happened?"

Marcy shook her head. "No. I was just glad it was over with."

"Okay, I'm sorry that happened," Weber told her. "Have you seen her since?"

"No, and I hope I never do again." Marcy looked around again and then confided in them, saying, "I've been working for Mr. Deferris for five years, and in all that time I think I've only missed two or three days of work. But if I find out that woman is coming in here for an appointment once he gets back, I'm calling in sick that day!"

Chapter 22

Their next stop was at Dean Wicklund's office. If he had a receptionist, she wasn't on duty. They found him with his arms buried inside a large copy machine.

"Are you taking it apart or putting it back together?" Weber asked.

"Well, I started out trying to clear a paper jam, and it's gone downhill from there. Inside here, there are four little plastic fingers that guide the paper through its path, or at least I think that's what they're for. I had to pull them up to get the paper loose and now I can't get them to go back into place."

"I'm pretty handy with things like that," Coop said, "Do you want me to take a look?"

"Sure, if you don't mind. It would save me having to call to have a tech from the office supply place over in Show Low come out. And who knows when he would get here?"

The deputy rolled up his sleeves and took the attorney's place. Wicklund wiped black toner from his hands with a paper towel, then shook Weber's hand and asked, "What can I do for you gentlemen, today?"

"I'd like to talk to Mrs. Duncan. I tried calling her cell phone number, but all I got was voicemail. Do you know where we might find her?"

"Can I ask what this is about?"

"We're just doing some follow up on her husband's death."

"Follow up?"

"Yes, sir. I got the autopsy report this morning and I wanted to tell her that. And she and Sonny Duncan are going to have to coordinate how they want to handle Mr. Duncan's funeral service. Just things like that."

"I'll be happy to pass that information along to her for you."

"That's fine," Weber said. "But I'd still like to speak to her myself. Is there a problem with that?"

"No, not a problem. But as her attorney, it's in her best interest that I serve as an intermediary. As we both know, you and Mrs.

Duncan have had a couple of encounters that haven't gone so well."

"Look, Mr. Wicklund, I'm not trying to jam your client up, or anything like that. I don't have anything against Mrs. Duncan. And while I'm sorry that things got off to a bad start between us, it's not like I went out there to the hog farm looking for trouble."

"I understand that," the attorney said. "However, Mrs. Duncan is in a rather fragile state at this moment, as I'm sure you can understand, given the circumstances. I just think it would be better to do things this way. You said you got her voicemail. Did you leave a message?"

"Yeah, I did. I just thought maybe..."

"Not to be rude, Sheriff Weber, but if she wants to talk to you I'm sure she'll call back. Otherwise, I'm not at liberty to give you her current location."

"I see."

"Got it," Coop said, closing the copy machine and plugging it back in.

"What was wrong with it?"

"Those little plastic guides or fingers you were having a problem with needed to be slid over just a tad bit to the right to click back into place. Once I did that they dropped right back down where they belonged."

"I appreciate that," Wicklund said. "You saved me some time and trouble there. Usually when I call the tech out it's three or four days before he shows up."

"Since we saved you some time and trouble, maybe you could see your way clear to doing the same for us and tell me how to get hold of Mrs. Duncan," Weber suggested, hoping the attorney might be a little more forthcoming in return for the favor Coop had done him. But Wicklund quickly shot him down.

"I'm sorry, that's not going to happen. Like I said, I'll pass the information on to her, and I'm sure if she wants to talk to you, she'll call."

It was obvious the attorney wasn't going to relent.

"Okay, thanks," Weber said. "Have her do that."

Back out in the Explorer, Coop said, "If I had known he was going to be such a jerk, I wouldn't have fixed his damn copy machine."

"It kinda makes you wonder, doesn't it?"

"Naa," Coop said, "most attorneys I've ever dealt with have been jerks."

"No, that's not what I mean," Weber replied. "It just makes me wonder why somebody who doesn't have anything to hide wants to avoid talking to us."

~***~

The New Light Christian Church was a large brick and glass building, and though nobody was around, a small card taped to the inside of the glass of the front door had emergency contact information. Weber dialed the number and Reverend Patrick Jacobson answered. When the sheriff told him who he was and that he and Coop were at the church, Jacobson said he was at the parsonage next door and would walk over.

The first thing Weber noticed when Jacobson arrived and shook their hands was that he was wearing the same heavy cologne he had when they had first met at the hog farm. Apparently he used that much every day.

"What can I do for you gentlemen today?"

"We are trying to locate Mrs. Duncan. Do you happen to know where she is?"

"Is there some problem?"

"No, sir. I wanted to let her know that we've got the autopsy report back on her husband, and that I spoke to Sonny already, and the two of them need to get together and figure out how they want to handle the funeral."

There was a look of distaste on the minister's face when he said, "The less Mrs. Duncan sees of that man, the better."

"Really? Why do you say that, sir?"

"You heard Roseanne say what kind of person he is. A drunkard who spends his nights carousing and his days sleeping instead of working."

"Yes, I did hear her say that. But I've met the man, and I've talked to several people who know him quite well, and that doesn't seem to be entirely accurate. Do you think it's possible that Mrs. Duncan's opinion of him might be somewhat slanted?"

"Sheriff Weber, if you drove all the way here from Big Lake just to disparage Mrs. Duncan, I'm afraid I don't appreciate it."

"Not at all, sir. I'm just saying that there are always two sides to every story. I would think as a minister you might be a little more open minded and give Sonny the benefit of the doubt."

"I think we're done here. Have a good day, Sheriff."

Weber found himself irritated at the little man's attitude, but he tried to hide it as he said, "Listen, whatever problems Sonny and Rosanne have between the two of them, it's not like she's the only one who has suffered a loss. He's the one who found his father out there in that hog pen all eaten up."

"Which wouldn't have happened if he would have been out of bed and helping like he should have been, instead of sleeping off another night of drinking."

"I've dealt with a lot of people who drink, Reverend Jacobson. And I've seen a lot of them after they got loaded and wound up spending a night in one of my jail cells. When I saw Sonny the morning his father had been killed, I didn't see any indications of him having a hangover or anything like that."

"Frankly, Sheriff, I don't really care what your impressions were of Sonny Duncan on that morning, or any other time, for that matter."

"Jesus, what is it with you?"

"Please don't take our Lord's name in vain."

"Okay, I apologize for that," Weber said. "But really, how can you be so close minded? Have you yourself ever seen Sonny Duncan drunk? Or even taking a drink?"

"I know what Mrs. Duncan has told me."

"Yeah, and I've seen how Mrs. Duncan can act. I'm not sure how reliable I would consider anything she says to be."

"Christians aren't perfect, Sheriff. We're just forgiven."

Weber hated platitudes like that. "But there's no forgiveness in your heart for Sonny Duncan, even if he was all the terrible things that Roseanne says he is? Why aren't you out there trying to comfort him, too? I mean, you and your church are here for Roseanne. But what about Sonny? Doesn't what he's experiencing matter?"

"God never gives us more than we can handle."

Weber looked coldly at the minister and said, "Sure he does. That's why people commit suicide."

"Good day, Sheriff," Reverend Jacobson said, turning and walking back towards the parsonage without another word. Weber wasn't done with the man yet and started to follow him, but Coop stepped in his path and held his hand up.

"Don't do it, Jimmy. I know how you're feeling, but you're not going to accomplish anything. Just let it go."

Weber knew his deputy was right, but he still seethed with anger.

"What's that woman hiding that she's got all these people throwing roadblocks in our way to keep us from talking to her, Coop?"

"I don't know, boss. The autopsy report says that she didn't kill him, but obviously there is something going on.

"Yeah, there is," Weber said. "And whatever it is, I'm going to get to the bottom of it!"

Chapter 23

The necropsy reports were in on the hogs that Sonny had shot the day his father died, and Weber felt his stomach churning as he read them. The stomachs of all of the hogs contained pieces of human flesh, and smaller bits were found in their mouths and on their teeth.

"I hate pigs," he said.

"Come on now, Jimmy, don't be that way. Just because they eat somebody now and then doesn't make them all bad."

"They're noisy and they stink."

"I'll admit they can be pretty loud. I think a jet engine taking off measures somewhere around 113 decibels, and a pig's squeal is about 115."

"Where do you come up with this information, Parks?"

"It's from growing up on a farm, Robyn."

Weber shook his head. "I'm not buying it. I think you make most of this crap up."

"Check it out if you don't believe me," the FBI agent said as he slathered mayonnaise on his hamburger. "Did you know that despite people saying that they're dirty, pigs are actually very clean animals? They roll in the dirt and mud because they can't sweat, and that's how they clean themselves. Did you know that when a piglet's only a few hours old, it will leave its nest to go to the bathroom. They're easier to house train than a dog. And they're smarter than dogs, too!"

"Can we not talk about pigs while we're eating? I can't get the picture of what happened out there at the hog farm out of my mind," Marsha said. "And you, mister, stop being such a pig!" She took the squeeze bottle of ketchup away from Parks while there was still anything left in it. "How can you even taste your food when you bury it under so much stuff?"

"It doesn't *bury* the taste," Parks argued, "it *enhances* it."

"The only thing I've seen enhanced around here is your waistline. I mean seriously, Larry, what are you gonna do if you can't pass your annual physical next month?"

"Are you kidding me? I'm in great shape."

"Yeah, round is a shape, I'm not denying that."

"Anyway," Robyn said, "moving right along, I talked to every beauty shop and nail salon and anyplace else like that here and in Springerville and Eagar, and nobody could recall Rosemary Duncan ever being a client. And from what I saw of her when you brought her in the other day, that didn't really surprise me. It seems like she went for the Plain Jane look."

"Was Dan able to drag anything else up on her?"

"Not a lot. He found the address she was living at in Springerville when she and Duncan met, and her driver's license comes back to that address. But that's it."

"No prior arrests or anything?"

"Nothing, Jimmy. She seems like most people who go through life day to day."

"No, she's not like most people, Weber said, shaking his head. "I know it in my gut. That woman has a history. There has to be something on her somewhere."

"If there is, Dan hasn't found it yet."

"So, what's your next step?"

"I don't know, Parks. I'm thinking maybe tomorrow I'll take a ride up to Holbrook and talk to José and Carmen Barela and see what they have to say."

"Now Carmen, that was a lady who liked to look good," Marsha said.

"Do you know her?"

"Oh, not real well. But I would see her over at the Golden Comb now and then and we'd say hello. I remember Allison saying that Carmen was always such a natural beauty that she didn't need much."

"Do you remember if she wore artificial nails?"

"I'm sure she did, but I can't say for certain. But honestly Jimmy, you don't think Carmen had anything to do with what happened to Duncan, do you?"

"At this point, I don't know what to think," he admitted. "But *somebody* put those marks on that man's body and left that piece of fingernail in his shirt. I want to know who."

"How are you folks doing this evening? Everything okay with your dinner?"

"Just fine, Sherry," Weber told her. "Looks like you got a pretty good crowd for a weeknight."

"It is! Mike's idea of holding dart tournaments is really working out great. Since we started them last month, Tuesdays and Thursdays are almost as busy as Friday and Saturday nights." Sherry Montgomery, who owned the Big Lake Brewpub with her husband Mike, was a pretty young woman in her mid-twenties, with an engaging smile and sparkling blue eyes.

"That's great," Weber told her. "I'm really happy for you guys. You're really making a success of this place."

"Not without more than a little bit of help from you," Sherry told him. "We will never forget what you did for us, Sheriff."

"Water under the bridge," Weber said, waving his hand. But he knew it was much more than that, remembering the evil man who had been their partner when the brewpub first opened, and how badly things could have turned out for the young couple.

"Well, I don't want to disturb your meal, but if you need anything at all, you just let me know."

"We'll do that," Weber promised.

As Sherry walked away, Robyn said, "I'm really happy for those kids. They are building a good life for themselves here in spite of everything they went through at first."

"You know what, Jimmy? We should get in on this dart tournament thing," Parks said.

"Oh yeah? Why is that?"

"Why not? It's fun, it's a challenge, and barbecued wings and nachos are half-price for the players on game nights."

"Why did I know that food was involved in this somehow?"

"Is not just about the food, baby," Parks said to Marsha. "Like I said, it's a lot of fun and a challenge."

"Uh huh."

"It may look easy throwing those darts, but it's not," he told her. "I did quite a bit of it when I was in the Navy. We should try it sometime."

"And?"

"And what?"

"And about the food?"

"It's not about the food, Marsha. It's about the camaraderie."

"So why can't we get a dartboard and play at my place? Or at Jimmy's?"

"We could. But don't you want to be out there playing with us instead of back in the kitchen cooking wings and making super nachos?"

"So it is all about the food? I knew it!"

"No" Parks protested. "I'm just looking out for you because I love you so much,"

"I should've worn my boots," Robyn said," because it's getting deep in here."

Their banter was interrupted when two men stopped at their table. "Evening, Jimmy. How y'all doing?"

"We're good, Mitch. How about you guys?"

"Can't complain. Nobody listens anyway."

"You two staying out of trouble?"

"Oh, yes, sir. We've been keeping our noses clean."

Weber doubted that. Mitchell Collins and his younger brother Rocky were good old boys who avoided work as much as possible and spent most of their time drinking, hunting, or fishing, without regard to silly things like seasons, licenses, or bag limits.

"That sure was a terrible thing that happened to Duncan, wasn't it?"

"Yes, it was," Weber said. He knew the hog farmer's ugly demise was being talked about all over town, but he didn't want to get into a discussion about it with these two.

"Is it really true that the only thing left of him was his head?"

"No, Rocky. That's not true."

"Well, how much did those hogs eat?"

"Enough."

"Did they get to his... ah, you know? Sorry ladies."

"No, when I said enough, I meant that's enough. This isn't exactly the kind of conversation to have while we're eating, guys."

"Oh, sorry, we didn't mean nothing," Mitch said. "There's just a lot of talk and..."

"Yeah. How about you boys go talk someplace else? We're trying to eat here."

"Yes, sir. I apologize. Y'all take care."

As the brothers walked off, Marsha pushed her plate away with distaste. "Okay, I guess I really wasn't all that hungry anyway."

"If you're not going to eat that..." Parks stopped and pulled his hands back from the table when he saw the withering look his girlfriend gave him. "What? My mama always taught us kids to waste not, want not." Marsha glared at him, and he said, "You're probably right. Like you keep saying, I need to cut down on the calories anyway."

Chapter 24

Before making the long drive to Holbrook, Weber called the number he had for José Barela the next morning.

"You don't have to come all the way out here," José said when Weber explained the purpose of his call. "We're just leaving for Show Low now. My wife's uncle Ernesto lives there and I'm going to be helping him put a new roof on his garage. We can meet you at his place."

"That sounds good," Weber said. "What time works for you?"

"We'll be at Ernesto's in an hour or so. Whenever you get there."

"I appreciate your time," Weber said, writing down the address the other man gave him. "I'll see you soon."

He was finishing his cup of coffee and attending to a few administrative details in the office before leaving when Mayor Wingate showed up.

"Sheriff Weber, I need a minute of your time."

Weber cursed himself for delaying his departure, but nodded and asked, "What's up, Chet?"

The blush of his romance with Councilwoman Smith-Abbott may have mellowed the pudgy little man for a while, but the theft of his mobility cart seemed to have wiped that away.

"I would really prefer that you address me by my title. Especially when we're around Town employees," the mayor said in a half whisper. "There's a certain formality that comes with my position in this town."

"Oh, sorry about that," Weber apologized in the same half whisper, then raised his voice as he called across the office. "Hey Mary, remind me not to call Chet Chet anymore, will you? I'm supposed to call him Mister Mayor. Something about formality."

"Okay, I'll do that," Mary Caitlin said. "Do you want a cup of coffee, Chet?"

"No, thank you, I'm fine."

"Okay Chet, I just wanted to be sure to offer you one."

The mayor frowned at her, and Buz held up his mug and said, "You're missing the boat, Chet. This is darn good coffee."

"He's not lying, Chet," Dolan added. "This is my second cup this morning."

"Can we go in your office?"

"Sure, Chet... I mean Mr. Mayor. We can do that."

Inside Weber's private office, the mayor plopped himself down into a chair and said, "You really enjoy that, don't you?"

"Enjoy what, Chet?"

"Making me look like a horse's patootie."

"Hey, don't blame me! Mother Nature's the one that made you look that way. And the fact that you choose to *act* that way is on you!"

"I don't have to come in here and be treated this way!"

"No you don't, Chet," Weber said, sitting down at his desk. "But you still do it. Why is that?"

"I keep hoping that just once I can come into this office and we can have a conversation in which you treat me with respect and do what I tell you to do, Sheriff."

"They say that the definition of insanity is doing the same thing over and over and expecting a different result. Maybe you need to give that some thought."

"Can we stop the banter and get down to business?"

"Is that what this is? Banter? Just a couple of guys shooting the bull?"

"The reason I'm here is because I want to know why you're wasting time and the Town's money running back and forth to Springerville and out there to Duncan's hog farm instead of focusing on my missing cart?"

"Really, Chet? You think you're stupid cart as an equal basis with what happened to Duncan?"

"No, I think it's more important! I mean, I'm sorry that Duncan is dead, but I'm alive and I need my cart back!"

"Has Deputy Northcutt been able to come up with anything yet?"

"Of course not. How do you expect somebody with so little time in this department to handle a major case like this? I want your most experienced deputies on this. I want all of them on this. It should be their number one priority. If the property of the mayor isn't safe, whose is?"

"I'm sorry you feel that way, but I think we're just going to keep on working on Duncan's death for a while, if it's all the same to you."

"No, it's not all the same to me! Why are you wasting so much time with this?"

"Because it's an open investigation, Chet."

"What is there to investigate? As I understand it, George Duncan was killed by a bull and then a bunch of his hogs ate his body. Are you planning to arrest the bull or the hogs?"

"No, Sonny Duncan killed them. By the way, is there a chance we can do that once in a while when we've got a real jerk who commits a crime? It just seems like it would speed things up a lot, instead of us wasting the Town's money investigating things."

"Stop it, Sheriff Weber! Neither one of us has time for this nonsense. Why are you wasting time and resources on what is obviously an open and shut case? I don't even understand why it's still open in the first place."

"Actually, there are a lot of things you don't understand, Chet. But as for this case in particular, we know how Duncan died, but there are still some questions about his death that remain unanswered. I need to get those answers."

"Such as?"

"I'm not at liberty to say right now. Like I said, it's still an open investigation."

"What? You don't think you can trust me with confidential information?"

"No, I don't."

"And just why not?"

"Look how you blabbed about Gretchen having that tattoo on her hind end."

"She doesn't have a tattoo on her..."

"See? You just don't know when to keep your mouth shut, Chet. Anything else you want to talk about? Where *does* she have a tattoo?"

"This conversation is over," the mayor said getting to his feet. "You get the answers you need and wrap this whole thing up quickly, Sheriff. The quicker this thing is over with and that hog farm is gone, the better!"

The mayor was reaching for the doorknob when Weber said, "Wait a minute, Chet. What do you mean the quicker the hog farm is gone the better?"

"I mean just what I said. That place is disgusting. I know four different developers who want to build out near there, but how can they? Would you want to have a house where you had to smell that all day long?"

"First of all, the hog farm was there long before any of these damn carpetbaggers ever showed up, building places on every square foot of open land they can get their hands on. And second..."

"Those developers have brought a lot of revenue to this town, Sheriff! Look at all the new businesses that are opening up. The number of new people who are coming up here these days."

"Yeah, that's fine and dandy for people who have a lot of money to spend," Weber said. "But what about the people who have been here forever and liked things the way they were? What about the way of life that is disappearing because all of these newcomers show up for a weekend or the summer and want to make Big Lake into the place they came here to get away from?"

"That's progress."

"You call it progress. A lot of people call it bullshit. And anyway, what makes you think just because Duncan is gone the hog farm is going to close up and go away?"

"Everybody knows Sonny Duncan has hated that place since the day he was born. He can't wait to get out of there. And even if he didn't, he doesn't have his father's head for business anyway. And Mrs. Duncan would be more than happy to sell out to any number of developers who've approached her husband over the last few years."

"How do you know that, Chet? Have you talked to Rosanne Duncan?"

"No, I haven't. But I have talked to her attorney, Mr. Wicklund, who by the way wants you to stay away from his client."

"Wicklund called you? When?"

"Yes, he called me. Yesterday after you were at his office and at the church where he and Mrs. Duncan worship. You stay away from that woman, Sheriff," the mayor said pointing his finger at Weber. "That's an order!"

Before Weber could tell him to stick his order where the sun didn't shine, the mayor opened the door and went through the main office and out the exit door, followed by a shower of "See you later, Chet" calls from the staff.

"It's always nice to have Chet stop in," Mary said, bringing Weber a fresh cup of coffee. "He just seems to spread happiness and cheer everywhere he goes, doesn't he?"

"He spreads something all right," Weber said as he took the coffee and nodded gratefully at her. "What it is is still open for debate."

"So what's his problem now?"

"He wants to know why I'm still investigating Duncan's death. And he ordered me to stay away from Roseanne Duncan."

"Why do you think that is, Jimmy?"

"I don't know," Weber admitted. "I've always thought that people who don't have anything to hide don't have any reason not to talk to the police."

"What do you think Roseanne Duncan is hiding?"

"I don't know that either, Mary. But I can tell you one thing, I damn sure intend to find out!"

Chapter 25

José Barela was a short statured, slim man who might have looked delicate from a distance. But on closer inspection there was no doubt that this was someone who had spent a lifetime doing hard work outside in all kinds of weather. It was evident in the crinkles around his eyes, the texture of his skin, and the missing middle finger on his calloused right hand when he extended it to shake Weber's.

"Nice to meet you, Sheriff."

"Thank you for making time for me," Weber said. "And you must be Mrs. Barela?"

"Just call me Carmen," said the young woman with a shy smile. Allison McBride from the Golden Comb beauty salon had been right. Carmen was a natural beauty, with long black hair that hung to her waist, large dark eyes, and what looked to be flawless light mocha-colored skin. When she extended her hand to the sheriff, Weber noticed that she wore purple polish on her nails, which extended just slightly past her fingertips.

They were standing in her uncle's yard on a back street near the high school in Show Low. Weber looked at the wooden skeleton of the large garage that had recently been erected.

"It looks like you've got quite a job ahead of you, and I don't want to take up any more of your time than I have to."

"It's no problem," José said with a slight accent. "Duncan meant a lot to us and we were both heartbroken when we heard what happened to him. He was a good man."

Carmen nodded in agreement with her husband.

"As I understand it, the two of you worked for Duncan for quite a while. Is that right?"

"Almost nine years," José told him.

"I'm curious. If Duncan was such a good man, and everything I know about him says that's true, and you were there for so long, why did you leave?"

The husband and wife looked at each other, clearly uncomfortable with the question and not sure how to answer.

"Did Duncan do something to upset you?"

"No," José said, shaking his head. "Like I told you, Duncan was a good man. One of the best I ever knew."

"What about Sonny? How was he?"

"Sonny, he's not his father, but he's good, too. In his own way. We never had a problem with him."

"You said he's not his father. I guess that's obvious. But what do you mean by that?"

"If you think Sonny had anything to do with what happened to Duncan, you're wrong," Carmen said. "He would never do anything to hurt his father."

"Oh, I didn't mean to imply that. Not at all," Weber assured her. "I'm just curious what your husband meant when he said that Sonny wasn't his father."

"He was just different," José said. "Duncan built that farm and he was proud of it. Like he should be. But Sonny, he didn't like it. He didn't want nothing to do with it."

"Was that a problem between the two of them?"

"Sometimes. I know that Sonny would always say he was going to go find another job someplace. But he never did. And he always worked hard around the farm."

"Why do you think he stayed there at the farm if he hated it so much, José?"

"Because he loved his father more than he hated those hogs."

Weber remembered Leonard Bowers and Sonny's ex-wife telling him the same thing. As much as Sonny wanted out, he felt the need to stay on and help his father. The sheriff felt a twinge of guilt because he had once been in Sonny Duncan's shoes. Weber may have grown up on a small ranch, but it was never the life he wanted for himself. Though he knew it broke his father's heart, soon after he graduated from high school he joined the Army and left Big Lake behind.

Military life suited him well and he enjoyed his assignment as a military policeman stationed at Fort Campbell, Kentucky. But everything changed after his parents were killed in a car accident six months into his second enlistment. He took an emergency leave to fly home to Arizona to settle his parents' affairs and make arrangements for his twelve year old sister. The young soldier faced an overwhelming task and he soon realized he couldn't run the ranch and raise his kid sister from afar. He applied for and received a hardship discharge. Try as he might to continue his father's legacy, he soon remembered why he had joined the Army in the first place. Before two years had passed, Weber had sold off the cattle, leased out the acreage, with the exception of the family home and surrounding ten acres, and taken a job with the Big Lake Sheriff's Office. When Pete Caitlan retired as sheriff, Weber was his handpicked successor.

Returning to the present, he asked, "Did you know Sonny's wife, Claudia?"

"Yes, we knew her," Carmen said. "Not well because she didn't stay out there that long after they got married. They got a place in town and..."

"Yeah, I heard that didn't end very well," Weber said.

"No, Sonny got railroaded on that," José said, and Weber detected a slight bitterness in the man's tone.

"What do you mean?"

"What he did, hitting her like he did, that was wrong. He knew it. But he didn't do it on purpose. He was fighting with that man she was with and she just got too close trying to break them up. Sonny felt terrible about that. I think knowing he had hurt her tore him up almost as much as finding her with that guy."

"How about the others out at the farm? Did you get along okay with Mona and Leonard and Carl?"

They both nodded their heads, and Carmen said, "Mona always treated me like I was her daughter. She was always so sweet to me. And Carl... he's nice. He's not, how you say, all there? But he can't help it."

"Can't help what, Carmen?"

She held her hands in front of herself, searching for the right words. "Carl is a big, strong man. But he is also like a little child in many ways. He doesn't always understand everything that's happening around him. Like when Sonny and Claudia broke up. He couldn't understand that. Claudia was always nice to him and Sonny was nice to him, so it didn't make sense to him that they couldn't be nice to each other. When she wasn't around anymore he kept asking Sonny where she went. How do you explain something like that to somebody like him?"

Weber knew the circumstances under which the Barelas had left the hog farm, but he always liked to hear things firsthand from the people involved, so he pressed on.

"Okay, you got along good with Duncan and Sonny and everybody else out there. I'm trying to get a picture of why you would leave. Mona told me you folks were all like a big family. What happened?"

Carmen hung her head and José's jaw tightened. Weber was afraid he had pushed them too far and that they would close up on him, but then José spoke again.

"My wife, she loved Duncan like he was her own father. And that's the way he felt about her, too. She cooked and cleaned house for him, but he never treated her like a maid or nothing like that. He never treated any of us like that. We were all the same. At least we were until *she* showed up."

"When you say she, who do you mean?"

"Mrs. Duncan."

"Rosanne? Is that who you're talking about?"

José nodded his head, and the look on his face told Weber that time and distance had not eased his anger toward Duncan's widow.

"As soon as she got there, everything began to change."

"How did things change?"

José told him about the communal dinners at the hog farm and how they had ended after Duncan got married. He told him how Roseanne had done nothing to hide her distaste for the hired help and made it very plain that she felt herself to be far superior to them. He related the story Sonny had told them about how she had reacted when Carl had innocently hugged her when they first met, and how after that she always ridiculed him and called him names. He talked about the wedge she had driven between Duncan and Sonny. And then he told the sheriff about the accusations Roseanne had made about the relationship between Duncan and Carmen.

"Nothing like that ever happened, Sheriff. It never would happen. Duncan and Carmen are both better people than that. Way better people than she ever was! What she said hurt us. It hurt us bad."

"I'm sure it did," Weber said. "And I imagine it hurt, too, when Duncan let it happen."

"Oh, he tried to make it better," Carmen said, looking up for the first time since José had started talking about their life at the hog farm. "We don't blame him or hold nothing against him for what he did. A man has to stand by his wife, right or wrong."

"And that's what I did, too," José said. "Duncan, he apologized to us over and over and was asking us to stay on. But how can we stay someplace when someone says those kinds of terrible things?"

"I understand," Weber told him. "I'd have done the same thing if I was in your place."

"I loved Duncan," Carmen said. "But not in a bad way. Not in the way that woman said. No, he was like my own Papa to me. He always said I was the daughter he never had. But she seemed to hate me from the first time we met and she made the way Duncan and I felt about each other seem so, so *filthy*!"

"Why do you think that was, Carmen?"

She shrugged her shoulders and shook her head. "I don't know. I really don't. I tried to tell her that it wasn't like that, and so did Duncan. But she just would not believe us."

"I can tell you why she acted the way she did," José said. "She was jealous, yes, but I think it was more than that."

"What do you mean?"

"Sheriff, I am not an educated man." He held up his hands. "These are my tools. From the time I was a boy I worked hard to help my family survive, and as a man I work hard to earn a living for myself and my wife. But because one is not educated does not mean one is ignorant. Do you understand what I am saying?"

"Yes, sir, I do," Weber said.

"Then I say this because I watch people and I see things. And what I saw out there was that Mrs. Duncan did not come to stay and make a home with her husband like a wife should do. No sir. She came to destroy."

"She came to destroy? What do you mean by that, José?"

148

"Some people are never happy, no matter how much they have. Yes, it may have smelled of hog shit, but that was the world we all lived in out there. That was the world Duncan brought her to. He did not force her to marry him. He did not force her to come to the farm. And the home he gave her was a good one. But that wasn't enough for her. No, she wanted more. And because she knew Duncan would never change, she wanted to destroy his world and rebuild a new one as she thought it should be."

"Let me ask you this José, and you, too, Carmen. Do you think Roseanne loved her husband."

Carmen didn't answer, but José shook his head adamantly. "That woman only loves two things, Sheriff. Money and being in charge. And when she married Duncan and had his money she wanted to be in charge of him and everything he owned. That is why she did what she did to us. That is why she treats Sonny the way she does. That is why she is so mean to Carl. She says she loves God, but I don't think so. I think she cares only for herself."

Divide and conquer. Weber knew it was the first thing that a control freak, man or woman, did when they entered a relationship. Isolate their partner from everyone and everything around them. And it seemed like that was exactly what Roseanne Duncan had been doing before her husband was killed.

"Listen, I know you have work to do, and I don't want to keep you from it," he said. "But before I go, do you think there's any possibility that anybody could have done anything to hurt Duncan?"

"Hurt him? The way we heard it, Montezuma attacked him and then the pigs..."

"Yeah, that's the way it happened," Weber said. "I'm just asking if you think there's any possibility that someone could have done something else. I don't know what, to be exact. I'm kind of just grasping at straws here, folks."

"We all told him to stay away from that bull all the time," José said. "But Duncan, he would go out there every morning to talk to it. I don't know why. But he seemed to like the beast for some reason. Not me! I was always afraid of it. I always feared something like this would happen."

"Okay, I'll let you get busy on that roof. Thank you for your time. And thank you for keeping me from driving all the way to Holbrook."

He shook their hands and as she held his, Carmen asked, "Sheriff Weber, we don't want to cause any trouble for anybody. But as we have told you, Duncan was like part of our family. And family is important to us. Do you suppose it would be okay for us to go to his funeral?"

"I don't see why not," Weber said. "I'm sure Sonny would appreciate you two being there."

"But Mrs. Duncan? Would she object to us coming to pay our respects?"

"Ma'am, from what I've seen of Roseanne Duncan, there's not much in life she doesn't object to," Weber told her. "You do what your heart tells you is right."

Chapter 26

As he often did, Weber had skipped breakfast that morning, and by the time he was done interviewing José and Carmen Barela he found his stomach growling. He went through the drive-through at the Jack-in-the-Box in Show Low for a sandwich and fries, washing them down with a soda as he drove east on State Highway 260. He stopped at the Game and Fish office in Pinetop-Lakeside and talked with Mark Santos, the game warden who usually worked the Big Lake area, about the upcoming big game season that would kick off at the end of the month.

Every year Arizona hunters, along with many from out of state, came to the White Mountains hoping to bag a trophy deer or elk. While the greatest majority of them were good citizens and responsible sportsmen, there was always a tiny minority that caused problems for law enforcement by violating the hunting regulations or getting into trouble in the local bars and saloons. The Big Lake Sheriff's Department and the Arizona Game and Fish Department worked closely together to keep things going smoothly.

Weber was just getting back in his Explorer when his cell phone rang. He looked at the caller ID but did not recognize the number.

"Sheriff Weber."

"Sheriff, this is Neil Deferris. I've been out of town and off the grid and I just got the news about George Duncan. My secretary said you need to talk to me."

"Yes, I do," Weber said. "Where are you, sir?"

"I'm on my way home now. I'm just coming into Show Low."

Bad timing. Weber wished the man had called thirty minutes earlier while he was still in Show Low.

"I was going to take Highway 60 back to Springerville, but I could go the other way and stop in Big Lake if you need me to. The only thing is, I've got my two grandsons with me and they are kind of tuckered out from trying to keep up with Grandpa. And I think their mom and dad are looking forward to having them home."

Two routes led from Show Low to Springerville, one of them US Highway 60 on the north, and State Route 260 a little further south that went through Pinetop-Lakeside and McNary, past the Big Lake turnoff, and on to the twin towns of Springerville and Eagar. The latter route was mostly all two lane road, more scenic but longer and slower due to the curves as it wound through the mountains.

"No, you go ahead and get those boys home," Weber said. "I'm actually just leaving Pinetop-Lakeside myself and I need to stop at my office on the way. Could we make it about 3 o'clock this afternoon at your office?"

"That would be fine," the attorney said. "I'll see you there."

~***~

Weber checked in at the office, got a status update from Jordan Northcutt on the mayor's missing mobility cart, and was trying to figure out how to avoid Mary Caitlin's latest barrage of paperwork when Judy Troutman buzzed his office from the dispatch desk.

"Sheriff, I've got Mrs. Taylor from the bank on the phone. She said she needs to talk to you and says it's important."

"Okay, I've got it." He picked up the phone, pushed the blinking light, and said, "Hello, Joyce. What's going on?"

"Can you get down here quick, Jimmy? I've got a customer here who I think is the victim of some kind of fraud."

"I'm on my way."

~***~

"I'm sure that this is all just a big mistake," an elderly woman was saying when Weber came to the door of the bank manager's office a few minutes later. "He seems like such a nice man, and I just want to help that little boy."

"What's going on?"

Joyce had a look of relief on her face when she saw Weber. "Sheriff, do you know Mrs. McKenzie?"

"Sure," he said, gently shaking the woman's frail hand, which was mottled with age spots. "I remember when I was a kid I used to trick-or-treat at your house. You always made caramel apples."

"That's right. I'm afraid I don't do that anymore. It just became too much work at my age. I'm 87, you know."

"Well, bless your heart. If you ever get around to making some of those apples again, I want one."

"The reason I asked you to come over, Sheriff, is because Mrs. McKenzie has a situation that concerns me."

"Okay, tell me about it."

"Like I was just telling Mrs. Taylor, I'm sure this is all a big mistake. I just don't know what the fuss is all about."

"What kind of mistake is that, Mrs. McKenzie?"

"Well, this nice young man who's been cutting my grass and doing some chores for me told me that his poor little boy is going to die if he doesn't get an operation. And do you know that the insurance company won't authorize it? Isn't that just despicable? How can they care more about profits than a child's life?"

"I see. Yes, that's pretty terrible. Who is this young man, Mrs. McKenzie?"

"The boy? His name is Albert. Did you know that was my husband's name before he passed on? What a coincidence? My Albert's been gone seventeen years now. We were married 52 years. And those were good years. He was such a nice man. Do you know I still talk to him, Sheriff? I tell him about my plans for the day when I'm making breakfast in the morning, I tell him about the flowers and the changing seasons, or sometimes I just talk about all of the wonderful times we shared together. You may think that's silly, but even though I know he's not there, it gives me comfort."

"Maybe you can't see him," Weber told her. "But you know what, Mrs. McKenzie? I think Albert is still there with you when you talk to him."

She smiled and nodded her head. "I like to think so, too."

"So Albert is the little boy who needs an operation. What's his father's name? The fellow who cuts your grass and does chores for you?"

"Oh, that's Thomas. He's such a loving father. And after all he's been through, he still has a smile on his face every day."

"So he's been through a lot, this Thomas?"

"Oh, yes sir. I don't remember when it happened, but his wife is that woman who was killed in that terrible house fire. Her and their little twin daughters. You must remember that,, Sheriff."

"No, I don't think I do," Weber said, shaking his head. "When did that happen?"

"I'm not exactly sure when," the woman said. "But Thomas said it was so terrible. He told me that's why he has all those tattoos on his arms. To cover up all the scars from when he got burned trying to save them. The poor man tells me he still blames himself for not being able to get them out of there."

Weber looked at Joyce, who shook her head slightly.

"And you say that now his little boy needs surgery?"

"Yes, he does, and the insurance company won't pay for it. I think that's just terrible."

"What kind of surgery does he need, Mrs. McKenzie?"

"I don't recall the name of it, but it's because his poor little lungs were ruined from breathing in all of the smoke from that fire. So he has to have one of those operations where they give him new lungs."

"A transplant?"

"Yes, that's it," she said. "A transplant. For artificial lungs. But the insurance company said it costs too much and they won't pay for it even though Thomas has made his premium payments every month, just like clockwork."

"So he asked you to help him out with the cost of the surgery?"

"Oh, heavens no! Thomas is too proud to ever take charity. That's what he called it, charity. No, I offered to give him the money for the surgery, but he said he couldn't take my money like that. So instead, he asked if I could just pay him in advance for mowing the grass and the chores he does around the house and then he would work it off over time. I told him that really wasn't necessary, I'd be happy to give him the money. But Thomas won't take charity."

"How much money is the surgery going to cost, Mrs. McKenzie?"

"$25,000. And do you know they will only take cash at the hospitals these days? What has become of this country, Sheriff Weber? Those hospitals are as bad as insurance companies. He has to give them the money up front before they will even admit poor little Albert for his surgery."

"$25,000 for a lung transplant. I don't know much about how much medical things cost these days, but does that sound about right to you, Mrs. McKenzie?"

"Oh, no," she said shaking her head. "That's only the down payment. There is another $25,000 due after the surgery is over with. Before they let Albert go home."

"So you're giving Thomas $50,000 for these medical bills, is that right?"

"I'm not *giving* him anything, Sheriff. I'm just paying him in advance for his work around the house. Thomas insists I let him work it off."

"By mowing the grass?"

"Well, not just mowing the grass. He's going to paint my house for me, too. And rake the pine needles and shovel the snow this winter."

"I see. When are you supposed to give Thomas this money, Mrs. McKenzie?"

"He's going to come by for it this evening at six o'clock. Mrs. Taylor here says that there's some kind of a problem, but I don't think so. It's not like Thomas is some sort of stranger or something. He's been cutting my grass for a month now, three times a week. He's such a nice man."

"Three times a week?"

"Yes, and we can thank the EPA for that!"

"The EPA?"

"Yes, the Environmental Protection Agency. I didn't know that they were mandating that grass be cut three times a week."

"I hadn't heard about that either," Weber told her.

"It' has something to do with greenhouse gases or some such. I'm not really sure. Thomas tried to explain it to me, but I'm afraid

I didn't follow all of it. I'm just glad he was driving by and saw that I hadn't been following the rules about all of that. He told me the government could have confiscated my house and put me out in the street."

"Yes, it sounds like you are lucky."

"What I want to know is, why is the government meddling in something like how often someone mows their grass, but they're allowing insurance companies to get away with letting little boys like Albert die when they need surgery so badly? Can somebody explain that to me?"

"May I ask what you're paying Thomas for cutting the grass every time he does it?"

"$100. He said he charges most people $200, but because I'm an old woman, and because my husband and his little boy have the same name, he only charges me half. Like I said, he's such a nice man."

"He sure sounds like a nice man," Weber said. "In fact, I'm really looking forward to meeting him."

Chapter 27

Neil Deferris was a big, broad shouldered man who looked like he would be more at home in a saddle on horseback or driving a tractor than he was behind his desk. His face was sunburned, and when he stood up to shake Weber's hand his grip was firm.

"Please, have a seat, Sheriff," he said, sitting back down himself.

"Thanks for adjusting your schedule to meet with me," Weber told him.

"No problem. Duncan was a good client and a good friend for many years. It broke my heart to hear he was gone. Especially the way he died." The attorney shuddered at the mental picture.

"I know there's attorney-client privilege and all that," Weber said, "so I don't really know what you can tell me about Duncan and his affairs. But I'm trying to get a picture of how things were for him."

"What do you mean, Sheriff? Do you think this was more than just an accident?"

"No, there's no reason to believe anything like that. It's just that there have been some problems between Mrs. Duncan and Sonny, and a lot of controversy over what happens to Duncan's assets."

Deferris scowled at the mention of Roseanne and shook his head. "That woman is the worst thing that ever happened to Duncan."

"Why do you say that, Mr. Deferris?"

"Because she's a lunatic. I guess Marcy told you what happened when she came in here."

"Yes, she did."

"I must have 15 or 20 messages on my cell phone from her wanting to know where I was and demanding that I get in contact with her immediately to settle his estate and evict Sonny from the hog farm."

"There's been a lot of chaos about that," Weber said.

"Then you know exactly how she is. I had a lot of misgivings when Duncan got together with her. I knew right from the start that it wasn't going to end well."

"What do you mean?"

The attorney looked at Weber for a long time without speaking, then sighed and said," I guess with Duncan gone, I'm not making any ethics violations with what I'm about to tell you. And if I am, maybe it's worth it."

"Whatever you say here doesn't have to leave this office if it's going to cause you trouble," Weber told him.

Deferris nodded and said, "When Duncan told me he was going to get married, and I found out they had only known each other for a few weeks, I strongly urged him to consider getting a prenuptial agreement. He wouldn't hear anything about that. If you knew Duncan very well, you knew that his word was his bond. I've seen him make deals for $100,000 or more based on a handshake. And sometimes those deals went sour. That's why he finally came to me years ago to help him with some bad debts. It went against everything he believed in to have to sign a contract for every business transaction. But unfortunately, that's just the way the world is these days. So the idea that he needed a contract between him and his fiancée? There was no way he was going to consider something like that. Not Duncan."

"And?"

"Apparently he mentioned to Rosanne that I had suggested it, and the next thing I know this crazy lady comes storming into the office calling me all kinds of names and telling me to mind my own business, and warning me that if I ever tried to come between her and Duncan again I would regret it. I mean she really threw a fit. I was just about to call the police when she finally left. "

"Wow. Did you tell Duncan about that?"

"I tried. I told you, Sheriff, besides having a business relationship, Duncan and I were friends. Good friends. When I told him about how Roseanne had acted, at first he just tried to brush it off, saying that sometimes she got a little excitable. I told him no, it was more than that. And I told him, as a friend, and I emphasized that I was speaking not only as his attorney but also *as a friend*, that he really needed to consider that prenup."

"What did he say to that?"

Deferris looked Weber in the eye and replied, "He told me to mind my own damn business, that's what he said. And if you knew Duncan, you know that was out of character for him. We'd never had a disagreement of any kind in all those years. I mean, sometimes I'd have to prod him to threaten to file a lawsuit against somebody who didn't pay their bill, or actually file suit a few times, but that was because he always wanted to believe the best of everybody. Let's face it, Sheriff, some people are deadbeats. And sometimes I think the food business has more than its fair share of them. But if a restaurant was behind on their bill, Duncan always wanted to believe they were just having hard times and was more than willing to work with them. Because he was so honest and upfront about everything, it was hard for him to accept that somebody would just stiff him. So sometimes I'd have to kind of ride his butt to get him to follow through on collections and things like that. But otherwise, we never had a harsh word between us until that day."

"How were things between you two after that?"

"Oh, Duncan wasn't one to hold a grudge. It went by a couple of weeks, maybe three, and the next thing I knew I was getting an invitation to his wedding. So I guess he got over it."

"He got over it. But what about Roseanne? Do you think she got over it?"

"No way! At the wedding she went out of her way to snub my wife and me. When we came through the reception line she purposely turned away and started talking to the people behind us, like we weren't even there. I just let it go, but my wife didn't appreciate that very much at all. I didn't see a lot of Duncan after that. He stopped in a few times after the wedding to drop off or pick up papers, things like that. Before he met her, we'd usually have lunch together, or at least a cup of coffee. But he never had time after he got married."

"And how did he act those times when he was in here?"

"Same old Duncan. Well, wait a minute, let me clarify that. He was the same old Duncan in the way that he was friendly and all, but there seemed to be something under the surface that was different. Something was bothering him."

"Did you ask what that something was?"

"I asked him how things are going, how married life was, just kind of making conversation. But whatever was getting to him, he wouldn't say."

"Mr. Deferris, I know that you referred Duncan to Roberta Jensen over in Big Lake a while back. Can you tell me what that was about?"

"He came in here asking me about wills. I'd suggested a few times over the years that he needed to get a will, but he never got around to it. He'd always say he didn't need one because he planned to live forever. So I was kind of surprised when he brought it up. I don't do wills, so I referred him to Miss Jensen."

"Can I ask why her and not one of the local attorneys?"

"Actually, I did refer him to Mike Masterson. But Duncan said if I couldn't do the will, he didn't want to work with anybody here in town. I had met Roberta Jensen a couple of times and was impressed with her, so I sent him to see her."

"I've only met her once, but she's a pretty impressive lady," Weber agreed. "Why do you think Duncan didn't want to work with somebody here in Springerville or Eagar?"

"He gave me some line about liking to spread his business around, but I don't think that had anything to do with it."

"So what do you think the real reason was?"

"To be honest, Sheriff, and please keep this between us if you will, I think it was because both Mike and Stefanie Masterson and Kate Whitney, the other attorney I recommended, all go to New Light Christian Church."

"The same church that Roseanne Duncan attends."

"That's right."

"What does that mean?"

"Your guess is as good as mine, Sheriff."

"Do you know Dean Wicklund?"

"It's a small town. Not as small as Big Lake, but small enough that everybody in this business knows everybody."

"Can I ask your impression of him?"

"I don't like him."

"Is there a reason for that?"

"Sheriff, did you ever hear the saying 'you're known by the company you keep'?"

"Sure."

"Let's just say that Dean represents a lot of people that I wouldn't want to be associated with."

"Would you care to explain that?"

"Look," Deferris said, "in theory, everybody deserves fair and equal legal representation, no matter how they do business or what they are accused of. That's one of the first things they teach you in law school. An attorney's job is not to judge, it is to represent his client in the best possible way. However, for me personally, there are some clients I just don't want to deal with for a variety of reasons. People who get DUIs, people who are involved in domestic violence cases, people who seem to make a habit of suing anyone they can in the hopes of collecting a few bucks, business owners who skate too close to the edge of what's legal on a regular basis. And those seem to be the kind of people who make up most of Dean Wicklund's clientele. In fact, I've represented Duncan in cases against two or three of them who didn't pay their bills."

"And as I understand it, he also goes to the same church as Rosanne and those other attorneys you talked about," Weber said. "That's an interesting coincidence."

"Oh, don't get me wrong, I'm not trying to put down New Light or anybody in its congregation. I know quite a few nice people who go there."

"How about the preacher there?"

"Reverend Jacobson? Yes, I know him, too. Like I said, it's a small town."

"What do you think about him."

"Do you really want me to get struck by lightning or something, Sheriff?"

"Don't worry. If you do, I know CPR."

Deferris laughed, then his face turned serious. "As a man of God, I believe he is dedicated to his church and to his following. On a personal level, I find him to be a pompous ass."

"Is there a reason for that?"

"Quite a few. But the one that comes to mind is that at the wedding, when Duncan married Roseanne, he treated Sonny like crap. And not just Sonny. A couple of Duncan's old friends were there and he treated them the same way. Like if they weren't part of his congregation he was better than them."

Something Deferris had said earlier had caught Weber's attention, and he asked, "How do you feel about Sonny Duncan. On a personal level?"

"What do you mean?"

"You said you don't like the kind of people that Dean Wicklund represents. People who have DUIs, people involved in domestic violence cases."

"I see where you're going, Sheriff. But Sonny's case is different. And not just because Duncan and I were friends or because of our business relationship. Sonny's had a rough time of it. I don't know if you know about his marriage falling apart and all that or not. I'm not excusing the things he's done, and maybe I'm a hypocrite because I don't know everybody's back story when I say I don't approve of the kind of people Dean represents, while at the same time I give Sonny a pass for doing the same things. So be it. But I like the guy. He knows he screwed up and he's taken responsibility for it every time. I'm sure in your line of work you've dealt with people who make the same mistakes over and over again and never learn from them because it's always somebody else's fault, not theirs."

There was a lot of truth to what the attorney said and Weber acknowledged it with a nod. "Miss Jensen called me after Duncan was killed," he said, and told Deferris about the three handwritten wills the hog farmer had dropped off at her office a few days before he was killed. "Do you have any idea why he would write up three different wills like that?"

The attorney shook his head. "I don't know, Sheriff. I'm sure Rosanne was putting a lot of pressure on him to make sure she was covered if something were to happen. And with the problems that were going on between her and Sonny, I'm sure she wanted to cut him out if she could. But as to why he would write three different wills with such different conditions like that is beyond me."

"I appreciate your time," Weber said. "Is there anything else you think I need to know before I get out of your way and let you get home to your wife?"

"Well, just that no matter what any will said, if Roseanne Duncan thinks she's going to take over the hog farm and get rid of Sonny, she's in for a rude awakening."

Weber's interest was instantly perked. "Why is that?"

"Keep in mind that I don't do probate law, Sheriff. But assuming none of those wills Duncan gave Miss Jensen are valid, and it doesn't sound like they were, if nobody comes up with a will that will stand up in court, Duncan died intestate, which means that she is entitled to half of anything that was acquired after their marriage, and a portion of what he owned before that."

"So she might get half of the place."

"Again, this isn't my area of expertise, so I don't know just what the percentages would be. And I don't know if there are any other heirs that might come into the picture. I know Duncan had a large extended family in this area. But here's the thing. The business itself is a separate entity."

"What do you mean?"

"I mean that a few years ago, back when Sonny and Claudia got married, Duncan wanted to provide for them. And, I think he was hoping to give Sonny some incentive to stick around. So he had me form a corporation. Duncan Pork Products. I'm the legal representative for that corporation and I sit on the board of directors, along with Sonny and Duncan."

"And?"

"And no matter what Roseanne Duncan thinks or wants, Sonny owns 48% of that corporation and Duncan's estate holds the other 52%. So no matter how it shakes out in probate, once Sonny gets his share of his father's estate he's going to be the majority stockholder. And a very well-to-do young man."

Chapter 28

It was almost dark by the time the rusty old sedan pulled into Elizabeth McKenzie's driveway, and the long-haired man behind the steering wheel was too busy finishing his joint and bobbing his head to the music booming from his stereo to notice the sheriff waiting in the shadows of the house next door. Moving quickly, Weber slipped around the back of the old Ford and stuck the barrel of his Kimber .45 semi-automatic pistol into the man's ear.

"Put your hands on the steering wheel and keep them there. Don't give me an excuse to pull the trigger."

"I'm not moving," the man assured him, gripping the top of the steering wheel as Weber opened the back door and slid into the seat behind him. The car was littered with fast food wrappers, empty plastic soda bottles, beer cans and other trash, and reeked of neglect and body odor.

"Man, if this is a rip off, you chose the wrong dude. I've got like ten bucks in my pocket, and enough pot to fill a bung. But you're welcome to it, just don't hurt me, okay?" His voice was high and shaky from fear.

"I'm not here to rob you," Weber said, pressing the barrel of the .45 into the back of the man's head, "You got a drivers license?"

"Yes, sir."

"Keep one hand on the steering wheel and use the other to haul it out and pass it back here. And do it slowly. Then get your hand back on the wheel. And if you move too fast, or your hand comes up with anything but a wallet in it, I'm gonna splatter your brains all over the windshield. Do you understand me?"

"Yes, sir. Don't worry, I don't want no trouble."

"A little too late for that," Weber said.

The drivers license said Richard Lee Grebberman, and the picture was the same as the man's face. Weber raised his handheld radio to his mouth and called Dispatch to check for wants and warrants. A moment later the dispatcher told him that while the subject had four priors for petty thefts and shoplifting, there were no active wants or warrants out for him at that time, and he was no longer on probation from his last offense.

"So, *Thomas*. It looks like we have a problem."

"I don't know what you're talking about, man."

"Sure you do. You've been ripping off that nice old lady in there. Three hundred bucks a week to cut her grass? Doesn't that seem a little excessive to you?"

"Hey, dude, whatever the market will bear, right?"

"Tell me about this little boy of yours. It seems like you've had a pretty rough time of it lately. Especially with your wife and your two little girls dying in that fire."

Grebberman had gotten over the initial shock of being accosted by a man with a gun, and once he realized that Weber was a lawman, he had become cocky.

"Don't know what you're talking about, man."

"Sure you do. I heard all about it. About how that fire killed most of your family, and about how poor little Albert needs a lung transplant and the insurance companies turned you down. Man, that just sucks."

"I don't know who you've been talking to, but whoever it was has a pretty vivid imagination or they're smoking some better shit than I am."

"I don't think so."

"Whatever, man. But just for the sake of argument, let's say there's something to this story of yours. So what? If somebody wants to pay me in advance for doing some work for them, that's not illegal, right?"

"Defrauding the elderly is illegal," Weber told him.

"My word against a senile old lady's. You don't have a case."

"Oh, so you're a jailhouse lawyer among your many talents, huh?"

The man leaned his head back against the seat rest and said, "Maybe I picked up a thing or two along the way. What of it?"

"You know, it pisses me off, but I have to admit that you're right. I talked to the judge and I talked to the Town's attorney, and they both say I don't have a case. I mean after all, you did say you are going to work off that $50,000, right?"

"Oh yeah, I'm a man of my word." Grebberman laughed sarcastically. "Of course, how much longer can an old bitch like her hang on, anyway? She'll probably croak before Christmas anyway."

"You're a real piece of shit, do you know that?"

"I don't think you can talk to me that way. That's abuse of a suspect or something, isn't it?"

"Oh, this isn't an official conversation," Weber told him.

"It's not? Well then get your ass out of my car, pig. Because I'm done conversing with you."

"Yeah, I'm done, too," Weber said. He leaned forward and wrapped his left arm around the man's neck and caught him in the crook of his elbow. Pulling backward, he jerked him off the seat. Grebberman started to resist and Weber squeezed tighter. As his air was cut off the man slapped his hands against the seat, struggling to breathe.

"Don't worry, I know how to use just enough pressure to get your attention, and how much it takes to kill you," Weber told him. "And I don't really have a problem doing either one. So here's how it's going to be, *Thomas*. I'm going to hang on to you like this for a couple of minutes just to make sure you really understand how serious I am. And then I'm going to let go of you, and I'm going to get out of your car, and you're going to get your ass out of my town and never come back. Do we understand each other?"

There was no response, so he tightened the pressure and Grebberman nodded his head frantically. The acrid smell of urine filled the car as the man in the front seat wet himself. Weber let up just a bit and said, "You're not going to pass Go, you're not going to collect $200, you're just going to drive and keep right on driving. Got it?"

He emphasized the question with another squeeze and got another head nod in response.

"What I'd really like to do is just pop a cap on your ass and be done with it. But the damn American Civil Liberties Union frowns on things like that. They are just about as bad as that Environmental Protection Agency you told Mrs. McKenzie about. But since I can't kill you, I'm going to make you a promise. If you ever call that woman, if you ever come around here again, if I ever hear that you're within 500 miles of Big Lake, you and I are going to have another visit. And when we do, I'm not going to be quite as friendly and nice as I am right now. You can count on that. Do we understand each other?"

Another frantic nod, and Weber kept the pressure on just as long as he could, to emphasize his point. When he let up, he said, "Don't come back, don't look back, just forget you were ever here. There's a great big forest out there, and by the time the coyotes and the bears get through with you and the smaller animals spread your bones around, no one's ever going to find whatever is left. And if they do, guess who gets to investigate the crime? You have yourself a nice life, *Thomas*. Just have it someplace far away from here."

Chapter 29

With winter coming, many Big Lake residents were splitting and stacking firewood to help heat their homes in the long, cold months ahead. Weber was one of them, using a maul and wedge to split stove-width lengths of shaggy bark juniper and alligator cedar in the back yard of his cabin on Saturday morning. He looked up when he saw a man approaching in his peripheral vision. Setting the maul down, he nodded and extended his hand to his visitor.

"How you doing, David? I haven't seen you in a while."

"Doing good Jimmy, doing good. Looks like you're getting ready for winter."

"I cut and split some when I can," Weber said. "I never seem to have enough time to get it all done before the snow falls."

"How do you like burning that shaggy bark?"

"Oh, it burns good. Only problem is it's messy and it makes a lot of soot. Which, of course, can lead to chimney fires if you're not careful."

"I'm glad I got a pellet stove. It's a lot cleaner and a lot less work."

"Yeah, Robyn has one at her place, too. I guess I'm just too old school."

"Have you heard anything about the plans for Duncan's funeral? I thought I'd hear from somebody by now."

"No, I haven't," Weber said. "I know the autopsy's done and the medical examiner was ready to release the body to the family. I told Sonny the other day. Have you talked to him?"

"I tried to call, but the phone only works about half the time out there. I know a lot of old-timers around here don't like the idea of the cell phone towers, but I have to tell you, Jimmy, they sure make life a lot easier."

"No question about it. I guess they've got three more going up next year." While he was old school in many ways, Weber did appreciate some of the changes that had come to Big Lake in recent years, including cell phone service. Coverage was still spotty outside of town, but getting better every year as new towers were erected.

"I guess I can drive out there. It's just..."

"Yeah, it smells bad," Weber said.

"Oh, that's not what I mean. I know this doesn't sound very Christian, but I'm really not looking forward to talking to Duncan's widow. Oh well, I guess I'll have to cross that bridge when I come to it. That's assuming that I *am* going to be the one officiating at his services. Like I said, I haven't heard a word from anybody."

The Reverend David Huntington had been a year ahead of Weber in high school, a tall geeky looking teenager with heavy acne and large ears that had earned him the nickname Jughead. After high school and college, he had attended divinity school and spent two years as a missionary working on the sprawling Navajo reservation that covered parts of northern Arizona and New Mexico. Returning to Big Lake, he had taken over the pulpit of the Trinity Lutheran Church when its longtime minister, Brian Garrett, had to step down to care for his wife, who was suffering from dementia. Some older members of the congregation had not been too sure about having someone so young at the helm of their church, but David had proven to be the right man for the job and had soon won everyone's confidence and respect.

"There's a total lack of communication between Mrs. Duncan and Sonny, but I told him the other day that they're going to have to put their differences aside for a little bit and work together on the funeral arrangements."

"At a time like this, families should pull together. But we both know that doesn't always happen, Jimmy."

"No, unfortunately it doesn't. I take it you've met Roseanne Duncan?"

"Not exactly," David said. "But I did speak to her on the phone once. And that was quite an experience."

"How so?"

The minister scratched behind one of his big ears and said, "I really don't want to gossip, but she didn't strike me as a very nice person."

"I think we share that opinion," Weber said. "She seems to have a way of stepping on toes and ruffling feathers wherever she goes. What happened in this telephone conversation you had with her?"

"Well, as you probably know, Duncan and I were second cousins."

"No, I didn't know that," Weber admitted, though he wasn't surprised because most of the families who had lived in and around Big Lake for generations were connected in some way.

"Yeah, though we didn't really interact as family members much at all. But Duncan was always a nice person, and generous to a fault. He always donated one of his hogs to our annual barbecue."

Weber wondered if there was any event that took place within 50 miles of Big Lake that didn't include a pig roast, courtesy of Duncan.

"We're not a very big congregation, as you know, Jimmy. None of the churches around here are. I think we were all hoping that as more people moved to the area or started staying here all summer long, our numbers would increase. But it hasn't happened for any of us. I guess the new folks aren't really here to worship, are they?"

"I guess not."

"Since we don't have a huge amount of people coming to our barbecue, we always have a lot of leftover pork, which we share among our congregation and donate to the food bank. Even with all of the big new places going up around here, Jimmy, there are still a lot of people who are just trying to get by and struggling to make ends meet. That meat helps a lot of them."

"I'm sure it does."

"Anyway, I called Duncan's place two weeks before the barbecue, like I always have in the past, to make arrangements for him to deliver the pig to us. This has been going on for as long as I can remember, way back before I came home to take over the church. And it's never been a problem. But when I told her what I was calling for, Mrs. Duncan came unglued. She started swearing at me and saying I was just another freeloader looking for a handout and I could forget all about getting any donation from them this year, or ever again. Then she slammed the phone down on me."

"I'm sorry to hear that, David."

172

"I was surprised by her reaction, to say the least."

"What happened after that?"

"We went ahead with the barbecue, but we had chicken instead. Then, a week later I was having lunch at the ButterCup Café when Duncan came in and saw me. He sat down across from me in the booth and said he'd read in the paper about our barbecue and wondered why I hadn't called him to get a pig, like I always did."

"Did you tell him what had happened?"

"Well, I tried to soften the blow as much as I could, Jimmy. I didn't go into all the details about how his wife had acted, calling me names and all that, I just said I'd called her and she turned us down."

"What did Duncan say about that?"

"I think he was embarrassed, to be honest with you. He just kind of hung his head and apologized and said there was some kind of miscommunication on their end and it wouldn't happen again. Then he reached in his pocket and pulled out this big roll of money that he had wrapped in a rubber band and he peeled off four $100 bills and gave them to me and said to use that to cover the cost of the chicken we had to buy, and to use whatever was left over for the needy. I tried to tell him that wasn't necessary, but he wouldn't take it back. He said yeah, it was necessary. Like I said, he was embarrassed."

"That's too bad," Weber said. "Let me ask you something, David. I don't go to church a lot, but I did when I was a kid growing up, and I have to tell you, Roseanne Duncan isn't like any of the Christians I knew back then. She talks about her church and her faith and all that, but when she gets mad she sounds like a drunken sailor. And the way she acts towards people, I just don't get it. And I've met that minister of hers from over there in Springerville, Patrick Jacobson. He didn't impress me much, either."

"The Good Book says ours is not to judge, Jimmy."

"Yeah, I know that. I just don't like hypocrites, and to me that's exactly what those two are. The way I hear it, at their wedding that Reverend Jacobson pretty much ignored anybody who was there that didn't belong to his church."

"I've met some folks like that in my time," David told him. "What can I say? It's not a perfect world we live in, and none of us are perfect."

"No, but it seems like a lot of people are less perfect than others."

David laughed and said, "I know God has a plan for everything, and we have to trust in him. But I have to admit, Jimmy, sometimes when I say my prayers I'm tempted to look up and ask him just what the heck he had in mind when he did some of the things he does."

Weber laughed with him. "Yeah, I guess if nothing else, he's got a sense of humor."

"Well, listen, that wood isn't going to split itself, so I had better let you get back to it. I'll take a drive out to the hog farm and see what I can find out about the funeral. Wish me luck."

"I still don't understand what Duncan ever saw in that woman, David."

"There's a reason for everything. And I guess sometimes it's not our place to know what that reason is. The last time I talked to Duncan, I could tell things weren't going well between the two of them. He even asked me to pray for them. That wasn't like him. I wish it could have been a happy union for both of them."

"Me, too," Weber said. "If anybody ever deserved some happiness in their life, it was Duncan."

Chapter 30

Weber's Sunday morning started early with an irate telephone call from Mayor Chet Wingate.

"Sheriff, I want Deputy Northcutt dismissed immediately!"

Weber looked at the digital alarm clock next to his bed. The red numbers showed 7:15. He yawned and asked, "Why is that, Chet?"

"Because the man is a nincompoop! Totally incompetent. I don't know why you put him on a major case like mine in the first place."

"What case is that, Chet?" Weber knew what the mayor was talking about, but he figured if he had to be irritated that early in the morning, the mayor should get the same thing in return.

"My cart, you idiot!"

"Oh yeah, I remember something about that. You can't find it or something, right?"

"I can't find it because it's been stolen! What kind of department are you running when you can't even keep track of the crimes that are happening all around you?"

"Calm down, Chet. What's Jason got to say about the investigation?"

"He says he can't find it, that's what he has to say. I told you I wanted one of the senior deputies on this case. Actually, I want you on it."

"Why me?"

"Because you're the sheriff and I'm the mayor, that's why! This is a priority case. The entire department should be involved in the search for whoever did this so we can bring him to justice."

"I don't know, Chet. According to you, Deputy Northcutt is incompetent and I'm an idiot. I don't know how we're going to get anything accomplished, given our shortcomings. But here's an idea; you keep telling everybody how smart Archer is and what a good cop he is, so how about I put *him* in charge of the investigation?"

"No. No, that won't work at all."

"Why not, Chet? I mean, to hear you talk, Archer's got all those detectives on TV and the movies beat all to hell. And here I've been holding him back by putting him on traffic duty or the high school. Yep, that's the thing to do. I'll pull Northcutt off your case right now and get that bloodhound son of yours on it. You know what? I bet he wraps everything up and has that cart of yours back in your garage by noon!"

"I don't want Archer on the case!"

"Why not?"

"Because the boy is as dumb as a rock! You know it and I know it, Sheriff."

"Can I quote you on that, Chet?"

"No, you can't quote me on anything! Just do what I said and go find my cart."

"Sorry, Chet, no can do. It's Northcutt's case and he's working it."

"He's not accomplishing anything!"

"What can I say? Crime is on the rise everywhere. All you have to do is watch the TV news to know that."

"So you're not going to go out and find my cart and catch the person who stole it?"

"Not right now, Chet."

"Why not?"

"Because it's not even 7:30 on Sunday morning, and I have other things to do right now that are more important."

"What could be more important than finding my cart?"

Robyn had been awakened by their conversation and snuggled up against Weber, her head on his chest. She raised up slightly and began to softly kiss his neck.

"I can think of at least one thing. Have a good day, Chet."

He hung up the phone while the mayor was still talking and turned his attention to more important things.

***

Jordan Northcutt was at the office having lunch when Weber came in four hours later.

"What in the world are you doing eating when we have a band of renegade mobility cart thieves pillaging the community?"

"I guess you heard from the mayor?"

"Bright and early this morning."

"I'm sorry, Sheriff," the young deputy said, putting down his homemade sandwich. "I was just coming on duty this morning when he pulled up beside me and started yelling at me, telling me to quit wasting time and go find his cart. He's been on my butt every day, two or three times a day, demanding I do something. The thing is, I don't know where to look!" He spread his hands in frustration. "I mean, I have nothing to go on. According to him, it was in his garage, plugged in so the battery could charge overnight, and when he came out the next morning it was gone. He said he didn't hear anything suspicious overnight, and I've talked to all of the neighbors and they don't know anything either. Nobody had any kind of security cameras that I could look at, nobody saw any strange vehicles in the area, nothing. The mayor wants me to dust for fingerprints, but I'm not sure what I'm supposed to dust, because there was no forced entry or anything like that. When I got there the garage door was open, and he said it had been all night long."

"Don't sweat it," Weber said. "I'm sure kids took the damn thing, and if we ever do find it, it's going to be somewhere in the woods."

"That was my thought, too, and I spent a lot of time walking around the woods near his house. I couldn't even find a tire track."

"Well, contrary to what our esteemed mayor may think, this isn't the crime of the century. And Chet has to carry some of the blame himself, leaving the garage door open like he did. That's an open invitation for somebody to come in and steal something. There was a time when nobody around here locked their doors, but those days are gone."

"I'm open to suggestions if you can think of anything I'm missing," Jordan said.

"I think you've done about all you can do at this point. You can try talking to some of the local kids, to see if one of them might rat out his buddies, but don't hold your breath."

"Thanks, Sheriff, I'll try that." Jordan shook his head, "I'm sorry to let you down. And I'm sorry to get you into trouble with the mayor."

"Don't worry about it," Weber said. "If Chet wasn't bitching to me about something every other day of the week I wouldn't feel complete. And trust me, if folks think he has heart problems now, they have no idea how much worse they would be if he didn't have something to complain about. Being happy would be way too stressful for him."

"Yes, sir."

"What is that you're eating anyway? Peanut butter and jelly?"

"Yeah, I'm brown bagging it."

Weber knew that a deputy's salary wasn't very much, and with a wife and baby to support, he knew Jordan was cutting corners to make ends meet.

"No. You can't fight crime and solve the Great Cart Caper on that. You need red meat, son. Let's go over to the Frontier Café and have us some real food."

"I'd better not. I've..."

"That wasn't a suggestion, Deputy, that was an order. I can't have you collapsing on me right in the middle of an important investigation like this because you're short on protein. Come on, I'm buying."

The diner was busy with the Sunday after church crowd and they had to wait a few minutes for a table to be cleared. Once they were seated and had ordered steak and eggs, Weber stirred cream and sugar into his coffee and said, "Here's the thing, Jordan. I think there's better than a 50-50 chance that Chet getting his cart ripped off is more of a prank than anything. He does tend to piss people off everywhere he goes on it, beeping his horn and going like a bat out of hell. So it may just turn up on its own. If not, and if you ever do catch who took the damn thing, it might be a tossup as to whether we should arrest him or give him an award for keeping the streets safe."

"You're probably right, Sheriff. I just feel like I let you down the first time you gave me a job like this."

"No, you didn't," Weber assured him. "If anything, I put you on the spot to start with. I should have told Dolan or Buz to handle it in the first place."

Seeing the look on the young deputy's face, Weber shook his head. "Don't get me wrong, kid. I don't mean because they are older and have more experience. What I meant was, they've been around long enough that neither one of them would have put up with his crap. The first time he started bitching at them, they'd have told him to stick it where the sun don't shine."

Jordan laughed and said, "I guess I've got a ways to go in that department."

"Look, Jordan, you may be young and you may be new to the job, but you're a good deputy. I don't have any doubt about that in my mind. But this whole thing with the mayor's cart is just a nuisance, so don't let it get to you. And don't let *him* get to you! Got it?"

"Yes, sir."

They were almost through with their meals when Joyce Taylor and her husband Ted came into the restaurant and were seated at a table next to them.

"Hey Jimmy, how you doing?"

"I'm good, Ted. How about you two?"

"Hanging in there."

"Well, that's about all any of us can do," the sheriff said.

"Jimmy, I want to thank you again for helping out Mrs. McKenzie," Joyce said. "I just knew something was up when she came in and wanted to withdraw so much money in cash."

"I'm glad you called me," he told her.

"I just hope he doesn't come around bothering her again."

"Don't worry about that. I'm pretty sure we've seen the last of that character around here."

"I wish I had known that was happening," said Ted. "We stopped by yesterday afternoon to check up on her and I told her not to worry about getting that grass mowed or the house painted, I'd take care of it for her and it wasn't going to cost her a dime."

The sheriff wasn't surprised to hear that. Ted Taylor, a bald round man known affectionately as T.T., owned a radiator repair shop and was one of the nicest people Weber had ever known.

"Were you able to convince Mrs. McKenzie that the EPA wasn't going to take her house away from her if the grass wasn't cut three times a week?"

"It took some talking, but I think so," Joyce replied. "We also talked about other ways that people might try to take advantage of her. I get so irritated when scam artists try to steal from good people, whether it's in person like that guy, or somebody calling or reaching out through the Internet to cheat them out of everything they worked so hard for all their lives."

A short, plump woman in her late 40s with dyed brown, shoulder length hair and sensible makeup, the Timber Savings Bank manager was a good businesswoman and a good judge of character. More than once the large corporation that owned the bank had offered her the opportunity for a transfer to Phoenix and advancement, but she was happy where she was in life. She had a nice house and a good family and wasn't willing to trade them for the rat race a promotion would throw her into.

"Well, if anything like that ever happens again, don't you hesitate for a minute to call me," Weber said.

"I won't," she promised, then shook her head. "I just wish Duncan would have listened to me."

The sheriff felt the hairs on the back of his neck stand up. "Duncan? What do you mean?"

Joyce looked around, then shook her head slightly. "We need to talk about this someplace else. Too many ears, if you know what I mean."

Weber knew very well what she meant. He didn't want to give the local gossips any more fodder for the rumor mill. "Could you stop by my office after you get done eating?"

Joyce nodded as the waitress came back to take their orders. Weber had a feeling that whatever the bank manager was going to tell him might take the case in a whole new direction.

Chapter 31

"Here's the thing," Joyce said when she sat down at the chair next to Weber's old roll top desk, "banks are real big on confidentiality and things like that. So what I'm about to tell you could get me fired. I'm trusting you to handle this the right way, Jimmy.

"You know I will," he assured her.

She nodded her head. "Duncan's been a customer at the bank for as long as I can remember. He's got half a dozen different accounts, CDs, things like that. And I don't think many people realize the extent of his wealth."

"Give me an idea,"

"Off the top of my head? I'd say close to $2 million. And that doesn't include his land. And you know the way real estate prices are around here these days."

The sheriff whistled. "You're right, I had no idea. I guess there's a lot of money in pigs. I knew Duncan wasn't hurting for money, and he paid cash for most things. But I didn't know he had that much socked away in the bank."

"Well, it wasn't all in one account or anything like that. Like I said he had several different accounts, and CDs and IRAs and things. He was one of our biggest depositors from this part of the state."

"From what you said at the restaurant, I get the feeling there was a problem?"

Joyce nodded her head. "Yes, I think there was."

"Tell me about it."

"Right after they got married, he came in and put Rosanne's name on his personal checking accounts as a signer."

"Is that uncommon?"

"No, not really," Joyce said. "Lots of married couples have joint accounts. But then a few weeks ago he added her to two of the business accounts. He said she was going to be handling some of the bookkeeping for him. Again, I didn't think a lot about it first. I mean, I'm a signer on Ted's business account for the radiator shop. I just figured it was nice that she was going to be helping Duncan out, taking some of the load off of him."

"But?"

"About three weeks ago I got a call from Duncan asking me if I could stop payment on a check that apparently got lost in the mail. But when I went to stop payment on it, it had already been cashed. He said okay, there must be some mistake on the other end and thanked me for my time. Then a couple of days later I got another call from him, asking if I was sure the check had cleared the bank. I looked at his account and it had been. Fast forward a day or two, and he called about two other checks that the payees never received. I looked them up and verified that both had been cashed. I asked him then if there was some kind of a problem and he said he was sure it was just a bookkeeping error somewhere. He blamed computers and said things were easier back in the days when you kept the books in an old ledger."

"Had things like that happened before?"

"Not with his account. I mean, sometimes things do get lost in the mail. And sometimes businesses receive a payment and for some reason it doesn't get credited to the customer's account. But three times in such a short time span makes you wonder. And these weren't small checks, Jimmy."

"How much were they for?"

"I don't have the exact numbers in front of me, but as I recall the first one was for $25,000, and the next two were both in the $12,000 to $15,000 range."

"That's a lot of money."

"Yes, it is. And then last week checks started bouncing."

"That doesn't sound like something Duncan would do."

"He *never* bounced a check in his life, Jimmy!"

"What happened?"

"Well, the first thing I did was cover them, of course. When you've got a customer like Duncan, with his history with the bank, there's no way we were going to return something for insufficient funds. I called him, or at least I tried to call him, but the darn phone wouldn't work. After the fourth check came in in two days, I took a drive out to the farm to talk to him about it."

"What did he say?"

"Nothing. He wasn't there. Mrs. Duncan said he was at a livestock auction down in Tucson, or someplace like that."

"Did you tell her about the bad checks?"

"I did. She said there must be some mistake on her end, that she was trying to make sense of the way he had been handling the bookkeeping, which was a mess, and she apologized and said that she would get it straightened out right away."

"And did she?"

Julie shook her head. "No, and Friday morning we had another bad check. I called again and that time Duncan answered the phone. When I explained what was going on he told me to transfer whatever kind of money I needed from one of his interest-bearing accounts into the checking accounts to cover things. I told him that would solve the immediate problem, but we needed to look at the underlying issue to figure out why this was happening."

"What did he say about that?"

"He said this was all news to him, that this was the first he'd heard about any problems with any of his accounts. He told me to hang on a minute and he would look at his checkbooks, and when he came back on the line he said that according to his numbers, the accounts in question should have several thousand dollars in each one. I told him both of the accounts were overdrawn and that I had already talked to his wife about it. But apparently she never told him about me coming out there. That's when I suggested that he and I needed to have a talk about what was going on. I told him this was raising some red flags and we needed to figure out why his accounts were coming up short."

"How did he respond to that?"

He said that his wife was over in Springerville at some church function, and that she was going to be tied up all day. He said he really wanted her there, too, and asked if we could get together sometime on Monday. I told him that would be fine, but that I was really concerned about the irregularities in his accounts and urged him to come in and see me as soon as possible so we can get to the bottom of things. But then the next thing I knew, Monday someone came into the bank to tell me that he had been killed."

"Damn. Do you think Roseanne was cooking the books?"

"No question about it, Jimmy. Do you remember those missing checks I told you about? The ones that the payees said they never received? I came in early Monday to have everything prepared for our meeting. Among other things, I looked up those three checks. They were cashed all right, but not by the businesses Duncan thought they went to."

"Where did they go?"

"All three of them were made out by Roseanne Duncan and deposited online into an account at a bank in New Mexico to a business called Fielding Enterprises."

The name Fielding sounded familiar to Weber, though he couldn't remember why.

"Is that somebody Duncan's business ever had anything to do with before?"

"Not to the best of my knowledge."

"Were you able to find out anything about this Fielding Enterprises?"

"No, I tried. They're not listed anywhere that I could find with a Google search, and when I called the manager of the bank, he wasn't very forthcoming at all. I understand that, what with all the privacy rules that we have to follow."

Alarm bells started going off in his head and Weber asked, "Where in New Mexico is this bank, Joyce?"

"It's called Bank of Southern New Mexico. It's a small bank in Deming."

"Damn!" Weber jumped to his feet and left the startled bank manager sitting next to his desk while he went out to the front office. "Is Dan Wright working today?"

"No," the dispatcher said, "It's his day off. You want me to see if I can reach him at home?"

"Yes, I do," Weber said. "Tell him I need to talk to him right away!"

~***~

"Here it is, right here," Dan said, pointing at his computer's screen. "Rosanne Duncan lived in Deming for eleven years before she moved to Benson, and then up here. And get this, Jimmy.

Remember I told you that her first husband passed away a while back? Seven years ago? His name was Christopher Fielding."

"As in Fielding Enterprises?"

"Your guess is as good as mine. If nothing else, it's a heck of a coincidence."

"No," Weber said shaking his head. "There's no coincidence here. I don't know what she had to do with Duncan's death, if anything. But that woman's been up to no good, and we're going to nail her for it!"

Chapter 32

It was mid-afternoon on Monday by the time Larry Parks was able to get a federal search warrant to access Duncan's banking records. When the FBI agent handed it to Joyce Taylor, the bank manager gave a sigh of relief, knowing that she was covered for whatever information she would reveal.

She had already done her homework and placed several printed sheets of account records on her desk. "As you can see, Roseanne Duncan wrote over $100,000 in checks to Fielding Enterprises, another $20,000 to herself, and $15,000 to her church."

"And Duncan didn't know about any of this?"

"Not that I'm aware of. I know that he thought these three here went to suppliers, and he said that's what it said in his check registers. And if you look at the numbers here in these checks," she indicated several lines under printouts, "these check numbers are totally out of sequence with the rest of the accounts. For example on this account here, the numbers of cashed checks go in sequence up to check number 2165. All those checks go to what look like legitimate payees. A propane company, credit cards used for the business, a tax bill. But now, look at these numbers here. Check number 4000 was for $500, written by Roseanne to herself. The next day check number 4001, again written by her to herself in the amount of $900. And it goes on like that in both accounts. I think she was taking checks from the back of the stack and using them, and not recording anything about them. This is why the accounts were coming up short and checks were bouncing, guys. Duncan never knew that money was missing from the account, so he was writing checks to pay bills and didn't know there weren't enough funds to cover them."

"What do you think, Parks? Can we make a case here?"

Parks studied the records carefully and nodded his head. "Oh yeah, I think so. I mean, it would be up to a federal prosecutor to make that decision, but this sure looks like bank fraud to me. And when she deposited that money online for those big checks into that account in New Mexico, she committed wire fraud. So we've got both bank fraud and wire fraud."

"If she gets convicted, what is she looking at?"

"Bank fraud can get you up to a million bucks in fines and 30 years federal prison, or both. And mail or wire fraud is worth a $250,000 fine for each violation."

"So what happens now? I know my people down in Phoenix are going to want some answers from me," Joyce said.

"Tell them that there are federal and local investigations going on, and that we're not keeping you in the loop," Weber said. "That way the heat's on us and not you. But off the record, we might not have known anything about this for a long time without your help. So we'll keep you updated as much as we can without compromising the case."

He looked at Parks and asked, "Got everything you need to get started?"

"I think so," Parks said, stacking the papers and putting them into a folder. "Let's go make it happen."

~***~

"She had him cremated! Never answered when I tried to call her to make arrangements for my dad's funeral, never said a word to me about it. She just went and did it! How can she do that, Sheriff? That's just not right!"

"No, it's not," Weber said, sitting back in his chair in disbelief at what he was being told. "How did you find out about it?"

"I called Carmichael's Funeral Home over in Show Low this morning after I couldn't get hold of Roseanne. That's who handled my mom's funeral when she died. I figured somebody had to do something to at least get the ball rolling. But then they called me back and said there was a problem and I needed to call the medical examiner's office down there in Tucson. I did and they said Friday morning some company from down there called Coronado Cremation Services came and picked up my dad's body. I called them and they said that Roseanne had taken care of all the arrangements and he had already been cremated. I asked how they could do that without my permission and they said she was technically his next of kin and could make that decision. She shouldn't have done that without at least talking to me about it, Sheriff."

"Legally, I guess she had the right," Weber said, "but you're right, that was no way to go about it. I'm sorry, Sonny."

"Do you know where that bitch is? Because I'm gonna find her and I'm gonna wring her goddamn neck!"

"Just calm down," Weber said. "I know how you feel, but you can't go around talking like that. Especially not to the Sheriff."

"I don't care! You can do whatever you need to do to me, but that bitch is going to pay for this."

Weber understood the man's rage, but the last thing he needed was for Sonny to do something stupid and compound the problems he already had.

"Listen Sonny, I can't tell you all the details right now. But she's not going to get away with the things she's done, okay?"

"You're damn right she's not going to get away with..." He stopped in midsentence and looked at Weber. "What do you mean she's not going to get away with the things she's done? What things? You just said it was her right to have my dad cremated. Do you know more than you're telling me about how he died? Did she have a hand in it?"

"No, she didn't kill him. We know that. I told you the other day, I talked to the medical examiner after the autopsy. There's no question about that. Your dad died from loss of blood because he bled out from that bull goring him."

"Then what are you talking about? What isn't she going to get away with?"

"Do you know much about your father's financial dealings? His bank accounts and things like that?"

Sonny shrugged his shoulders. "Not really. We've always banked at Timber Savings here in town. Why?"

"I was talking to Joyce Taylor, the bank manager, today. You're not a signer on any of those accounts. Why is that?"

"Because I didn't want to be. I told you before, I never gave a damn about the business. I didn't want to be a part of it from the start. My dad kept trying to get me to take a bigger interest in that end of things, and I wouldn't do it. Just flat-out wouldn't do it. Because I knew as that soon as I did, I'd be stuck out there on that damn hog farm forever."

"That must have been frustrating for your father."

"It was," Sonny acknowledged. "And looking back, I kind of kick my ass for that now. I mean, I know it really hurt him that I didn't want to take over and run things someday. But I wanted nothing to do with it. Hell, Claudia took more of an interest in the business side of things than I did."

"Claudia? Your ex-wife?"

Sonny nodded. "Yeah, she started taking classes in bookkeeping and small business and things like that at the community college. I asked her why she was messing with all that and she said that someday my dad was going to be gone and it was going to be up to us to at least know something about the business and how it ran."

"How did your dad feel about that?"

"Oh, he was thrilled. He even paid for her tuition. I think maybe he figured in his mind that with her handling the numbers, I might decide to keep the place running down the line, even if I wasn't out here working with the hogs myself. But of course, that all went to hell when me and her broke up. Just one more time I let him down."

Weber wanted to offer some consolation to the man and tell him that whatever had happened in the past belonged in the past and to stop beating himself up about it. But as much as he hated to see Sonny chastising himself over his failures as a son, at least he had calmed down a bit and wasn't looking for blood at the expense of his stepmother.

"Listen to me, Sonny. I know this is a terrible time and you're going through a lot of stuff right now. But here's what I need you to do. I need you to go home and I need you to just continue taking care of things like you've been doing for now, okay? You do your thing and let me do my thing."

"I may not be as sharp as my old man, but I'm not an idiot, either. You're onto something, Sheriff. What's going on?"

"I'm not trying to jerk you around, Sonny, but I can't tell you anything else right now. I will say that some developments have come up that I'm looking into. And again, this doesn't have anything to do with your father's death. Rosanne did not kill him. I want to emphasize that again. I don't want you to go off thinking that and doing something that's going to get you into trouble. You know what they say about karma. Just trust me, okay? Hold on and let this play out."

Sonny nodded his head. "Okay, we'll do it your way. For now at least. But I'm telling you right now, Sheriff, that woman better not cross my path and start any crap with me. Because if she does, I'm not gonna be responsible for what happens!"

Chapter 33

"Yeah, I knew Rosanne Fielding," Detective Pete Willis of the Deming Police Department told Weber. "I knew her husband, Christopher, too. He was a standup guy. Really terrible, what happened to him."

"What happened?"

"He got killed. Terrible accident."

"Accident, as in traffic accident?"

"No. That would have been bad enough. He was killed when he was working on his car. Damnedest thing anybody around here ever saw."

"Tell me about it."

"Well, the best anybody could determine, he was under his car changing the oil and the jack slipped and a couple tons of Oldsmobile fell on him."

"Oh, man. I hope he went fast."

"Nope, afraid not. His wife had gone out of town for the weekend, some kind of church thing, and she found him when she came back Sunday night. The best anybody could determine, the car fell on him sometime Saturday morning and there was just enough weight to compress his chest so he couldn't breathe very much at all. The ME said it was slow and painful and probably took him a long time to die."

"Damn. Let me ask you something, Detective. Do you think his wife had anything to do with it?"

"Officially, Christopher Fielding died of an accident. There's no evidence to show anything else happened. It says so right there in the records."

"I'm hearing a *but* somewhere in there," Weber said.

"But, like I said, I knew Christopher. He was a hell of a shade tree mechanic. He and I used to race stock cars together. The guy knew his way around tools and cars. And jacks."

"And you think something else happened besides a simple accident?"

194

"What I think and what the record says are two different things. And when it comes down to it, my opinion don't count for diddly squat against the official findings."

"So, one cop to another, what's your opinion?"

"In all the time I knew Christopher, all the hours we spent working on cars together, and racing together, and hanging out together, never once did I see him crawl under a car to do anything unless he had jack stands under it."

"So maybe he got careless and forgot?"

"Maybe. But let me ask you this, Sheriff Weber. How careful are you with your weapons?"

"Damned careful."

"Have you ever gotten careless and forgot and had an accident?"

"No, I never have."

"Me either. Because both of us have seen the damage a bullet can do. I told you Christopher was a good shade tree mechanic. Hell, he was better than good. When it came to turning a wrench, he was one of the best I've ever seen. He came from a long line of car nuts. As I recall, his dad hauled home an old wrecked Model T or something like that when *he* was just a kid, and him and his brothers rebuilt it. That was his first car. When Christopher was fourteen, his Uncle Buddy got his head crushed working under a car when the cinderblocks he was using to hold it up collapsed. So he knew the damage something like that could do. Are you following me?"

"Yes, I am," Weber said.

"Christopher was just as careful around cars and tools and things like that as you and I are with our weapons. But there weren't any jack stands under the car that fell on him. You tell me how that happened? And there were some other things that made me call bullshit on the whole accident story. When they got the car lifted back up and got Christopher out from under it, there was a crescent wrench there on the floor next to him, along with the plastic tub he used to drain oil into."

"Okay. I'm not sure where you're going with this."

"A crescent wrench. The guy had every tool in the world in his garage, SAE, metric, you name it, he had it. The plug on the oil pan was a 3/4 inch. So the guy's got every tool known to man and he works on cars all the time. Why did he get under there with a crescent wrench instead of the proper wrench?"

"I see your point. What else looked out of place to you?"

"I said the plastic tub was under the car with Christopher and that crescent wrench. But there was no new oil filter. Not under the car and not sitting on his workbench. And there was a case of oil in a cabinet in the back of the garage, but he didn't have any out. Why would a guy like him who grew up working on cars not have the oil filter if he was going to change oil? And why didn't he have any oil out there where he was working on the car? It just didn't add up. If you have ever been involved in small track racing, you would know that seconds count not only on the track, but in the pits. Every wasted movement when you come in can cost you time and laps. Christopher was the most efficient guy you ever met when it came to that. He didn't start a job until he had everything ready to complete it as quickly as possible. We all used to tease him about being so anal about things like that. But nobody teased him when he took on the trophies at the end of the race."

"But you were never able to prove anything?"

"Nope. Rosanne was never an easy person to get along with, but she was a good churchgoing woman who was well known in the community. I tried to tell my boss something was wrong about the whole thing, but he wouldn't listen to me. He kept telling me I was letting my grief over the loss of my friend cloud my judgment."

"That does happen sometimes," Weber said.

"Not to me," Detective Willis said. "Look, Sheriff, we're both small town cops. You know how it is. We know everybody. The good and the bad, and those in between. Sometimes when we answer a call we have to lock up somebody we went to school with. Or tell some girl we dated back in the day that her kid just died of an overdose. Or pull a relative out of what's left of a car when some drunk T-boned them. We know how to put our emotions aside and do our jobs. Otherwise we wouldn't last very long. Am I right?"

Weber had to admit that what the man was saying was true, and he acknowledged it.

"So tell me what you think really happened?"

"Christopher's chest was compressed. He had some cracked ribs and a cracked sternum. All that came from the car sitting on top of him. But he also had a contusion on the back of his head. The medical examiner said that probably happened when the car fell. That it forced his head backward onto the concrete floor of the garage."

"But you don't think it happened that way?"

"I can't prove it, but no, I don't. I think somebody hit Christopher in the back of the head with something and knocked him out. Then I think that person jacked the car up and shoved his body underneath it and then let the jack back down and knocked it over so it looked like it was an accident. I think that person expected him to die right then, and probably didn't stay around long enough to find out if he did or not."

"And that person would be Rosanne?"

"I wasn't there, I can't say. But Christopher was a pretty solid guy, so if it was her, I would think she had to have had some help."

"Do you have any idea who that might have been?"

"No, I really don't."

"Were they having trouble, Christopher and Rosanne?"

"I know he was getting fed up with her constant nagging all the time. Nothing was ever good enough for her. And he wouldn't go to church with her, which to her was a mortal sin. More than once he said he thought they should just end it. Go their separate ways and get it over with instead of making each other miserable. He was a good old boy and he wasn't going to change. And Rosanne damn sure wasn't going to change either."

"It doesn't sound like the perfect marriage," Weber admitted. "But then again, is that worth killing somebody over?"

"Maybe. Maybe not. I guess it depends how upset you are by all of it. But there is one thing that a lot of people would consider worth killing somebody over."

"What's that?"

"A $75,000 life insurance policy with a double indemnity accident clause."

Chapter 34

"Yeah, people have been killed for a lot less than 150 grand," Parks said when Weber related his conversation with Detective Willis. "It's entirely possible that kind of money got this Christopher Fielding fellow wasted."

"Are you guys saying we've got a black widow on our hands?"

"I don't know, Coop," Weber said. "Willis sounds pretty sharp, and whether Rosanne had anything to do with her first husband's death or not, he's convinced it wasn't an accident. But he was never able to convince his bosses that it was more than speculation on his part."

"And now it's a cold case, and they probably don't have the time or the money to dig into it without some kind of solid evidence," Parks said.

"This is all really interesting, but none of it changes the fact that the medical examiner said Duncan died from what that bull did to him," Robyn said.

"No, but there's still the thing with the broken fingernail and those marks on his side. And we still don't know how the hell he got in there with those hogs. That woman had something to do with it," Weber said. "I don't know what, but she had something to do with it."

"Everybody keeps telling you how dangerous that bull was, and how Duncan still kept going out and messing around with it every morning. Didn't someone say the bull would paw the ground and shake his horns or something like that?"

"Yeah. And?"

"But nothing ever happened before. So why did it attack him that morning, Jimmy?"

"I'm not following you, Robyn. Where are you going with this?"

She shrugged her shoulders. "I'm not sure, to be honest with you. I'm just thinking out loud. Did Duncan do something to antagonize the bull?"

"Leonard Bowers said Duncan would wave a handkerchief at it sometimes. Like he was playing matador or something."

"Maybe the bull got tired of playing the game? Or he just caught it on a bad day? Who knows? I think animals have got personalities, too. What set the bull off that day instead of any other day?"

"I don't know, it's hard to say."

"What if it wasn't the bull that was different that morning?"

"Now you've really lost me. What are you getting at?"

"What if Duncan was different? It's like they played this game every day, but that morning something different happened. What was it, and why?"

"I grew up around livestock," Weber said. "Including bulls. I'd never trust any of them for a minute."

"I know, I'm just trying to look at all the angles, Jimmy. And I keep asking myself, what set the bull off that morning instead of the day before, or the next day?"

"Like I said, you can't trust them. I've been around bulls that were pretty docile most of the time, but some little thing, or nothing at all, can get them all riled up when you least expect it."

"But what if it *was* something? What if something was different about Duncan that morning?"

"Like what?"

"I don't know," Robyn admitted. "What about toxicology tests? Did they find any evidence of him being drugged?"

"Drugged?"

"Let's play *what if*? What if Duncan was impaired in some way that morning? Something that slowed him down or changed his judgment a little bit. And when the bull got to snorting and carrying on like it did, he wasn't able to get out of its way?"

"Damn! I never thought of that," Weber said. "What's the number for the Medical Examiner's office in Tucson?"

Five minutes later he had Doctor Hurtado on the telephone. When Weber asked him about any evidence of drugs in Duncan's system the ME put him on hold for a short time and then returned.

"Sheriff, keep in mind that Mr. Duncan had bled out long before we got him, so there wasn't much left to do a blood test on. And a lot of the soft tissue organs in his abdomen were gone, thanks to the hogs. But in analyzing what we could, I didn't see anything that raised any red flags. The bit of liver we could recover didn't show any signs of alcohol abuse, or any of the common things we look for. I'm sorry."

"Thanks anyway, Doc. It was worth a shot," Weber said.

"If I can think of anything else, I'll sure get back to you with it."

"I appreciate it," Weber told him, ending the call.

"Sorry for wasting your time with that," Robyn said.

"Hey, never apologize for looking at things from every direction or thinking outside the box," Coop told her. "Sometimes the things we think are totally off-the-wall are just what it takes to break a case wide open."

"I really want to talk to that woman again," Weber said.

"That's going to be hard to do with her attorney and that preacher of hers blocking the path," Coop said.

"Just play it cool, Bubba," Parks advised. "Once the federal prosecutor's office takes a look at those bank records there's no doubt in my mind that we'll be spending a lot of time talking to Roseanne Duncan."

When the FBI agent said that, neither he nor the sheriff knew how soon they would be talking to Duncan's widow, or under what circumstances.

~***~

"You want Sonny arrested for *what*?"

"Federal law clearly states that anyone who has been convicted of domestic violence is prohibited from possessing a firearm," Dean Wicklund said. "By his own admission, Sonny used a rifle to shoot several hogs and the bull the morning his father was found dead. And Mrs. Duncan here witnessed the shooting."

"My God, those animals had just killed his father and were eating his body!"

"Don't use the Lord's name in vain," Roseanne snapped.

"I wasn't using..."

"It doesn't matter why he was doing it," Wicklund cut the sheriff off, saying, "the fact is that Sonny Duncan was in possession of a firearm, and he's been convicted of domestic violence for beating his ex-wife."

"He didn't *beat* her." Weber said. "I've talked to Claudia and even she says it was an accident."

"That's neither here nor there. He broke the law and it's your job to arrest him."

Weber looked from the attorney to Roseanne and said, "I can't believe you. I absolutely cannot believe anybody could be as cold and heartless as you are."

"Sheriff, your prejudice is showing. Stop haranguing my client. Are you going to do your job and arrest Sonny, or do I have to take this matter to the state Attorney General's office?"

Weber wanted nothing more than to slap the smug look from the attorney's face, but instead he said, "You want me to do my job? Okay, you got it. Let's go back to the interview room so you can make out a full report, Mrs. Duncan."

"I've already told you what she saw that day, and I know Sonny himself told you he shot those animals," Wicklund objected. "That's all you need."

"No, sir," Weber said, shaking his head. "If you want to do this, we're going to do it by the book. After all, I wouldn't want to slip up somewhere and have the Attorney General on my back, would I?"

In the interview room he handed Roseanne a yellow legal pad and pen and said, "Write it all down. And don't forget anything."

"You have a report from the morning her husband was killed," Wicklund said.

"This is a separate case. I need a separate statement. Write it down and I'll be back in a minute."

When Weber returned, he had Coop and Parks with him. "I believe you've both met Deputy Cooper. And this is FBI Special Agent Parks. You may remember him, Mrs. Duncan. He's the guy who took the shovel away from you out at the farm when you were going to hit Sonny with it."

"Don't even go there, Sheriff," Wicklund warned.

"Go where? I was just making introductions."

"I don't want that man in this room," Roseanne said, glaring at Parks.

"Unfortunately, you don't have a lot of say in that matter," Weber told her. "What you've accused Sonny of is a federal crime. I'm just a small town sheriff. I have to refer this to the FBI."

"Fine, whatever," Roseanne said.

"Let me take a look at what you've got here." Parks picked up the legal pad and read what Rosanne had written, then passed it to Weber for his review.

"There, you have her statement. Are we done here?"

"So you really want to push this? In spite of Sonny losing his father, and you having Duncan's body cremated so he couldn't even hold a funeral for him? That's not enough for you? What's it going to take to make you happy?"

"That's enough, Sheriff," Wicklund said heatedly. "I told you before to stop abusing my client!"

"I'm just making conversation," Weber said innocently. "I just don't understand why she is so vindictive towards Sonny. What's he ever done to you to make you hate him that much, Rosanne?"

"We're done here," Wicklund said, standing up. "Come on, Mrs. Duncan. You don't have to take this."

"No, you go on back to Springerville and you gloat all the way about how you're ruining a good man's life," Weber said. "But what the hell, maybe if you get a minute or two you'll say a prayer for him, right?"

"Enough, Sheriff!"

"I'm going to nail you, lady. One way or the other, you're going down!"

"Why? Because I'm making life hard for that worthless excuse for a human being out there? This could all have been avoided, Sheriff. All you had to do was do your job and get Sonny out of there when I told you to. But no, you good old boys all stick together! Well, guess what? It's not going to work this time! I told you Sonny was leaving there no matter what." Roseanne was shouting at that point, pounding her fist on the long interview table in anger.

Wicklund pulled her to her feet and Rosanne struggled to break free. "That's enough, Rosanne! You're doing exactly what they want you to do. Stop it. The law is on our side. Sonny is going to be sitting in a jail cell tonight."

Rosanne gave Weber a look of hatred as her attorney hustled her out the door and down the hall.

"Well that was fun," Coop said.

Chapter 35

"You've got to be shitting me? This can't be happening."

"I'm sorry, Sonny. I really am. But we don't have any choice in the matter, our hands are tied."

"You can't do this, Sheriff," Leonard Bowers said. "It's just not right!"

"I know it's not," Weber replied. "But like I said, we have to do our job. Mrs. Duncan came into our office yesterday and filed a complaint. We can't just ignore that, as much as we'd like to."

"What happens now?"

"I've already talked to Judge Ryman. He wants us to bring Sonny before him and he's going to release him on his own recognizance. From there it's up to the federal prosecutor as to whether or not he wants to go forward with anything. Look, we are going to work this out, okay?"

"So I go to jail because I shot that damn bull and some stupid hogs after what they were doing to my dad?"

"No, you're being arrested for being in possession of a firearm and having a conviction for domestic violence. We know it's bullshit, you know it's bullshit, everybody knows it's bullshit. But that's the law. You're not going to be sitting in a cell or anything like that. But we have to go through the motions. Deputy Wright here is going to take you in and book you, take you to see the judge, and then he is going to bring you back home. Okay?"

"And who's going to feed the hogs and everything else while I'm gone?"

"I'll do it, Sonny. I promise, I won't let you down," Carl Turner said, visibly upset by what was happening but trying to reassure his friend.

"Don't worry about the hogs or anything else out here," Leonard added. "Just go do what you gotta do and come back, Sonny. We'll handle things here."

"Okay, whatever." He held out his hands to be cuffed.

"No need for that," Weber said. "You're just taking a ride with Deputy Wright, here. There's no way any of us are putting handcuffs on you, Sonny."

The younger man nodded his head in appreciation.

"Now, I do have a search warrant to seize any firearms that are in your possession or that you have access to. And I know that sucks, too. I'm sorry."

"Yeah, do what you gotta do," Sonny said. "I've got a Winchester next to the front door and a pump shotgun in the bedroom closet in my trailer."

"Is that what you shot the hogs with, the Winchester?"

"Yeah."

"Anything else in your trailer, or your truck, or anything?"

Sonny shook his head.

"Besides the guns, are we going to find anything else we shouldn't?"

"Like what?"

"Like drugs?"

"Hell no! I'll have a beer now and then, but I don't mess with that stuff. I never have."

"Okay, we just have to ask. How about in the main house? Are there any firearms in there?"

"Yeah, my dad had some guns. But they're not mine."

"I know, but technically you have access to them. So we have to search there, too. Do you know what all is in there, and where they are?"

"There's a gun cabinet in the room on the first floor that he used for his office. It's got some rifles and shotguns in it."

"Anything else?"

"He had a Colt .357 and a Ruger .22 single-action somewhere, but I don't know where. If they're not in his desk drawer or the gun cabinet, they may be in the bedroom."

"Your dad's bedroom?"

"Yeah. Sheriff, I'd hate to see my dad's guns go away and get chopped up or whatever you guys do to confiscated guns. I didn't even know I couldn't have one. I guess maybe they told me about it when I pled guilty to hitting Claudia, but I was such a basket case right then that I really don't remember. Honest."

"I understand," Weber told him. He knew how people who made their living off the land in the west depended on their firearms, not just for sport but also for protecting their livestock from predators. Coyotes roamed freely through the mountains, as did black bear, and though it didn't happen all that often, it wasn't unknown for a mountain lion to stray too close to a farm or ranch looking for an easy meal. Plus, there was emotional attachment. Weber had not hunted for many years, but he still owned the rifles and shotguns he and his father had used on the ranch. Some of them had been passed down all the way from his great grandfather, and their sentimental value was much more than any dollar amount they might be worth.

"All right," Weber said. "Dan, take him in and get things rolling."

They walked to Dan's cruiser and he opened the front passenger door. It was obvious Sonny appreciated the courtesy instead of being put in the back like a suspect. Weber leaned in the open door and put his hand in the man's shoulder.

"Look, Sonny, we're not here to bust your balls. I don't like this any more than you do. But I'm asking you to trust me, okay?"

"That's what you said yesterday when I told you about her having my old man cremated. And now today I'm getting arrested on something that even you say is a bullshit charge. How long am I supposed to trust you, Sheriff?"

Weber wished he could tell Sonny something else, but he didn't know himself what or how he was going to bring Roseanne to justice for embezzling the company's money, even if she didn't play a role in Duncan's death. And no matter what the medical examiner said, and what Weber had told Sonny about his father's cause of death, the sheriff still believed there was more going on than met the eye. He just had to find some way to prove it. But all he could do at that time was tell him to hang in there. As he watched Dan's car drive away, Weber wondered how much more Sonny was going to be able to take.

"Okay, let's get to it," he said. "Dolan, you and Buz search Sonny's trailer and seize the long guns. Parks, Coop, let's go check out the house.

They walked past Leonard Bowers, who stared at them in anger with his arms folded across his chest. Weber thought the farmhand might have something to say, but whatever he was thinking, he kept it to himself. Carl just shrugged his shoulders and said, "Guess I'll go take care of the hogs."

~***~

There were nine long guns in a glass fronted gun cabinet in Duncan's office. Three of them were bolt-action high-powered hunting rifles with telescopic sites, one was an ancient lever action Winchester .30-30 carbine like the millions that rode in saddle scabbards and pickup truck gun racks across the west. There were three shotguns that had obviously seen a lot of use hunting birds and small game, and two .22 rifles. Two drawers in the bottom of the gun cabinet held boxes of ammunition, gun cleaning supplies, and the Ruger revolver Sonny had told them about, in a holster on a gun belt.

"No .357," Coop said.

"Is not in the desk, either," Parks added. "But I sure wish I had the warrant back from the federal prosecutor, because there's all kinds of checkbooks and financial paperwork that I really want to get my hands on."

"Leave it all alone for now," Weber advised. "We don't want to blow the case based on improper search. This warrant just covers guns."

"I guess we look upstairs next?"

"Sounds like a plan to me."

There were four bedrooms on the second level of the house, three of which obviously had not been used in a while. The top of a mirrored dresser in the master bedroom was covered with books and agricultural magazines, while the surface of the one across from it was empty.

Coop started to open the drawer of one of the nightstands next to the bed, but Weber stopped him.

"Not yet."

"Why not?"

"If you kept a gun in your bedroom, where would it be?"

"I *do* keep a gun in my bedroom, and it's in the nightstand next to the bed, just like this one."

"Right, and if you open that drawer and find that .357 Sonny told us about, we're done here. Who knows? That gun might just as well be in one of these dresser drawers or a closet. Don't you think we should look in them first?"

Coop smiled at him and nodded. "Yeah, you're right. That damn gun could be anywhere."

The dresser with the magazines on top of it had obviously been Duncan's, and the drawers were filled with jumbles of socks and underwear, things you would find in a man's dresser. The one on the opposite wall held Rosanne's clothing. The first drawer held bras and underpants, pantyhose, and handkerchiefs, all neatly folded.

The second and third drawer revealed blouses, again all neatly folded and stacked. Parks whistled when he opened the bottom drawer.

"Well, well, this is interesting!"

"What?"

"You know what they say about church ladies," the FBI agent said, holding up a short red see-through négligée. "I guess you never know what goes on behind closed doors."

"I don't want to know," Weber said shaking his head.

Parks rummaged through the drawer carefully, chuckling at the seductive things he was finding.

"Are you about done getting your jollies there?"

"Hey, I'm just looking for a gun."

"Well, it's not here in the closet, either," Weber said. "Let's check out the nightstands."

The one on the left side of the bed contained a Bible, a small flashlight, and a hairbrush. They found a four-inch barreled Colt Trooper inside a zippered case in the other nightstand.

"Bingo," Weber said, unzipping the case and unloading the revolver. He looked around the room and said, "I guess we're done here. At least for now."

"Looks like it," Parks said.

"Guys, I've really got to take a leak," Coop said. "Do you suppose I would be violating the warrant if I used the bathroom there?"

"I don't see how," Weber said. "When you gotta go, you gotta go. Just be sure to put the seat back down when you're done."

When Coop closed the bathroom door behind him Parks looked around the bedroom. "So seriously, Jimmy, can you picture Roseanne Duncan dressing up in something flimsy and prancing around here?"

"That's not a picture I want in my mind," Weber said.

A moment later they heard the toilet flush, then water running in the bathroom sink. A moment later there was the sound of something small hitting the floor and Coop saying, "Damn." There was a long pause, and then he opened the door and said, "This is interesting."

"Whatever it is, unless it's a gun, don't touch it."

"No, it's not a gun, Jimmy. It's pills."

"None of our business," Weber said.

"Yeah, there may be a day when you need Viagra, too," Parks added.

"It's not Viagra. These are blood pressure pills. I knocked them off the sink when I was reaching for the towel to dry my hands. The cap wasn't fastened down all the way, it was just sitting on top and I had to pick up the pills that spilled out."

He handed Weber the small brown bottle.

"So Duncan had high blood pressure. What's that got to do with anything, Coop?"

"Read the label from the pharmacy, Jimmy. This prescription was filled three weeks ago. It says here Duncan was supposed to take one pill a day. And it says there were 60 pills in it when it left the pharmacy. That's a two month supply. But there are no more than 30 pills in it now. And that's not all," Coop said. "A couple of the pills ended up in the little trashcan next to the vanity. And when I looked at them, guess what else I found?"

He held up his palm, and when Weber saw the remains of the red acrylic fingernails in his deputy's hand he couldn't resist shouting out loud.

"Son of a bitch," he said with a grin. "We've got her!"

Chapter 36

"Yeah, Duncan's been on blood pressure meds for years," Kirby Templeton said from behind the counter at Mountaintop Pharmacy. "Doc Johnson kept telling him he needed to slow down and start taking life a little easier. But that wasn't going to happen. You know how Duncan was. He'd just laugh and say he planned to be one of the pallbearers at the doctor's funeral."

"According to what we saw on the pill bottle at his house, Duncan was supposed to take one pill a day, right?"

Kirby looked at his computer and nodded. "That's what it says here."

"If the prescription was filled three weeks ago, and Duncan's been dead over a week, that would mean there should have been about 45 or 46 pills left if he was taking one a day. But there were only 29."

"That can't be right," Kirby said.

"I counted them myself," Weber assured him.

"So what happened to the rest of them?"

"I don't know? What kind of pills were they, Kirby? I mean, I know they were for his blood pressure, but were they something that someone might be sneaking to abuse?"

The pharmacist shook his head. "No, I don't see that happening. They were beta-blockers. They slow the pulse rate down to lower a person's blood pressure."

"What would happen if somebody took more than they were supposed to, Kirby?"

"Oh, that wouldn't be good at all."

"What could some of the symptoms be?"

"It depends on how many more they were taking than were prescribed. Normal side effects can include insomnia, fatigue, shortness of breath, dizziness, disorientation, weakness, and muscle cramps. Even heart failure. And those could all be exacerbated by overdosing. What are you getting at here, Jimmy?"

"If Duncan was OD-ing on this stuff, could that make him woozy or out of it enough that he might get too close to that bull, or do something like that? Could that be what got him killed?"

"Sure, it's possible," Kirby said. "But Duncan was no fool. He wouldn't double up on his dosage like that."

"Probably not. But those pills went somewhere. And I think they went into his body."

"What are you saying?"

"I'm saying this changes everything," the sheriff told him. "Thanks Kirby, I've got things to do."

~***~

"It's entirely possible," Doctor Hurtado said when Weber told him his suspicions. "If he was lethargic or disoriented, or suffering some other effect from an increase in beta-blockers, sure."

"Is there any way you can determine that from your autopsy results?"

"Not really," the medical examiner said. "Like I told you before, he was pretty much drained of blood by the time we got to him. And we didn't have any reason to check for anything like that. I wish I could help you more, Sheriff, but I'm afraid not."

"That's fine," Weber told him. "This helps me a lot."

~***~

"I've got to admit that part of me figured once you got me into the jail I was gonna sit there forever," Sonny Duncan said that afternoon when Weber and Parks returned to the hog farm. "You're a man of your word, and I appreciate that, Sheriff. And I swear, I wasn't trying to break the law or anything. I've had that rifle and shotgun since I was a kid and I never thought anything about them. I mean, the rifle sat behind the door loaded like it always had. Once in a while we get a coyote hanging around hoping to grab one of the shoats, and I use it for that. I never even thought about the damned domestic violence thing."

"It's okay," Weber told him. "I believe you. Like I said, we just have to go through the motions."

"What happens now? Am I going to go to prison or something?"

"No, you're not going to prison," Weber assured him. "We'll get this worked out. I think that the worst that might happen is you'll have to pay a fine. Let's cross that bridge when we come to it. In the meantime, how had your dad been feeling lately?"

"What do you mean?"

"Was he complaining about not feeling well, anything like that?"

"Not really," Sonny said. "I mean, he was getting up there in years and I guess it might've been starting to show a little bit."

"Show how?"

"Oh, I don't know off the top of my head. Wait, there was a while back we were unloading a truckload of feed and he had to take a break. It comes in 70 pound sacks, and there was a time when my old man could outwork me and two other guys. So I had a good time pulling his leg about the fact that he had to stop and sit down to catch his breath."

"What did he say about that?"

"What do you think he would say? He called me an asshole and got back to work."

"Anything else like that ever happen that you know of?"

"Not really. I'd see him yawning once in a while the middle of the day, and I didn't remember him doing that before. To be honest I thought maybe him and Rosanne were, well, you know. I figured he just wasn't getting as much sleep as he used to."

When Weber talked to Leonard and Mona, it was obvious that the longtime employee still did not appreciate seeing Sonny arrested on what he considered to be a trumped up charge. But Leonard did say that he also remembered the incident when they were unloading the feed sacks a little over a week earlier. "Yeah, Sonny had a good time with that. I mean, nothing bad, just him and Duncan horsing around."

"Now that you mention it, I did notice something a little bit different about Duncan about a week or so before he died," Mona said.

"What?"

"I went out to the mailbox to bring in the mail, and as I was walking back down the lane I saw Duncan leaning against the fence alongside the road. I asked if he was okay, and he kind of looked at me strange."

"Strange in what way, Mona?"

"I don't know. Like he was confused or something. Almost like he wasn't sure who I was, or who he was. It was just for a few seconds, Sheriff. And then he kind of grinned and said something about he must have had a brain fart, or something like that."

"Anything else?"

"No, not that I can remember. How about you, honey?"

Leonard shook his head. "Duncan was Duncan. He could always outwork anybody on the place. I never really noticed anything different about him, except for that thing with the feed sacks. And hell, everybody needs to take a break now and then."

Carl wasn't very forthcoming when Weber tried to talk to him. "I'm mad at you!"

"Why are you mad at me, Carl?"

"Because you took Sonny away and was gonna lock him up in jail. Sonny's my friend and he didn't do nothin' bad."

"No, he didn't," Weber said, sitting down next to the farmhand on the couch in his trailer. An animated movie was playing on the television screen about some kind of fish that was talking to what looked to be a mermaid.

"Then why did you take him to jail?"

"Like you said, Sonny didn't do anything bad. But sometimes people make mistakes that causes them problems. Sometimes they do things they don't mean to do because it's a mistake. Right?"

"Like when Sonny hit Claudia and got in trouble?"

"Yeah, just like that," Weber told him. "We all know Sonny didn't mean to hit her, but it happened and he got in a little bit of trouble for it."

"But that was before, and he hasn't done nothin' bad for a long time."

"No, he didn't. Not like hitting anybody, anyway. But see, because he got in trouble that one time, he's not supposed to be using any guns. So, we had to take care of that. But now he's back home where he belongs."

"I don't like guns," Carl said. "When they shoot the guns it hurts my ears."

"Yeah, it hurts my ears, too. That's why I wear earplugs when I practice shooting."

"Sonny shot a coyote one time. It was trying to get to the baby pigs. Is he going to get in trouble for that, too?"

"No, because he was protecting those pigs. Remember when I told you it's okay to defend yourself?"

"Yeah."

"Well, it's okay to protect somebody else, too, if they're in danger. And it sounds like those little pigs were sure in danger from that coyote."

Carl nodded his head, his attention divided between the sheriff and the TV screen.

"Listen, I know you want to watch your show, but I've got to ask you a couple more questions and then I'll go away."

"Okay."

"Carl, did you ever see Duncan act like he didn't feel good? Like maybe he was sick to his stomach or really, really tired? Or anything like that? Or maybe acting like we do sometimes when we just wake up and we're not wide-awake yet? Maybe kind of clumsy or something like that?"

"No. I miss Duncan. The hogs ate him."

"I know they did, and that was a terrible thing."

"Sonny shot those hogs. And he shot Montezuma, too. Just like he did that coyote."

"Yes, he did," Weber said. "And he shot them for the same reason he shot that coyote, he was trying to protect Duncan and everybody else."

"I miss Duncan."

"Yeah, I know. I miss him, too."

Weber stood up and asked, "So, are we still friends, Carl? Even though I had to make Sonny go away for a few hours today?"

The farmhand thought about it for a minute and then nodded his head. "Okay, we're still friends. I'm not mad at you anymore."

"That's good," Weber said, "because I need all the friends I can get."

He stuck out his hand to shake, but instead Carl stood up and hugged him with arms that were strengthened by years of hard labor.

Weber hugged him back, then said, "I'll leave you to your movie. Thanks for your time, Carl." But the other man was already focused back on the TV screen, and if he heard the sheriff, he didn't acknowledge it.

Chapter 37

"Jimmy, nice to see you. I can't remember the last time you've been inside my church."

"Sorry about that. I guess I have been doing some backsliding."

"Well, like they always say, better late than never."

"Thanks for seeing me on such short notice," Weber said, "I appreciate it."

"No problem at all," Reverend David Huntington replied. "What can I do for you?"

"When you were at my place the other day and we were talking, you said something about the last time you talked to Duncan, he asked you to pray for him and his family?"

"That's right."

"Do you remember when that was? Was that when he saw you at the restaurant and gave you that money because of the mix up about the donated pig for your barbecue?"

"Oh, no. The thing with the money was quite a while ago. The other happened two Sundays ago."

"Two Sundays ago? Like, the day before he died?"

"Yeah. To be honest I was surprised to see him. It's been quite a while since Duncan came to church. I guess he used to attend all the time back when Eleanor was still alive. But after that he pretty much stopped coming."

"Do you know why?"

The preacher nodded his head and said. "I'm ashamed to say I do."

"Tell me about it."

"This all happened back when Brother Garrett was still at the church. I guess a couple of the women objected to the way he smelled. You know, from the hogs and all."

"You're kidding me?"

"I wish I was. Apparently he overheard somebody saying something snotty about him, about how back when his wife was alive at least she made sure his clothes didn't smell of hogs. The way I heard it, Duncan didn't say a word. He just got up from the pew and walked out, and never came back."

"That's a shame."

"Yes, it was. As you know by now, Christians aren't perfect. We've had an old biddy or two among us who I think only show up on Sunday so they can know who didn't. But I will say that most of the congregation here are wonderful, wonderful people Jimmy. In fact, I know that after that happened, several of the ladies went out to the farm to talk to Duncan. To apologize and tell him that he was welcome anytime."

"But he never came back?"

"No. But he made sure we had a hog every year for our barbecue. And if Duncan knew of somebody who was having hard times or was sick or whatever, it was not uncommon for him to just show up and hand me an envelope with some money in it and tell me to make sure they had what they needed, and there was more where that came from. And every year, a couple of weeks before Christmas he'd show up with the back end of his truck loaded with brand new toys. He said every kid deserved to have a nice Christmas."

"Do you know why Duncan came to church that day, when he hadn't been in so long?"

"He stayed around after the services were over and said he needed to talk to me if I had time. I told him I would always have time for him, and we sat and talked for an hour or so."

"Can I ask what about?"

"He told me that he was having some problems at home and with his business. I asked him what kind of problems and he didn't go into a lot of detail. He just said that his son and his wife were not getting along at all, and that he was worried about what would happen between them, and to the business if something happened to him."

"Did he go into any detail about what these problems were?"

"Not really. But he asked me something that didn't make a lot of sense to me."

"What was that?"

"Jimmy, do you remember the story of King Solomon and the two women who came to him, each claiming that they were the mother of the same baby?"

"Vaguely," Weber said. "Something about cutting the baby in half?"

"Right. Both women had a child and they lived in the same house. One child died and they both laid claim to the other. So they went to the king to settle it. Solomon listened to both of them tell their story, and then he drew his sword and said that he would cut the baby in two and give each woman half. One of the women didn't object, but the other one dropped to her knees and begged him not to kill the baby. She said to give it to the other woman instead. Solomon knew that was the real mother, because she would rather have the baby alive even if she had to give him up."

"I remember that from Sunday School," Weber said. "As I recall, I think it gave me nightmares for a while."

"Yeah, there are some stories in the Bible that will do that to a kid. I remember when I was in divinity school one of the instructors saying *Read the Bible, it will scare the hell out of you!* Anyway, Duncan asked me about that story. He said he knew he wasn't going to live forever and he was thinking that if he presented his wife and son with the same scenario, maybe they would come together. Then he asked me to pray for all of them, asked for the wisdom of Solomon."

Chapter 38

Weber left the church almost bouncing with excitement. He called Dispatch and asked where Coop was.

"He's out on a disturbance on Agate Lane with Robyn," the dispatcher told him. "At Councilwoman Smith-Abbott's house."

"What's going on there?"

"I don't know, but it involves Tami Gaylord."

"That can't be good," Weber said. "I'd better head over that way."

Tami Gaylord, who owned a local boutique that sold overpriced Native American artwork to gullible tourists, favored heavy makeup and multicolored shift dresses that hid her bulk. She always had her eye out for a new man, and despite her size and her often brash attitude, she had managed to snag an assortment of husbands along the way. The unions never lasted long, but Tami was able to comfort her broken heart with the large settlements she got in the divorce decrees. A while back she had set her sights on Mayor Chet Wingate, and for a brief time the couple made a spectacle of themselves as they paraded around town groping each other in public. But that all ended when Councilwoman Gretchen Smith-Abbott could not contain her jealousy any longer and faced off with the boutique shop owner in a dispute that was still talked about in the beauty shops and stores around town. Since then, the mayor and the councilwoman had been almost inseparable. Weber wondered if Tami had shown up at the councilwoman's house to resume the feud, though for the life of him he couldn't understand why anybody would want to fight over the likes of Chet.

When he got to Agate Lane, he pulled up behind the two police cars already there and made his way through a crowd of gleeful onlookers to the front yard, where he could hear shouting. Pushing his way through the last of the looky-lous, he saw Coop standing between the councilwoman and Tami, arms extended outward like a referee separating two boxers before the bell rang to begin a match.

Tami Gaylord would never be called a pretty woman under the best of circumstances, and this day, with her face red with anger and her mascara smeared, she certainly wasn't going to win any prizes. Not that the councilwoman was likely to walk off with a crown, either. Her hair had come undone and was hanging over the side of her face, and the front of her gray suit was dirty. A stray pine needle or two clung to the fabric.

"Okay, what's going on now?" Weber demanded, wondering if Chet had been foolish enough to try to carry on liaisons with both women at once. As it turned out, that wasn't the case at all.

"I'll tell you what's going on," Tami shouted. "This dried up old prune is trying to get even with me for having anything to do with her boyfriend, and she's using her position on the Town Council to do it!"

"Who are you calling a dried up old prune, you fat slut?"

"Slut? You're calling *me* a slut? But what does that make you, miss fancy-dancy Councilwoman? Not only are you screwing Chet Wingate, now you're trying to screw me, too! Well, it's not going to happen, bitch!"

Gretchen started to respond, but Weber cut her off. "Okay, both of you, that's enough! One more comment like that out of either one of you and I'm going to throw you both in a cell. He pointed to the garage door, which was splintered and hanging halfway off its track. "What the hell happened there?"

"This *woman* hit my car when she came roaring into the driveway, uninvited I might add, and pushed it into the garage door."

"It's a big wide driveway," Tami said. "Why were you parked right in the middle of it so there was no room for anybody else?"

"It's my driveway, I'll park wherever I want," Gretchen shouted. "And besides if you weren't driving such a big tank, there'd be room for two vehicles. But I guess a woman your size needs something that big just so she can fit into it, don't you?"

"Stop it," Weber said. "Look at the two of you, acting like crazy women out here for the whole world to see. Don't you have any shame?"

"She's the one that should be ashamed," Tami said. "She's trying to put me out of business because she's so petty about Chet."

"I'm not trying to put you out of business," Gretchen retorted. "That new sign you put up violates the code. All I did was send you the letter saying it had to come down."

"That sign cost me almost $3,000, and I'm not taking it down because of some stupid sign code. We never had that before."

"Well, we do now. It went into effect last year. Don't blame me because you never attend Town Council meetings or read the newspaper. Or because you were too lazy to even come into Town Hall to get a permit before you had it put up!"

"That's what this is about? A stupid sign?"

"A $3,000 sign," Tami said.

"That you didn't get a permit for," Gretchen shot back. "I was only doing my job. It's not my fault you didn't do yours."

Tami took a step forward and Coop blocked her path.

"Okay, enough of this nonsense. Tami, you get in your car and go home right now. And Gretchen, not another word out of you. This needs to be settled with the Town Council, not here in front of half the community."

"What about my car, and my garage? Look at the damage she's done to them!"

"This is private property. It's a civil matter."

"She can come onto my property and maliciously destroy things and just drive away like nothing ever happened?"

"Then sue her," Weber said, "or let your insurance companies work it out. I don't care. But this ends right now. Got it? Tami, go. Now! Before I arrest you for disturbing the peace."

"I want her arrested. She assaulted me!"

"I was defending myself on my own property."

"Shut up!" Both women stepped backward when the sheriff roared at them. "I said that's enough! Tami, get out of here. That's your last warning."

The big woman glared at him, then gave Gretchen the finger as she made her way past and climbed behind the wheel of her big SUV. She backed out and burned rubber speeding away.

"Just look at my Prius! It's ruined."

Weber had to admit that the little hybrid had certainly gotten the worst of the encounter. The back end was dented, and the front was crumpled where it had hit the garage door.

"See if it will start so you can back it up a little bit," Weber said. "Otherwise that door is liable to fall down the rest of the way and completely crush it."

Gretchen looked at him in alarm.

"Don't worry, Deputy Cooper and I will hold it up so it doesn't fall on you when you are in the car. Then we'll either prop it up or take it off the track so it doesn't come down on top of somebody."

"No, that's all right. I'll call somebody to come out and fix it."

"Yeah, you're going to have to call somebody. No question about that. But in the meantime, we need to secure it. It's a hazard. That thing could come down at any minute."

"It's okay, Sheriff. I'll get somebody out here. You all can run along. Thank you for your help."

"Really, it's no bother. It will just take us a couple minutes. And like I said, we can't leave with it hanging halfway down like that. If it were to fall and hurt somebody we'd be liable. I'm sure the Town Council doesn't want a lawsuit on its hands because we didn't do our job."

The councilwoman started to protest, then sighed with resignation and got into her battered car. Weber and Coop held the garage door as she started the Prius and backed up a few feet. Grunting, the two men were able to push the door partly open.

"Go inside and see if you can find something to prop this side up with until she can get somebody to come out and fix it," Weber said.

Coop slipped under the door, and a moment later emerged with a folding metal stepladder. They managed to shove the door a little further up and wedged the stepladder under it.

"That should do it," Weber said, stepping backward.

"Uh, Jimmy, there's something in here you need to see."

"What's that?"

"Come here and take a look."

Weber followed him into the garage and stared in disbelief. Then he looked at his deputy and said, "Damn, you need to go buy yourself a lottery ticket or something, Coop. That's two mysteries you've solved today"!

Chapter 39

"Please don't tell Chet," Councilwoman Smith Abbott begged.

"How am I not supposed to tell him? He's been on my back since this damned thing came up missing. I can't pretend we don't see it sitting here."

"This could ruin our relationship."

"What am I supposed to do? You stole his damn cart!"

"I didn't exactly steal it... I just.... took it."

"Yeah, but you took it without his permission, or his knowledge. Unless somebody changed the law and hasn't told me about it, that's stealing."

"Please, Sheriff Weber, you have to understand."

"Understand what, Gretchen? Help me out here, because I'm at a loss. Why did you take the stupid thing in the first place?"

"Why? You've seen how he drives it down the sidewalk beeping the horn and waving at people like a madman. He's a danger to himself and everybody else. And an embarrassment! How do you think it looks for the town when our mayor does that? How do you think it looks for me as his... you know?"

"I'm not disagreeing with what you're saying. I've tried to get him to stay off that thing since the day he got it," Weber said. "Even the Doc says he doesn't need it. Just like he doesn't need that stupid oxygen bottle he totes around everywhere with him. But Chet likes playing the invalid for some reason."

"He certainly didn't play the invalid when he was with Tami Gaylord," Gretchen said bitterly. "Parading around town with that ugly toupée on his head and wearing those disgusting clothes, like they were on their way to a disco or something."

Weber remembered the previous summer, when the mayor's affair with Tami was going on hot and heavy. Chet had come into a local restaurant with Tami clinging to his arm, wearing tight jeans that bulged over his protruding belly and a black silk shirt open halfway down his chest, showing a sparse patch of gray hair and excess rolls of flesh, while three gold chains hung around his flabby neck. It had not been a pleasant sight.

"Yeah, she brought out a side of Chet none of us had ever seen." He wanted to add that nobody ever wanted to see it again either, but he held his tongue.

"I just don't see what she has that I don't. With her, he was running around like he was some kind of Lothario, and with me he wants to sit on the couch and hold hands like we're two old people at a senior citizens rest home or something. I mean, I'm happy to have him, but there are times I really want what Tami had with him, too. I don't mean the weird clothes and the way they were hanging all over each other in public. There is a time and a place for everything. But at the right time, in the right place, I'd like something more, Sheriff. Is that too much to ask?"

"Look Gretchen, I'm not a marriage counselor or anything like that. But I guess if you want something, you have to make it known. Let's face it, Chet's not exactly Einstein. My dad used to say that if you want to teach a mule something, the first thing you have to do is hit it in the head with a 2x4 to get its attention. Not that I'm saying you should hit Chet with a 2x4. Then again, maybe that might be the best idea. But whatever the problems between the two of you are or how you feel about this goofy cart of his, you can't just go around stealing things. You've put me in a really awkward position."

The sheriff's position got even more awkward a moment later when a horn beeped and they turned to see the mayor's white Cadillac Escalade pulling into the driveway.

"What happened here? Somebody said there was a disturbance."

"Oh, it was awful," Gretchen said, suddenly turning into a willowy maiden whose handsome knight had come to her rescue. "Tami Gaillard attacked me. Physically *attacked* me! She hit me and knocked me down and..."

"Oh, my poor dear. I'm so sorry!" He started to say more, then stopped when he saw his mobility cart inside the garage.

"My cart! What's it doing here?"

Gretchen hung her head in defeat. "I'm really sorry, Chet. I...."

"We're all sorry," Weber said, cutting her off. "Gretchen found it over there in the woods behind her house. I think some kids stole it and went joy riding on it. She pushed it in here and I think she even strained her back doing it. In spite of her pain, she plugged it in, hoping it would charge. But apparently they trashed the thing completely. She called us to report it, but by the time we got here Tami had shown up and things had turned ugly"

"What? It looks like new!"

"No, Deputy Cooper here is pretty good with electronics and things like that. He checked it all out and said the motor is shorted out and the gears are stripped. Isn't that right, Coop?"

"Yeah, that's right. I'm sorry, Mr. Mayor but you'd probably be better off buying a new one than trying to get this one running again."

The mayor started toward the garage and Coop stopped him. "Don't touch it! Like the sheriff said, the motor is shorted out. It about knocked me on my butt when I tried to start it. The Framus coil is back feeding through the McCartney condenser, which sent an electromagnetic pulse to the frame and eradicated the safety bypass. Which of course means that the heavy earth magnets in the motor backed up and fried the windings."

"That sounds bad."

"It is bad," Coop assured the mayor. "Very bad."

"Can it be fixed?"

"No, sir. That thing is dangerous. It needs to go to the junkyard. The high isotopes from the back feeding have obviously weakened the structural integrity of the frame itself. There's not anything on it we can even salvage."

"But that cart cost me almost $3,500 the way I had it outfitted! Not including shipping and handling. And it took over six weeks to get it up here."

"I know. That just sucks. But besides the possibility of getting electrocuted, with those gears stripped out like Coop was telling me, you could be going down the sidewalk and it might take off and drive right through the side of a building or something. I can't let you back on it, Chet. It's a liability issue for the whole town."

"I want the hooligans who did this caught and punished, Sheriff Weber! And I'm putting that responsibility directly on your shoulders. It's your job to bring them to justice. Do you understand me?"

"Yes, sir, I do. And I promise you, Chet, we're going to do everything we can to get to the bottom of this as soon as possible. You have my word on that."

"Well, see that you do!"

"Chet, I'm feeling a little lightheaded from my ordeal. Could you help me inside, please?"

"Oh, sure. I'm sorry," he said, taking her arm. "Let's get you inside and settled down."

"Don't leave your car running," she said. "The last thing we want is for those kids to come back and steal it, too."

As Chet went to his Escalade to turn it off and lock the doors, Gretchen appeared to stumble toward the sheriff. Weber caught her before she fell, and she whispered, "Thank you, Sheriff. I owe you."

"Whatever you do, don't let him start wearing that damn toupée again," Weber whispered back. "Do that and we're even."

Seeing his damsel in distress, the mayor quickly rushed to her side and said, "I've got her, Sheriff. Thank you. Now get out there and find those thieves who stole my cart and ruined it. Come on, my darling," he said to Gretchen, leading her toward the doorway of her home, "Your Chet's here, and he's going to take very good care of you."

As Weber and his two deputies watched the mayor and Councilwoman make their way into the house, the sheriff asked, "Coop, was any of that bullshit you were feeding the mayor true? Framus coils and McCartney condensers and isotopes? Are they even real?"

"Would I lie to you, boss?"

"No, not for a second," Weber said, shaking his head. "I'm sorry I even doubted you. But Robyn, remind me never to play poker with this guy."

~***~

"I'm pretty sure I know what Duncan planned to do with the three wills," Weber said when they were back in his office. "It all makes sense to me now."

"I'm glad it makes sense to you, because I'm still not getting it," Parks said. "Run it by me again.

"When David Huntington said Duncan asked him to pray for his family and said he needed the wisdom of Solomon, it hit me. I think Duncan wrote up all three of those wills because he planned to show Roseanne the one giving everything to Sonny, and to show his son the one giving everything to her. When it looked like neither one of them was going to get the whole place, he hoped that they would both seize the third option he presented in that third will, splitting it right down the middle, and learn to work the hog farm together."

"But they both hated each other and they both hated the hog farm."

"I know. And Duncan loved them both and he loved the hog farm. It was his legacy, and I guess he just thought that sooner or later they'd get on board with it."

"Jimmy, I can understand the emotional attachment to the place, and maybe even Duncan thinking the two of them would come around, on some level. But he wasn't a fool by any means. How realistic was that?"

"From our perspective, probably not at all. But if he was doubling up on those blood pressure pills, maybe he was befuddled enough to think he could pull it off."

Chad Summers shook his head. "I'm still not buying that part, either. Duncan didn't like taking medicine of any kind. I remember once when I bumped into him when he was in town and we were having lunch together, he was complaining about a headache. The waitress offered him a couple of aspirins and he said no, it would go away. He said it was bad enough he had to take blood pressure pills, he didn't need any more chemicals in his body."

"I don't think he was taking them," Weber said. "At least, I don't think he knew he was. I think Roseanne was crushing them and slipping them into his food or his coffee or something."

"That makes sense," Parks acknowledged.

"So what brought this all to a head?" Robyn asked. "Like I said before, why that morning in particular?"

"I think a couple of things triggered it," Weber said. "I think the increased meds were messing with Duncan, maybe leading him to believe that there was something serious wrong with him. From everything I've heard about him, he didn't like going to the doctor if he didn't have to. My old man was the same way. And, I think when Joyce Taylor at the bank told him about the discrepancies in his checking accounts he may have gotten suspicious. Or, maybe not, and he just told Roseanne that they needed to go to the bank to get things straightened out on Monday. And that's when she knew she had to do something before that happened."

"I guess it could have gone down that way," Coop said. "But how do we prove it? The ME didn't find anything in the toxicology reports, and the body's been cremated. Where does that leave us?"

"Do you remember when I talked about playing poker over there at Gretchen's house, Coop?"

"Yeah?"

"Sometimes I like to play a hand or two myself. Let's see if my bluff is as good as yours."

Chapter 40

"I cannot believe you let Sonny out of jail when you had him dead to rights." Roseanne said when she arrived at the Sheriff's Office the next morning.

"What can I say? We screwed up and dropped the ball. That's why we had to have you come all the way back over here, Mrs. Duncan."

"Because his stupid name was wrong? That's ridiculous."

"I know it seems that way," Weber said. "But I'm sure if Mr. Wicklund were here, he'd tell you the same thing. The federal prosecutor says we can't make an arrest that will hold up in court without a valid complaint. Did you call him?"

"No, I did not call him," she snapped. "I'm not going to pay him $150 an hour to ride over here with me to fill out another report. Let's get this over with."

"Sure thing," Parks said, handing her the original complaint she had lodged against Sonny for possession of firearms. "What we need you to do is just rewrite the whole thing, but everywhere you have Sonny Duncan, replace that with his full name, George Samuel Duncan, Junior."

She quickly wrote up a new complaint and signed it. "There, are we done now? I have better things to do than sit here talking to you people."

"I'm sorry we got off to such a bad start," Weber said. "But I guess we are going to have to learn to work together."

"What do you mean?"

"Well, we've got your report and we're going to go out and re-arrest Sonny like you want us to. But that's just the start. I mean, you're going to have to testify at his trial if we're going to get a conviction."

"Gladly. I hope they put him away for a long time."

"Have you ever been a witness in a criminal trial, Mrs. Duncan?"

"No, Sheriff, I have not," she said testily. "I don't make a habit of associating with criminals."

"I'm sure you don't. Usually the prosecutor is going to want to talk to you ahead of time, kind of walk you through the whole process before trial. Don't get offended, but sometimes they even suggest what kind of clothing you should wear. Nothing too flashy, like bright colors or big jewelry, or things like that."

"I assure you I know how to dress properly, Sheriff Weber," she replied sarcastically. "And flashy is not my style."

"No, ma'am, probably not. Just out of curiosity, do you wear those fake fingernails like some of the ladies do?"

"What?"

"You know. Those fake fingernails. The ones that they glue on to make their fingers look longer?"

"No, I do not."

"That's strange. Because when they did your husband's autopsy they found something odd. Turn that laptop computer around, Deputy Cooper. Show her that picture."

Cooper turned the laptop's screen toward her and showed her the photograph of the small lacerations on Duncan's torso.

"Do you know what those are, ma'am?"

"I have no idea."

"I didn't either, not at first. Then they found this. Show her that other picture, Coop."

Coop brought up the photograph of the piece of fingernail.

"That medical examiner, he's pretty sharp. He knew right away what those little cuts on your husband's body were from. But he didn't know what this was until one of the ladies that works there saw it. How about you? Do you know what they are?"

"No, I don't know. What does this have to do with anything?"

"Well, ma'am, the little marks are from someone's fingernails digging into his skin. And that little red thing there? That's a piece from an acrylic fingernail that they found in his shirt. But you said you don't wear those, right?"

"That's what I said."

"So then how did your husband get those marks, Mrs. Duncan? I talked to Mona Bowers, but she doesn't wear those artificial fingernails either. And you two were the only women out there? Can you explain that?"

"I think I can."

"Great. I'd sure like to hear it."

Rosanne sighed heavily, as if she was about to say something that would take a heavy load off of her heart. "It hurts me to say this, but my husband was far from perfect. Only after we were married did I find out that he had been having an affair."

"An affair? Who with, ma'am?"

"A woman named Carmen Barela."

"Carmen? José Barela's wife?"

Rosanne wiped a tear from her eye and nodded. Cooper pushed a box of Kleenex across the table and she took one out and dabbed at her eyes.

"I never would have thought George was capable of something like that. Not in a million years. He always put on this persona of the good old easy-going farmer. But that was all an act. Underneath all that, he was a lecherous, dirty old man. And I didn't find out until it was too late. I know what you're thinking, George couldn't be like that. It's probably hard for you to believe. I didn't believe it myself until I caught them in the act."

"You caught them? Together?"

"Yes, I did, and it was horrible. Right there in our bed."

"What did you do, Mrs. Duncan?"

"What do you think I did? I ordered that harlot out of my home and told George I wanted a divorce."

"You two were getting divorced?"

She sighed again and closed her eyes, shaking her head. "Looking back, I probably should have stood my ground. But he was apologetic and crying and asking me to forgive him. So once I had time to calm down and think about the situation, and after talking to my minister, I did what the Bible tells us to do, Sheriff. I turned the other cheek. We had a long talk about it and decided that it was best if the Barelas left, and George and I would pick up the pieces and start over."

"I see. And that's the last you saw of them?"

"I thought so. But I became suspicious that George was still seeing her."

"Why is that?"

"A lot of little things. He would say he was making a quick trip to town for something and be gone half the day. When I'd ask him where he'd been, he'd always say he ran into somebody and they got to talking and he forgot about the time. And I noticed the smell of perfume on him several times. I don't wear perfume."

"Did you confront him about these suspicions of yours, Mrs. Duncan?"

"Not at first. At first I prayed for guidance. And then I talked to George about it. Of course, he denied it, but then I caught them again."

"Your husband and Carmen Barela?"

"Yes. They were parked in his truck a mile down the road from the farm in a little pull off. I walked right up on them doing their filthy business in the front seat of the truck."

"And when was this?"

"I don't know exactly, maybe a week or so before George died. I'm sure that's when he got the marks on his body. A decent woman wouldn't do something like that. A decent woman submits to her husband but she doesn't become an animal."

"It didn't happen that way. Those marks were fresh, not a week old."

"Then I don't know. Maybe he saw her again. For all I know, they were doing something out in the barn or something before he got killed."

"Maybe. Or maybe there's another scenario," Weber said. "Maybe you put those marks on him."

"I told you, Sheriff, a decent woman doesn't do things like that."

"Maybe he didn't get them in bed."

"What are you suggesting?"

"I'm suggesting that after the bull gored Duncan you were trying to help him back to the house or something. I think you had your arm around him and were trying to hold him up and that's when he got those marks and when you broke off the fingernail."

"I told you, I don't wear those."

"You probably don't wear sexy lingerie either, do you?"

"How dare you speak to me that way!"

She started to stand up, and Weber said, "Sit down. I'm not done with you yet."

She gave him a hateful look and sat back down.

"We were in your house, Mrs. Duncan."

"What? You have no right to be in my house!"

"Actually, we did. Pursuant to the search warrant to seize any firearms Sonny might have had access to, we searched his mobile home and your house. And I've got to say we were kind of surprised by some of the outfits we found in your dresser drawer. And those fake fingernails in the wastebasket in your bathroom. Do you suppose Carmen Barela left them there? Maybe she kept a stash of sexy nighties right there in your bedroom to make things quick and easy when she and your husband wanted to take a tumble?"

"I have nothing more to say to you."

"That's fine, but I've got a lot more to say to *you*. I know you were drugging your husband by overdosing him on his blood pressure meds. That's why he was acting weird lately. That's why he couldn't react fast enough when he got too close to Montezuma. I know you're the one that put those marks on him and left that piece of fingernail in his shirt. I'm pretty sure we can get DNA to prove it came from you. I know you tried to help him after he got hurt. I don't know why you did that. And I don't know why you stopped. Did you push him into the hog pen so they could finish the job? Like I said, I don't know right now, but I'm going to prove it."

"You can't prove anything," Roseanne snarled. "All right, maybe those were my négligée's. So what? It's not illegal for a woman to have clothing like that. And maybe I did put those scratches on my husband and left that broken fingernail. We were married. Maybe I was trying to spice up our sex life so he wouldn't go back to that whore of his. But maybe José Barela found out that the affair between my husband and his wife was still going on. Maybe he came out to the farm to confront George about it that morning. Maybe he did something that caused the bull to attack him. Maybe he put my husband in that hog pen."

"Or maybe your husband confronted you about the missing money from his checking accounts. Maybe you knew he was going to divorce you over them. He might even have been planning to prosecute you."

"Prosecute me for what? I didn't do anything wrong. I'm a signer on those accounts, so I had every right to write checks on them. I didn't break the law."

"You misdirected funds. I'm pretty sure that's illegal some way or another."

"So who's going to file a charge against me? George? He's dead, remember. And since I own at least a part of the business, all I did was put some of *my* money from *my* business into *my* account!

"Well, you've got a problem there," Weber told her. "You didn't own any part of the business at the time. It's a corporation and you didn't hold any of the stock. Duncan put you on the payroll as an employee, but until his estate is settled, that's all you are to the corporation. Just an employee. An employee who ripped off funds. That's fraud, lady."

"I'm not saying anything else," Roseanne said. "I want my attorney."

Chapter 41

"I really hope you can make this stick," said Bob Bennett, Big Lake's Town Attorney. "I'm not sure the judge is going to go for it. When I called him about the search warrant this morning, he said you're really reaching here, Jimmy."

"Those pills went somewhere, and I think they went into Duncan," Weber said. "And I think the way she was doing it was by putting them in his coffee every day. Leonard Bowers, one of the guys who works out there at the hog farm, said every morning Duncan would go outside early and have a cup of coffee and watch the sunrise. There'd been a couple of times when he acted strange, and taking too much of the blood pressure medicine could have caused that."

"What was her motive?"

"She knew Duncan was never going to throw Sonny out of there, and she wanted him gone so she could control the hog farm. I think she was hoping he'd have a heart attack or something from the increased dosages. But it wasn't happening fast enough. So I think she really gave him a bunch that morning when he got killed."

"Why not just keep doing what she was doing and wait it out?"

"Because they had an appointment at the bank that Monday. I think she knew that when Duncan found out just how much she had been ripping him off, it was all going to be over with. So she gave him a super dose in his coffee, hoping he'd have a heart attack right there and die. But that didn't happen for whatever reason. Then when he got out there messing around with the bull like he always did, either he collapsed or got too close or something that set it off. At first Roseanne tried to get him away. Maybe she was going to get him help, I don't know. But for whatever reason, she steered him over to the hog pen and rolled him inside and let them finish the job. Then she went back to the house and acted like she didn't know anything about what was happening until Sonny came running in the house trying to get the telephone to work so he could call for help."

"Where is Roseanne Duncan now?"

"Probably back in Springerville. When she lawyered up last night her attorney came and took her out of here, since I didn't have enough to charge her with yet. That's why I need that search warrant, Bob. I want to be able to tear that place inside out looking for any kind of evidence."

"Like what?"

"I don't know. Maybe residue from the medication in the coffee cup or the coffee pot. Maybe we can find something on the computer out there that shows she was researching the effects the meds can have on someone if they took too much. Maybe something about the banking stuff."

"I can tell you right now, Jimmy, Judge Ryman isn't going to issue a search warrant with such a broad paint roller. You know that as well as I do. You're going to have to be very specific about what you're looking for. So I can put down drug residue or anything having to do with Duncan's medication. And I can probably get him to go with a search of any computers out there to see if she was looking things like that up. But the financial things? I don't think that's going to fly. Best to leave that for the FBI's investigation."

"I'll take what I can get," Weber said.

"All right then, let's go see the judge."

~***~

An air of gloom hung over the hog farm like a thick fog when Weber and his deputies arrived. Leonard Bowers had the hood up on a truck and was leaning inside the engine compartment. He stood up and scowled when he saw Weber getting out of his Explorer.

"Don't tell me you're back here to hassle Sonny again. Can't you let the poor guy have some peace?"

"We're not here for that."

"Sonny didn't do anything! Just leave him alone."

Weber was surprised to detect the smell of beer on the man's breath, and noticed four empty cans on the ground.

"It's a little early in the day to be drinking, isn't it, Leonard?"

Mona came to the door of their mobile home and looked at the sheriff with red rimmed eyes, but didn't greet him like she normally did.

"Listen, I know this has been tough on everybody, and I imagine it's really hitting home now. I'm sorry about that. But we're not here to give Sonny any more grief. I promise. But I do need to talk to him."

"He's not here."

"Do you know where he is?"

"I said he's not here."

"Hey Leonard, what's with the attitude? I told you, I'm not here to arrest him or give him any problems. I just need to talk to him about something."

"I've got work to do, I don't have time to stand here jawing with you all morning."

Weber knew Leonard had been unhappy about them arresting Sonny before, but they had kept their word and returned him within a short time, so the man's rudeness surprised him. He started to reply when Coop asked, "Isn't that his truck over there? The blue Ford?"

"There's lots of vehicles around here. I don't know who drives what all the time."

"Maybe he left and came back and you missed him," Weber said. "I think I'll go knock on his door, just to be sure."

"Okay, okay he's there! But leave him alone. He's not feeling good right now."

"Why not?"

"Why not? Christ, after everything he's been through, why should he feel good? Why do you have to keep coming out here bothering him and causing problems? Hasn't he been through enough already?"

Weber ignored him and walked over to Sonny's trailer and knocked on the door. When there was no response, he knocked harder. Eventually he heard a sound on the other side of the door and Sonny asked, "What?"

"Sonny, it's Jim Weber. I need to talk to you for a minute."

"What do you want?"

"Well, first I want you to open the door. How about we start there."

There was silence for a long moment, and Weber started to say something again when he heard the knob turning.

"What the hell happened to you?"

"It's nothing."

"Bullshit. That's a lot more than nothing. What's going on, Sonny?"

"I just got banged up a little bit. It happens all the time. You grew up on a ranch, you know that."

"Yeah, I got some bumps and bruises over the years, but this was more than that. Come out here so I can get a good look at you."

Sonny came out onto the porch, blinking in the sunlight, and Weber said, "You look like you went ten rounds with a heavyweight boxer. Who did this to you?"

"I told you, I got banged up working out there."

Weber had seen a lot of people who had been beaten up in his time as a lawman. Everything from women who had been assaulted by drunken husbands and boyfriends, to men who had mouthed off to the wrong guy in a bar, to deputies who had suffered the worst of it when taking prisoners into custody. There was no question in his mind that someone had worked Sonny over good. Both eyes were blackened and swollen, there were bruises on the left side of his head, and he had a deep gash in his forehead that had been crudely taped together.

"Stop lying to me. Somebody worked you over good. Who was it?"

"Just let it go. Okay, Sheriff?"

"I've been up front and honest with you all along, Sonny. I don't appreciate you jerking me around like this. I want to know what happened to you, and I want to know right now."

"Okay, I got stupid. I went to a bar and had a few drinks and got into it with a couple of guys."

"Who were these guys?"

"I don't know, just a couple of rednecks."

"What bar were you at when this happened?

"I don't remember."

"You don't remember? Do I look like an idiot to you, Sonny?"

"Look, I was drinking and running around raising hell. I hit two or three different bars, and I was so wasted by then that I don't remember which one I was at when I got my ass kicked. But knowing me when I drink, I deserved it. So can we just drop it?"

"So why did you lie to me and say you got banged up out here on the farm?"

"I didn't want to say anything about the drinking, what with that federal charge about the guns pending. I was afraid it would make me look bad when I got to court and I got scared. I'm sorry."

Weber looked at him for a long time, not buying the story, but he decided not to push the issue at the moment.

"Okay, fair enough. The reason I'm here is that we have a search warrant for the house."

"I thought you already did that when you took the guns."

"This is for something else," Weber said.

"Whatever, I don't have anything to hide."

"All right. Do you need the paramedics to come out and take a look at you? That cut on your head looks pretty nasty."

"No, I'm fine. I've just got a headache."

"You might have a concussion."

"Not with this hard head of mine. Go search and find whatever you need to find, Sheriff. This sunlight's making my headache worse."

"Okay, I'll check in with you before we leave." Weber turned to his deputies and said, "Let's go, guys."

They fanned out through the house, Dolan and Buz checking the kitchen, seizing the coffee pot, a stainless steel thermos, and two thick coffee mugs in the sink. Coop and Chad went upstairs to the master bathroom to retrieve the box of blood pressure medication and the used acrylic fingernails from the wastebasket, and to search the medicine cabinet and bedrooms for any other evidence.

Parks looked longingly at Duncan's desk, but Weber said, "Not yet, buddy. Any idea when that prosecutor is going to give you a yay or nay on the search warrant?"

"I'm hoping today, Jimmy. This is all coming to a head and I don't want Rosanne Duncan running away before we can get her."

"I don't really think that's going to happen," Weber said. "I think she's too greedy to give up a chance for the big money. And she thinks she's a lot smarter than us because she got away with whatever she did to her first husband over there in New Mexico."

"Hey Jimmy," Coop called from upstairs. "You'd better come up here."

"Where are you," he asked when he got to the second floor.

"Back bedroom, end of the hall on the right."

"What have you got," Weber asked when he entered the small bedroom.

"What kind of car was Rosanne Duncan driving yesterday when she came in?"

"I don't remember. Some kind of SUV?"

"Yeah. And you remember what color it was?"

"What is this? 20 Questions?"

"Think about it, what color was it."

"Maybe some kind of light gray or silver. What are you getting at, Coop?"

He pointed out the window and asked, "Like that silver Hyundai Santa Fe?"

Chapter 42

Weber pounded on the mobile home door and shouted, "Open up, Sonny. Right now."

When the door opened Sonny Duncan had a look of defeat on his face.

"No more bullshit, you tell me what happened to you. And I want the truth this time."

"I told you, I got into a fight at a bar."

"You're lying," Weber said. "You know it and I know it, so just stop. Did Rosanne do that to you?"

"I told you..."

"And I told you to stop lying to me. Where is she? Why are you covering up for her after everything she's done to you?"

"I haven't seen her."

"You haven't, huh? Then how do you explain the fact that her SUV is parked over there in those trees out of sight?"

"I told you, I haven't seen her. I don't know how her car got there. It's news to me."

"Jimmy? Get over here."

Dolan and Buz were standing by the tool shed.

"You stay right here on the front porch, and don't you even think about taking a step off of it or back inside," Weber ordered Sonny.

He crossed the yard to the tool shed near the hog pens. "What have you got?"

"It looks like dried blood on the blade of this shovel."

Weber looked closely at it. "Yeah, it does. I think we know how Sonny got beat to hell, don't we?"

"So where's Rosanne, and how did her car get stashed back there in the trees? If Coop hadn't spotted it from that bedroom window we would have never known it was there."

"Spread out and start looking for her, guys. And when you do, put the cuffs on tight. I'm going to go find out why Sonny is covering up for her."

But Sonny wasn't saying anything except, "I want an attorney."

"For what? You're the victim here if she beat you like that."

There was no response.

"Okay, have it your way. He walked over to Carl's trailer and knocked on the door, but there was no response. So he made his way down to the Bowers'. Mona open the door wordlessly.

"Where is she?"

The woman just shook her head.

"I don't understand what's going on here," Weber said. "Why is everybody covering for Roseanne?" But when he saw the look on the woman's face, suddenly he understood.

He left her standing in her doorway and walked quickly back to Sonny's trailer, pulling out his handcuffs as he stepped up onto the porch. "Turn around and put your hands behind you."

Once the cuffs were on, he said, "What did you do to her?"

Sonny just shook his head and didn't reply.

"Damn it, Sonny. If she was beating you like that, you had a right to defend yourself, no matter what you did. But don't play these games with me, okay?"

Nothing. No response.

"All right, if that's the way you want it. Let's go."

He led Sonny to the back of Coop's car, opened the rear door and put him inside. As he turned away he noticed movement out of the corner of his eye as the door to Carl's trailer closed. Weber went back to it and knocked on the door again.

"Carl, open up."

There was only silence from the other side.

"Carl, it's Sheriff Weber. I'm coming in."

He pushed the door open. The small living room and kitchen were empty.

"Carl? Where are you?"

Weber went down the hall, poking his head into the bathroom, then into the bedroom.

"Carl, come out of the closet."

When there was no response, he said, "Come out, Carl. We need to talk."

The door slid sideways and the big farmhand came out, his head down and tears on his face.

"Please don't take Sonny away again."

"Let's go in the living room and talk, okay?"

"Sonny didn't do nothin'"

"That's what we need to talk about," Weber told him.

"He didn't do nothin'."

"Yeah, that's what you said. But somebody beat Sonny up real bad. Do you know who did that?"

"Sonny's my friend."

"I know he is, Carl. I'd kinda like to think he's my friend, too. But he's not telling me what happened out here and who did that to him."

"Sonny didn't do nothin'."

"Maybe he didn't do nothing bad, but somebody did something bad to him, and I need to hear about it."

"I'm supposed to keep my mouth shut. That's what Sonny said."

"Well, Sonny may be wrong about that. Do you remember what I told you? About how if somebody is hurting you, you have a right to defend yourself? If that's what happened and Sonny defended himself, he's not going to be in trouble."

"Sonny didn't do nothin'."

"No, Carl, if he was defending himself he didn't do anything wrong."

The big man just looked at him with anguished eyes.

"That mean lady said I'm stupid. But I ain't as stupid as she thinks I am."

"I don't think you're stupid at all," Weber told him.

"No, I'm stupid. But I'm not stupid like she said. I used to go to Sunday school when I was a kid so I know about that Bible stuff."

"That's a good thing," Weber said.

"I know about do onto others like you want them to do onto you. And I know about how you're not supposed to sin and stuff like that."

"You do know a lot," Weber said.

"And I remember what you said about how if somebody is hurting you or someone else, it's okay to hurt them back to make them stop. Does it say that in the Bible, too? I don't remember that part."

Weber felt goosebumps on his arms. "Carl, is there something else you want to tell me?"

The big man walked to the open door of his trailer and looked across to the hog pens, where fifty huge animals with voracious appetites were grunting and squealing.

"I remember something else from the Bible. I remember about an eye for an eye and a tooth for a tooth. But that's okay when someone's trying to hurt somebody and you're defending them, right, Sheriff?"

Weber looked at the hog pens in horror, then back at the simple man who loved to watch cartoons at the end of a long hard workday, and said, "Oh my God, Carl. What did you do?"

Chapter 43

"I didn't expect Roseanne to pull a disappearing act with that much money on the table, but I sure didn't expect her to go out to the farm again, either. If I would have seen that coming, I would have figured out some way to keep her in custody when that shyster lawyer of hers came to get her."

"Don't beat yourself up about it, Jimmy," Bob Bennett said. "It's not like you had a crystal ball."

"I know, but I still feel responsible."

"Just let it go. She's the one that started it, and she's the one that caused things to end up the way they did."

"What's going to happen with Carl?"

"Technically, it was legal for him to step in to save Sonny. There's no question in my mind that Roseanne Duncan went out there to settle the score with Sonny once and for all, or that she was in the process of beating him to death when Carl stopped her. And she would have. As for the other, I guess a prosecutor could make a case for abuse of a corpse or improperly disposing of the body or something. But there was no premeditation here on Carl's part. And if anybody were to try to push it any farther than that, all they would have to do is talk to him to realize how he is. I'm sure he'll have to have a psychological evaluation, but aside from that, this isn't going anywhere."

"How about Sonny and the Bowers? Is any of this going to come down on them?"

"Can you prove Sonny had recovered consciousness by the time Carl disposed of her? Or that the Bowers saw it happen or colluded in any way?"

"No, but there's no question in my mind that they knew something had ..."

The Town's Attorney held up his hand. "Stop it, Jimmy. You're a good lawman, and a good man in a lot of other respects, too. But that crystal ball I said you don't have? Well, you don't. And I don't believe you can read minds, either. Did you ever hear that saying about letting sleeping dogs lie? No good can come from you dwelling on this. Okay?"

"Yeah, I guess you're right."

"You know I am. Some good people got hurt by this, Jimmy. It's time for the hurting to be over and for the healing to start."

Chapter 44

In spite of the fact that November had come and snow was falling, it seemed like over half the town attended Duncan's memorial service. The Boy Scouts were there in uniform, along with an honor guard from the VFW. There were people from across the region who had done business with him, members of every church congregation and volunteer group that he had supported by donating hogs and money to their efforts over the years, and many others.

Duncan's second cousin, Reverend David Huntington spoke about the man's good work, his generosity, and his love for his fellow man. He talked about how Duncan had paid utility bills and back rent and provided groceries for so many of those who had fallen on hard times. Never doing it in person, never wanting any recognition, just keeping in the background while trying to make life better for others.

"I know that it's easy to focus on the bad in this situation," the preacher said, "to dwell on the losses, and the terrible price that's been paid and will continue to be paid in the wake of this tragedy. But Duncan wouldn't want that. If he were here with us, and I believe he is, he would want us to smile and remember the good times. He would want us to carry on his work by taking care of one another, by accepting one another based on who we are, not what we look like or sound like or talk like, or even smell like. And mostly, he would want us to carry on his work by loving one another. And now, let us bow our heads in prayer."

After the memorial service, David invited everybody next door to the church's community hall, where refreshments would be served. The bruises had faded away, but Sonny Duncan would carry the scar on his forehead from where Roseanne had hit him with a shovel for the rest of his life, a grim reminder of what had happened that terrible day she made her last visit to the hog farm.

Weber shook his hand and asked, "How are you doing, Sonny?"

"I'm good, Sheriff. Getting things back on track."

Weber smiled at the woman by his side and said, "Claudia, it's nice to see you here."

"I wouldn't have missed it for the world. I loved Duncan. He was a good man."

"Yes, he was, no question about that. And this fellow here, he may not want to admit it, but he's a chip off the old block."

With her arm linked through Sonny's, Claudia smiled and said, "Yeah, he is."

"I'm glad to see you two together. It warms my heart. And I think it would've warmed Duncan's, too."

"We've been through a lot," Sonny said. "But no matter what, I don't think either one of us ever stopped loving the other one. So we're putting the past behind us and moving forward, one day at a time."

"That's the way to do it," Weber said.

"The only thing that's really bothering me right now is that gun charge hanging over my head. I haven't heard a word about that."

"You know, that's a funny thing," Weber told him. "Larry Parks is usually on the ball about things, but what with everything that happened out there at the farm, he flat-out forgot to follow up on that charge until it was too late."

"What do you mean?

"I don't know, typical government red tape, I guess. But he was just telling me that the charges weren't filed in a timely matter or some paperwork got lost, or something. At any rate, he said the whole thing's been dropped. That's a bureaucrat for you. That's why they call the FBI Famous But Inefficient."

"You're kidding me?"

"Nope. Of course, I can't release those firearms back to you, or to Claudia here if you guys are together. But if you wanted to sell them to somebody like, say Leonard Bowers, for five bucks apiece or whatever, he's welcome to come by my office with a receipt and take them off my hands. I sure don't have room to store them forever."

Weber smiled at the young couple.

"Thank you, Sheriff. Thank you for everything."

"No need to thank me. I'm just doing my job. How's Carl doing?"

"He's okay. I don't think he really realizes what he did. I mean, he knows he did it, but he doesn't quite understand it all the way. Does that make any sense?"

"Yeah, it does," Weber said. "And I think that's probably for the better, don't you?"

"I do. I was talking to the shrinks down at that place where they have him for evaluation. They all agree that he's not a danger to himself or anyone else, but they also are in agreement that he's not competent to stand trial. They tell me he will probably be released into our custody by the end of the month. And he's sure looking forward to getting back home."

"Speaking of getting back home, I hear that José and Carmen Barela are back out there, too."

Sonny nodded his head and looked at the couple standing across the room talking to Leonard and Mona Bowers. "The guy they were working for up there in Holbrook couldn't afford to keep them on. And we needed the help. It just worked out best for everybody."

"So what are your plans, if I can ask,"

Sonny grinned ruefully and said, "Well, with Claudia handling the books and so many people depending on me, I guess I'm still in the hog business, Sheriff."

Weber laughed and said, "At least tell me you bought a place in town somewhere."

Claudia shook her head and replied, "No, a husband and wife need to be together. And to tell you the truth, I'm getting to where I don't notice the smell out there anymore."

Weber laughed and said, "Life is a funny thing, isn't it?"

Someone came to pay their respects to Sonny and Claudia, and the sheriff excused himself. He chatted with a few people for a while, then Robyn caught his eye.

"Are you ready to go?"

"Yeah. Just about. Give me a minute."

He walked to the little table on the side of the room where they had placed two photos of Duncan, one from his wedding day with Eleanor, a smiling young man in an ill fitting suit standing next to a pretty girl in a white dress; and the other of Duncan leaning against the bed of his pickup truck with the hog pens in the background, that same easy-going grin on his face that Weber would always remember. The sheriff gently touched the urn that held his ashes and said, "They are all going to be all right. Don't you worry about them. Rest in peace, my friend."

Here's A Sneak Preview Of Nick Russell's Next Big Lake Book, *Big Lake Snowdaze,* Coming Soon!

"Oh, Jimmy, in the long list of crazy things we've done since I met you, this one tops them all. Let's just forget about this whole thing while we can."

"Stop being such a wuss, Parks. How bad could it possibly be?"

"Bad, Robyn. Real bad."

"I'm going to do it, too."

"Yeah, but you've already got internal plumbing. When my junk hits that cold water, it's gonna go places it was never intended to be!"

"Well, if you're going to act like a little girl, you might as well be one."

"I swear, Marsha, if you do something like locking the doors when we try to get back in, or driving away and leaving us standing there, I'm going to hunt you down if it's the last thing I ever do."

"Relax, will you? I promise I'll have all the doors unlocked, and the heater going full blast. And here," the woman behind the steering wheel of the Chrysler Pacifica held up a big stainless steel thermos and said, "this hot buttered rum will be right here waiting for you."

"Whose idea was this, anyway?"

"It damn sure wasn't mine," Sheriff Jim Weber said. "You can blame Juliette Murdoch at the Chamber of Commerce for this one. She's the one that dreamed up the challenge between us and the volunteer fire department."

"Yeah, but that was between the Sheriff's Office and the fire guys. How the hell did I get roped into it?"

"When the FBI gave you this cushy job up here, part of it was to assist the local police agencies, right? That's what you're doing.

Besides, I had to keep one deputy dressed and on-duty to hold back the crowd when they see that good-looking body of yours."

"No, man," Parks said, shaking his head. "They never covered this in training at Quantico."

"Just quit your sniveling," Robyn said. "Okay guys, get ready, they're ready to start the countdown!"

Outside the minivan, Town Councilman Kirby Templeton, wearing a heavy parka with a fur-lined hood, was using a bullhorn to address the gathered crowd.

"Okay folks, are you ready?"

There was applause from the crowd, and Kirby shook his head.

"No, that's not going to cut it. I asked, *are you ready*?"

This time there were hoots and hollers and cheers from the audience.

"That's more like it," Kirby said. "Now, you all heard the rules, right? When Councilman Gauger fires the shotgun, ten representatives from the Big Lake Fire Department over here on the left, and ten representatives from the Sheriff's Department there on the right are all going to run down the boat ramp and into that icy water. They have to get at least chest deep and they all have to duck themselves under at least once. This is an endurance contest folks, and whoever has somebody stay in the water longest is the winner. Will it be the big brawny men of the Fire Department?"

There were loud cheers from the crowd.

"Or will it be those brave men and one daring lady from the Sheriff's Department?"

More cheers and applause as fans of the Sheriff's Department showed their support.

"Okay then, I guess we'll know pretty soon, won't we?"

"Chief Harper, if your firemen are ready, honk your horns."

Horns blasted on the two vehicles holding the firemen, signifying they were ready to go.

"Sheriff Weber, how about you?"

Marsha held her hand down on the Pacifica's horn, and next to them Meghan Northcutt, wife of Deputy Jordan Northcutt, blew her SUV's horn.

"All right! Councilman Gauger, are you ready?"

Standing on the shore of the lake, Frank Gauger nodded and shouldered his Ithaca 20 gauge over and under shotgun, aiming it out over the ice covered lake. "Okay, on three. Everybody, help me count it down," Kirby said over the bullhorn.

"One," shouted the crowd.

"Oh, this is crazy," Parks said.

"Two."

"I don't want to do this!"

"Three!"

Gauger pulled the trigger and the shotgun roared. Car doors flew open and nineteen men, along with Deputy Robyn Fuchette, poured out of their vehicles and ran the few feet to the concrete boat ramp, slipping and sliding as they made their way down to the ice cold water. There were hoots and hollers from the crowd, and whistles at Robyn in her one piece bathing suit.

Those were quickly followed by shrieks from the contestants as they plunged into the icy water.

"Oh-My-God! I'm gonna die!"

"Damn, it's cold!"

"No way!"

"I think my nuts just fell off!"

"Stop being such sissies. Get those heads under!"

The water was so cold that it burned, and Weber felt his whole body clench by the time it had reached his knees. He knew he had to go out further and duck under, but there was nothing he wanted more than to turn tail and run back to the warmth of Marsha's van. As it turned out, he didn't have to force himself to go on, because Dale Portwood, a string bean of a man who spent his working hours mowing grass and laying sod in the summer for a landscaping company and driving a snowplow in the wintertime when he wasn't answering calls as a volunteer fireman, slipped on the icy ramp. He landed on his rear end and slid into the water, knocking four or five people off their feet like some kind of human scythe as he went.

With his back turned away from shore, Weber hadn't seen that coming and swallowed a mouthful of cold water on the way down. He bobbed to the surface, coughing and choking and managed to get his feet under him. The water was up to his armpits and he was surprised that once he had been totally immersed it didn't feel nearly as bad as the cold night air did. All around him people were yelling and shouting, and at least half of the contestants had already admitted defeat and ran for the warmth of the waiting cars.

Weber looked over at Steve Harper, Big Lake's Fire Chief, who was standing in the water chastising his men as they fled. "You're all a bunch of chickens. You gonna let these guys beat us?"

"Not me, I quit," Robyn yelled as she pushed past him and ran up the ramp.

"Traitor!" Weber yelled after her.

"You gonna follow your girlfriend, Jimmy?"

"Not until you're outta here," Weber told him.

"Hell, son, I plan on staying here until the spring thaw so I'll be the first person to catch a fish next year!"

There was a yell from over his shoulder, and Weber turned to see if it was one of his deputies giving up or a fireman who had had enough. He was surprised to discover that it was Kevin Upchurch, Harper's best friend. While Upchurch, who worked as a maintenance man for the school system and stood head and shoulders above his shorter friend, had always been unerringly loyal to Harper, it looked like he was about to betray the Fire Chief as he made his way toward the ramp. But then Weber realize there was something different about the tone of his voice. Upchurch had a look that was almost terror on his face, and he was dragging something behind him. Weber looked again and realized it wasn't *something*, it was someone. At first he thought one of the participants in the Polar Bear plunge had collapsed, but then he realized it was a woman. A naked woman. A very obviously dead naked woman.

The sheriff looked at Steve Harper and said, "And I thought the worst thing that was going to happen this weekend was when the mayor killed Santa Claus!"

Made in the USA
Las Vegas, NV
18 March 2021